THE BODY

IN THE

SLEIGH

A FAITH FAIRCHILD MYSTERY

KATHERINE
HALL PAGE

wm

WILLIAM MORROW
An Imprint of HarperCollins*Publishers*

THE BODY IN THE SLEIGH. Copyright © 2009 by Katherine Hall Page. All rights reserved. Printed in the United States of America. No part of this book may be used or reproduced in any manner whatsoever without written permission except in the case of brief quotations embodied in critical articles and reviews. For information address HarperCollins Publishers, 10 East 53rd Street, New York, NY 10022.

HarperCollins books may be purchased for educational, business, or sales promotional use. For information please write: Special Markets Department, HarperCollins Publishers, 10 East 53rd Street, New York, NY 10022.

FIRST EDITION

Designed by Rosa Chae

Library of Congress Cataloging-in-Publication Data

Page, Katherine Hall.
  The body in the sleigh : a Faith Fairchild mystery / Katherine Hall Page. — 1st ed.
    p. cm.
  ISBN 978-0-06-147425-5
    1. Fairchild, Faith Sibley (Fictitious character)—Fiction. 2. Spouses of clergy—Fiction. 3. Caterers and catering—Fiction. 4. Massachusetts—Fiction. I. Title.

PS3566.A334B673 2009
813'.54—dc22   2009001000

---

09 10 11 12 13   OV/RRD   10 9 8 7 6 5 4 3 2 1

To Librarians Everywhere
Especially the late Inabeth Miller
and the late Ruth Rockwood;
Jeanne Bracken, Emily Howie, Micheline Jedrey,
Dottie MacKeen, Carol Mahoney, Barbara Myles,
Virginia Stanley, Ruth Rogers,
and Anne Walker-Hennessy Cifelli

Myrrh is mine, its bitter perfume
Breathes a life of gathering gloom;
Sorrowing, sighing, bleeding, dying,
Sealed in the stone-cold tomb

—REVEREND JOHN HENRY HOPKINS JR.,
"WE THREE KINGS"

Acknowledgments

Many thanks to the following for help on subjects ranging from iceboating, tattoos, and Christmas on Deer Isle, Maine, to postmortems, pancreatitis, and recipes: Kyra Alex, Helen Barer, Diana Davis, Dr. Robert DeMartino, Kevin Grindle, Kimberly Grindle, Forrest and Margie Nevells.

For goat expertise, including cheese making and milking with an infant strapped close: Anne Bossi and Bob Bowen of Sunset Acres Farm, Brooksville, Maine; Karen Valentine and baby Benjamin of Burden Creek Dairy, Johns Island, South Carolina.

Special thanks to my new editor, Wendy Lee; my gifted Morrow publicist, Danielle Bartlett; and my agent, Faith Hamlin, as we celebrate twenty-one years together.

The Body in the Sleigh

PROLOGUE

The Christmas Eve sky was filled with stars when Mary Bethany found a baby in her barn. They hadn't had a real snow yet; the island never got the kind of accumulation the mainland did, but it was cold. She had pulled a woolen overcoat that had belonged to her father over her winter jacket and grabbed an old shawl of her mother's, draping it around her head. Her small herd of goats was letting her know that it was milking time, holiday or no holiday.

Mary hadn't been leaving a festive gathering. She hadn't been leaving any gathering at all. Just a cup of hot cider, a slice of the fruitcake sent by her cousin Elizabeth, and a few cats for company and to keep the rodent population down. Walking the short distance from the old farmhouse to the small barn she'd built when the herd got too large for the shed, Mary had remembered the legend about animals being able to speak on Christmas Eve. She'd allowed herself to speculate about what her goats would have to say. They were Nubians, pretty, long-eared goats that gave rich milk with the highest butterfat content and protein of any breed. Her pretty nannies. Her neurotic nannies. Temperamental, easily miffed divas, they let her know with resounding bleats when something was even the slightest bit wrong. She was afraid that given human voices, their conversation would be a litany of slights and sorrows. Or perhaps not. Perhaps they would tell her how much they depended on her, how much they loved her. She had entered the warm barn smiling, and her smile grew broader when she saw the large basket with a big red bow, nestled against a bale of hay. It must be a gift from a neighbor. She hadn't thought she would be getting any presents. Even her sister Martha's yearly Swiss Colony cheese log had not arrived. A tag hung from the bow: "For Mary Bethany." She ignored the goats for a moment and knelt down before the gift.

It was an afghan in soft pastel colors. That would be Arlene Harvey who crocheted so beautifully. The summer people always snapped up her work at the Sewing Circle's annual fair in August. How kind, Mary thought. It would be just the thing to throw across her lap at night when she sat up late reading. But so unexpected. She hadn't seen or spoken to the Harveys since she'd brought some of her rose-hip jelly over in early September. It had been a wonderful summer for the *Rosa rugosa* bushes that surrounded the house and had seeded in what passed for a lawn and, beyond it, the pasture. Mary had gathered the large, bulbous bright orange hips and put up jelly, made soup, even dried some for tea. Looking at the gleaming jars on the pantry shelf, she had decided to bring some to Arlene and Doug—her nearest neighbors, a mere six acres of fields and woods away.

But this was too much! It must have taken Arlene a long time to make; the stitch was intricate and the wool so fine. Then she heard a tiny sneeze. The merest whisper of a sneeze. She pulled back the blanket and she uncovered—a baby! Eyes squeezed shut, a newborn—tiny—about the size of a kid. She rocked back on her heels in amazement, letting the cover drop from her hands. A baby?

The goats were crying louder, insistently. There was nothing human about their speech, but Mary knew what they were say-ing. She would have to milk them or they would wake the child. Whose child? And what was it doing here in her barn? Mary touched the baby's face gently. It was soft and warm. A beautiful child with rosy cheeks—*Rosa rugosa* cheeks—and shiny dark fine hair, like cormorant feathers, escaping from the hooded snowsuit. A blue snowsuit, new, not a hand-me-down. It must be a boy. His eyelids fluttered at her touch, but he slept on. Mary stood up shakily. She would milk the goats, then take the baby inside. That was as far ahead as she could think at the moment. In all her forty-seven years, nothing remotely like this had ever happened. Nothing unusual at all, unless you thought an old maid who kept to herself, raised goats, and made cheese was unusual—or odd—as some did. But nothing really unusual.

Automatically she milked the six goats and put out fresh water, more hay, and the grain mixture of oats, corn, and molasses she fed them. They complained at her haste and voiced their irrita-tion. "I don't have time to coddle you tonight," she told them, and something in her voice seemed to chasten them. At least, the noise level dropped. "Besides," she added, "if anyone should be upset, it should be me. It's Christmas Eve. You're supposed to be able to tell me what happened here tonight."

She brought the baby into the house, setting the basket down by the woodstove in the kitchen, then ran back for the milk, which went into the shed in the second refrigerator. She'd had to buy it after she'd started making cheese.

When she closed the barn door and let the latch drop, Mary looked up into the night sky. It was clear and the stars seemed close enough to touch. There was a large one directly overhead. She blinked and it was gone. Turning at the back door for a last look before she went into the house, she saw the star was back.

In the kitchen, Mary took off her coat and jacket, wrapping the shawl around her shoulders. The baby was awake and making little mewing sounds like a kitten. He must be hungry, she thought, and reached in to pick him up. He settled into the crook of her arm, as if it had been carved just for him.

"You poor thing," she said aloud. "Who are you? And how could anyone bear to give you up?"

Holding him tight, she pulled the afghan out of the basket. Underneath it were an envelope with her name on it, some baby clothes, cloth diapers, two bottles, and a package wrapped in brown paper—not the kind you buy on a roll, but cut from a paper bag. The letter wasn't sealed; the flap was tucked in, easy to open with one hand. Mary knew then that the baby's mother had tried to think of everything, even this small detail—that Mary would be holding the baby when she read the letter. It was short and typewritten:

> Dear Mary,
>
> Keep him safe and raise him to be a good man. His name is Christopher.

That was it. No signature. No further explanation. Mary picked up the package and peeled the tape from one end. A packet of bills fell out. She shook it, and more followed. Packets of hundred-dollar bills. A lot of hundred-dollar bills.

CHAPTER 1

Faith Sibley Fairchild slipped quietly out of bed, although nothing short of a sonic boom—or conversely a whimper from one of the children—would awaken her husband, the Reverend Thomas Fairchild, from his deep winter slumber. She walked to the window overlooking the cove. The tide was high and the surface of the water was ablaze with the light from the moon. It had been full the night before, and tonight, Christmas Eve, it was just as luminous. It was so bright out that the snow covering the pines along the shore looked like frosted gingerbread cookies and the meadow in front of the cottage sparkled. Mainers considered their seasons fall, winter, mud, and July. Faith was glad to be experiencing winter, the one she'd missed. She turned from the scene and put on her robe and slippers. Sleep had eluded her. Perhaps a warm drink would help.

Downstairs in the kitchen that opened onto the living room with its row of plate-glass windows, Faith filled the kettle without turning on the lights. There was something magical about the way the moonbeams were streaming in, lighting her way.

A mug of chamomile tea soon in hand, she settled onto the

couch in front of the windows. Christmas Eve—or rather Christmas Day. She'd seen that it was past midnight by the clock on the stove.

They'd gone to the early children's service at the Congregational church in Granville and spent the rest of the night watching a video of Alastair Sim in *A Christmas Carol*. Although granddaughter, daughter, and wife of men of the cloth, she realized it was the first Christmas Eve service she'd attended where she had not been related to the robed figure in the pulpit. The experience had been oddly disconcerting, like visiting a foreign country, but one that spoke the same language as she did—"'And it came to pass in those days, that there went out a decree from Caesar Augustus, that all the world should be taxed.'"

It must have been a night like this, a starry, brilliant night. Poor Mary, so young and no doubt quite uncomfortable after the long journey on the donkey that ended not in a comfy queen-size bed, but a pile of straw. No midwife save Joseph and then all that company—shepherds, the Wise Men. They, at least, had an entourage and Mary didn't have to think what to serve them, one hoped. The shepherds, though, would have been ravenous after a cold night watching their flocks. Faith had been older than Mary when her firstborn was brought forth, but she well remembered being sore afraid in those last few hours and completely overwhelmed by the thought of the awesome responsibility she and Tom had taken on. Over the last twelve years, she'd continued to feel this way at times, but oh, the joy! For a moment she was tempted to get up and peek in on Ben and his sister, Amy, three years younger. She knew what she'd find. Her son, in his room, would be sprawled across the bed, having thrown off all his covers. Amy, on the other hand, would lie tucked securely under the covers like a letter in an envelope, in the exact position she'd been in when her eyes closed. Faith was sure that visions of sugarplums were dancing in both their wee heads. Her offspring would be up in a very few hours, yet she stayed where she was, drinking the tea.

Her thoughts drifted back to the chain of events that had brought them to Maine over a week ago—specifically to Sanpere Island in Penobscot Bay—from their home in Aleford, outside Boston. It was an unseasonable time of the year for the Fairchilds to be here. As usual, they'd closed up Columbus Day weekend, not expecting to return until May to air the place out, sweep up the dead flies, and resist the temptation to plant the garden too soon. Tonight, ghostly mounds gave indications of the perennial border in front of the house and she could just make out the raised vegetable beds to one side. They'd put away the fence that kept the deer from destroying their efforts.

She sipped some more tea, enjoying the sensation the warm liquid made as it traveled down her throat. How did we get here? How did *I* get here? Life took detours and she had yet to meet someone who hadn't faced them in some form or another—in varying degrees.

Everything had started just after Thanksgiving—and, despite the tranquil scene in front of her, the time on the island, meant to heal, had also not been without incident. She wasn't sleepy at all, but her gaze was blurring, and the events of these last weeks began to stream across her mind like a Technicolor dream.

It had been a difficult fall—they'd lost a good friend under tragic circumstances and Ben had had a very tough time adjusting to middle school—so when Tom started to have stomachaches and had no appetite, they'd told each other, "Stress." It was also that time of year—the holidays. Early in their marriage they'd talked about how much they loved the Christmas season, starting with the lighting of the first Advent candle and continuing on to the joys of Christmas Day with its message of hope and peace. Loved it—and hated it. As a preacher's kid, albeit in a parish on Manhattan's East Side, Faith knew all about the tension Christmas brought. This was not simply due to the increase in the number of church services—or the lack of private family time (a year-round dilemma)—but the problems that surfaced as lonely people compared their lives to television specials, and harried parents tried to combine work and assembling Notre Dame in gingerbread with their overstimulated offspring. Stress, they'd told each other. That was the trouble. Tom swigged Maalox and crunched Tums. They promised each other some time off in January. Then the pains moved to his back, and one bright picture-perfect winter morning complete with a cloudless blue sky and a shimmering dusting of snow, Faith got a call at Have Faith, her catering firm, from Emerson Hospital. Her husband was in the emergency ward. He hadn't wanted to worry her and had actually driven himself the few miles from the parsonage in Aleford to the hospital before collapsing in pain upon arrival.

It was pancreatitis, and the sight of him hooked up to an IV and heart monitor, pale as Marley's ghost, was almost more than she could bear. He tried for a grin, but it turned into a grimace. His doctor was reassuring in that ambiguous manner some doctors employ. Lucky to have caught it—but. Sound metabolism—but. They just needed to figure out why he'd developed it in the first place. Was her husband a heavy drinker? The shocked look on Faith's face had provided the answer to that one. Tom wasn't a teetotaler by any means, but the parish hadn't been going through an unusual amount of communion wine during his tenure. Family history? A quick call to her mother-in-law, who then promptly set out for the hospital, confirmed that Tom's was the only case so far as she knew. "Ah," said the doctor. "Must be gallstones."

And gallstones they were. After the CAT scan confirmed the diagnosis, they'd treated Tom for the pain and waited a week for the inflammation to subside before operating. Faith—and Tom—learned that there were an amazing number of things in life that could be put on hold, that one simply didn't have to do. Things other people—Faith's assistant at her catering business, Niki Constantine; Tom's associate minister; the divinity school intern; the vestry—would do for you, or things one really hadn't needed to do at all. Postsurgical instructions were rest, a high-carb, high-fiber, low-fat diet—and "stay off the sauce for a while." The doctor's bedside manner was similar to Groucho Marx's. So long as Tom watched for symptoms, he'd be better than ever—probably. The pancreas would repair itself—probably. It was just one of those things. The doctor slipped into Cole Porter mode and Faith had been unable to stop herself from retorting, "Hey, we're not talking about a trip to the moon on gossamer wings! Is my husband going to be all right or not?" He had smiled in that patronizing way some doctors do and patted her hand in that patronizing way some doctors do. "Time will tell." Which, of course, was no answer at all.

Time had told, though. And whatever jolly old St. Nick delivered, Tom's steady improvement—what was she saying? Tom *himself*—would be the best present under the tree, now and forever.

She'd been stunned by his illness. Tom Fairchild was the picture of health, one of those perennially big hungry boys whose tall, rangy frame burned calories as fast as the woodstove across the room consumed logs. At the thought, she got up to add some more to the sturdy Vermont Castings Defiant model—she liked the name: "Take that, Cold!" They didn't really need the stove anymore, since they'd put in a furnace when they'd remodeled the cottage several summers ago. But the crackling birch smelled heavenly and filled the room with the kind of warmth no furnace could duplicate. She'd been opposed to putting a furnace in—why spend the money when they would never be on Sanpere Island in the wintertime? She'd suspected it was Tom's idea of the proverbial thin end of the wedge. He'd spend every vacation on Sanpere if he could. While Faith loved the island too, there were others called Saint Barts and Mustique that beckoned more seductively in cold weather.

But here they were. Thank God. It was, of course, where Tom wanted to recuperate, and it had been a perfect choice. The days they'd been here and the days that stretched out ahead filled with nothing more taxing than the *New York Times* daily crossword puzzles and the Audubon Christmas Bird Count made her slightly giddy with relief. Tom would be fine, better than ever. The words had become a kind of mantra she repeated to herself whenever her husband looked tired or she thought there was a new crease on his forehead. They'd pulled the kids out of school over a week early and she'd expected them to object to the notion of being so isolated—no friends, a TV that only played DVDs and videos. In fact, they'd quickly adapted to the slower pace. She had a feeling it was a respite, particularly for Ben. Their teachers had supplied them with work and it was finished in the first two days, leaving the rest to spend almost totally outdoors—they'd brought their snowshoes and cross-country skis. Inside the kids curled up with *Swallows and Amazons* and Jane Langton's captivating chronicles of the Hall family. Faith never wanted the reason for all this to happen again—she planned that she and Tom would go gently into that good night someday far, far in the future at the exact same moment. She couldn't bear to think of life without him, but now that he was on the mend, she knew she would always treasure this Christmas and the time the four of them were spending together. The kids had been worried about him too, of course, and watching him return to his good, old Daddy self was reassuring.

Coming to Sanpere: a perfect choice, yes—until she'd come upon the body in the sleigh.

She pushed the scene fast-forward and instead struggled to concentrate on others. The Christmas season on Sanpere Island was similar only in the barest outlines to Christmas in Aleford, or New York City—the standard by which Faith gauged most things. Holiday decorations, the guy in the red suit, Jesus, Mary, Joseph, the manger, and presents were accounted for in all three places. In Aleford, people put up wreaths in late November, which remained securely in place until Easter, never out of synch with the weather. Some of the town's more jovial residents strung a few lights on their yews, which the less jovial viewed as commercial-izing Christmas and, worse, a waste of electricity just when the planet was teetering on the edge of destruction.

In Sanpere, however, every yard was crowded with snowmen, reindeer, elves, and Santa, of course. Colored lights outlined every house, glowing "icicles" dripped from the roofs, and even more wattage lit up the trees. Faith knew there was a contest each year for Best Holiday Display, but she'd never suspected the contestants would rival Rockefeller Center. They'd had to make several tours of the island to revisit the kids' favorites—the basketball hoop that had sprouted a fully trimmed tree outside a bedecked trailer; lob-ster boats in and out of the water outlined in lights and looped with fir garlands. The hands-down favorite was the "tree" con-structed of fifty lobster traps, trimmed with pot buoys and topped with a huge star in one of the fishermen's front yard. At night, its rope lighting could be seen from miles away.

The merchants in Granville and Sanpere Village, the smaller of the island's two main towns, had given over their windows to the season, even stores that were closed in the winter. The photo studio, a fixture for at least two generations, featured a ginger-bread village made by the island's kindergarten class. A local artist had created a Nativity scene in another store, and a life-size Santa stood on the roof of the bank. Sanpere's lone electrician, whose business had formerly housed one of the small markets that used to dot the island, had filled the front window with a cozy scene of Santa in a rocker sitting in front of a colorfully trimmed tree, all bathed in soft orange lighting that mimicked firelight. Sanpere's paper, *The Island Crier,* ran its annual "What Christmas and the Holidays Mean to Me" supplement filled with artwork, poems, and prose from the island's schoolchildren. This year many focused on what one's cat and/or dog would do or had done in the past—"Lucky will probably knock the tree down. He will also probably shred the presents." "Inkspot left paw prints all over the icing on the cake my grandma made." One fourth-grader had been refreshingly frank: "Easter is really my favorite holiday, then Halloween, but I like Christmas all right too." Must be something about being in fourth grade; another cut straight to the chase: "Christmas means my uncle Roger coming. He once played football and could have gone pro, but he turned down his chance."

Holiday flags fluttered, and having spent many hours making the fragrant balsam wreaths that were shipped all over the country, islanders had also turned out plenty for themselves. Everywhere one looked there was some sort of decoration. There was nothing restrained about celebrating the season on Sanpere, culminating in the biggest difference between a Down East Christmas and Aleford's: Santa arrived via lobster boat.

On Friday evening Faith and Tom had taken the kids to the town pier in Granville to greet him along with most of the island—population 3,134 in the winter. They'd cheered Santa ashore along with everyone else and joined the crowd for cocoa and cookies in the Grange hall. With no school the next day for the children and, sadly, most of the boats out of the water for the fishermen, due to the economy, not weather, the night took on a leisurely character. It was only the women, Faith had noted, who had that to-do-list look. She'd felt a bit guilty at how short hers was, but remembering previous years, decided she was owed.

The Fairchilds had hung a wreath on their own front door and bought a small, living tree in a tub. It was trimmed with ornaments they'd made during the week from pinecones and clam and mussel shells. So it would look as pretty at night, they'd added a string of tiny white lights purchased at the Island Variety Store. The only decoration Faith had brought from home was the exquisite Gladys Boalt Treetop Angel figure Tom had given her their first Christmas together. She always put it on the top of the tree even before they put the lights on—that normally tedious job. The angel had become a kind of talisman and Faith had promised herself that no tree they'd ever have would be without it. She glanced over at it now. The angel's deftly painted smile looked enigmatic—or perhaps it was Faith's imagination.

Yes, everything had been perfect until she'd found the body in the sleigh. And now in this early-morning hour, the scene played, unbidden, as sharply focused as when it had occurred.

Tom had been napping and she was taking the kids on their first tour of the island decorations. They'd stopped at the market to pick up some things for supper and were greeted by Santa handing out candy canes. He turned out to be Sonny Prescott underneath the beard. Sonny would normally be found at his dock; he was a seafood dealer. Mostly lobster these days, since there were no ground fish near enough to speak of. He'd explained he was doing the occasional stint as Santa at the store in exchange for the use of the "rig" Christmas Eve and Christmas Day for various family parties. Faith had duly admired the lush velvet outfit and realistic silky white beard and wig. In return, Sonny told them to be sure to stop at the display on the Sanpere Historical Society's front lawn, promising it was "some pretty."

The society was housed in the oldest farmhouse on the island and attracted people from the time it opened in May through the fall, especially those who were researching their roots. The former barn had been restored a few years ago and served as the setting for the society's collection of antique farm machinery, carriages, and other modes of transportation. Another outbuilding was filled with glass cases of ship models.

They'd driven straight over and were not disappointed. The

house itself boasted a fir wreath at every window. Set in front of the door was one of the sleighs that had provided the only means of transportation during the winter months before four-wheel drive and Ski-Doos. It was filled with gaily wrapped presents, and three mannequin passengers peeked out from beneath a carriage robe. It was all very Currier & Ives. Faith had brought the camera and had been taking pictures of Ben and Amy in front of all their favorites. She hadn't sent out cards this year—another reprieve, although she liked catching up with friends and family. The sleigh would be a wonderful backdrop for a shot of the two children, fortuitously dressed—Amy in a red parka, Ben in forest green. She could have prints made at the Rite Aid in Blue Hill and send them to family and a few close friends at least. Others must have had the same photo-op idea; there were several sets of footprints leading to the sleigh, stopping alongside. The kids hadn't been as willing to pose for this picture as the others. They were getting tired—and besides, they liked the lobster-pot tree better. She'd urged them on, walking ahead.

Then she stopped.

"Ben, Amy, go back to the car. I'll be there in a minute."

"But, Mom, I thought you wanted to take a picture of us," Ben had protested. He was out of the car and cooperating and now his mother was telling him to get back in? Adults never knew what they wanted.

"Another time. Please, get in the car right now."

Both kids had been quick to pick up on the tone of her second request. They'd obeyed without hesitating.

Faith herself stood frozen. Not sure at first that what she was seeing was real, she was very sure now. There were three figures— a male and two females—in the sleigh, but only two mannequins. One female was not an example of Sanpere's Christmas cheer, but the polar opposite.

The girl was dead.

There was no question about that, but how did she come to die? How long had she been in the sleigh? It was late morning. Most of the island was at work, and school was still in session. No one would have been out taking holiday photos except someone with Faith's free time.

The girl was young, but looked college, not high school, aged. Her face was waxy white and there were no signs of violence other than the contorted mouth. Her eyes were closed. Faith felt for a pulse on her neck. Her skin was freezing and it was like touching a marble statue. There was no pulse; there was no life left at all.

Cell phones only worked on the shores that faced Swan's Island to the north, where there was a cell tower. The historical society was inland. She'd have to knock on a neighbor's door. She looked for signs of smoke from a nearby chimney. Someone was home across the road. She stepped carefully away from the footprints by the sleigh and took a final look back at the scene. The mannequins had not been disturbed, nor the presents—although there was a brown paper bag with some words stamped on it shoved next to the gifts. It didn't look as if it had been an original part of the display.

Just as the girl hadn't.

She sat between the two other lifeless figures, carefully placed—or perhaps she had climbed in herself? She, or someone else, had pulled the heavy woolen lap robe that was part of the display almost up to her chin. Faith couldn't see much of what she was wearing, just the top of a thin flowered blouse—not exactly winter garb. Her hair was short, very blond, white-blond like Marilyn's. Her ears, an eyebrow, and her nose were pierced, sporting an array of small rings and studs. Faith realized she was still holding her camera in readiness and took pictures of the tracks in the snow, the sleigh, and its contents. She had to force herself, hating the notion that they would join her holiday snaps—for a time anyway.

She stopped briefly at the car and told the kids it would be a little longer. At the market, she'd given in to their pleas and bought a half-dozen store-baked, sugar-shock cupcakes, iced red and green with plenty of sprinkles. She told the kids they could each have one now while they waited. On no account were they to get out of the car.

Then she walked across the road and knocked on the front door. There hadn't been a doorbell in sight. An elderly woman answered so quickly that Faith was sure she must have been watching the scene from her window.

"There's been some kind of accident. There's a dead girl in the sleigh across the street and we need to call 911."

The woman nodded. "My eyes aren't what they were—cataracts. My daughter wants me to have that surgery, but I don't want anything stuck in there. Anyway, I thought there'd only been two dolls, or whatever they are, in the sleigh yesterday. The phone's in the kitchen."

She led the way into what was undoubtedly the warmest room in the house. It was a blend of two, perhaps three, centuries. The linoleum on the floor and the Magic Chef stove were mid-twentieth. The Kelvinator fridge looked to be the same vintage. The walls were covered with the old house's original beadboard and plaster; the heat source was an Empire Crawford wood cookstove, blackened and its chrome gleaming—all these dating from the nineteenth century. There was a Hoosier as well. But there was also a brand-new stainless dishwasher, and a large flat-screen TV dominated the room. Following Faith's glance, the woman told her, "My grandson gave it to me so's I could watch my shows. Gave me the dishwasher too. Didn't really need that, though. Here's the phone."

Faith made the call and was relieved to hear that there was a cruiser on the island. An officer would be there immediately. With no police on Sanpere, except for the Field Troopers who periodically patrolled from the Maine State Police branch in Ellsworth,

she'd been afraid she'd have to wait with the kids for a long time
or call someone to take them back to the cottage. She knew from
previous experience that she couldn't leave the scene.

"My children are in the car. I have to go back outside. I'll wait
for the police there. Thank you so much."

"You're that Mrs. Fairchild who lives on the Point in the summer. Friends with the Marshalls."

It wasn't a question, but a statement of fact—and a vetting.

Faith nodded. "We're here for Christmas. My husband has
been ill and we came up here so he could rest."

This seemed like information the woman already had, which,
given the nature of the island grapevine, didn't surprise Faith.

"I like Christmas. Got my first present last night. My grandson,
same one, came by late—he knows I don't sleep much anymore—
and handed me one of those things you put your feet into. Water
bubbles around and my bunions feel a treat this morning."

Hard to think of a comment other than a murmured, "How
nice for you." Faith moved toward the door to the hallway. The
woman followed her.

"I'm Daisy Sanford, by the way," she said.

Ursula Rowe, the mother of Faith's friend and neighbor Pix
Miller, had once told Faith that you could figure out a woman's
age by her name, particularly with flower names. "Born sometime
in the twenties or thirties, although I hear they're coming back
into fashion now. But introduce me to an 'Iris,' 'Rose,' or 'Daisy'
and I'll be looking at a woman in her seventies or older."

Faith remembered the remark; this Daisy looked as if she'd
earned all her wrinkles over the course of at least seventy-five
years.

"Sorry to meet you under these circumstances." Faith was at
the front door. Daisy nodded.

"I knew something was wrong. Looks like we're heading toward a white Christmas for sure and that always fills the church-

yard. Should have gone out to check, but I promised my family I wouldn't tackle the walk without one of them being next to me. Did you know her?"

The girl's face was not one she would ever forget, but no, Faith didn't know her. Had not, she was almost certain, ever even seen her.

She shook her head. "She's young, no more than late teens or early twenties, and unless she worked someplace—waitressing at Lily's or in one of the stores open in the summer, I wouldn't have run across her anywhere."

People the girl's age tended to hang out on Main Street in Granville or in the old ball field also in Granville on summer nights—not places Faith frequented. If you drove by, you'd see the red glow from their cigarettes and maybe catch one of them heading for a car and a clandestine beer. There wasn't a whole lot for teenagers to do on the island.

"Why don't you send your little ones in here where it's warm? I baked this morning."

Faith had been aware of the aroma of bread and something sweet like molasses filling the kitchen. The offer was tempting, but she wanted to keep Ben and Amy close, speak to the police, and leave as fast as possible.

"Thank you, that's very kind, but I'm hoping this won't take long and I can get them home."

"Change your mind, just knock." Daisy sighed heavily. "There's going to be broken hearts on this island soon."

Someone's daughter, granddaughter, niece, cousin, friend—the web of connectedness on the island left almost no one untouched in good times and bad.

Faith saw the cruiser coming down the road and hastened across before her children could be startled. She was very happy to see that it was Sergeant Earl Dickinson in the driver's seat. The Fairchilds had known Earl since their first days on Sanpere and he was married to Faith's good friend Jill Merriwether, owner of the Blueberry Patch, a seasonal gift and book store in Sanpere Village.

She told the kids, whose mouths were stained bright red and green, everything was all right—that she just had to speak to Earl for a moment—and greeted him as he stepped out of the car, the little notebook he always carried flipped open to a blank page.

"Tell me what happened," he said in his calm voice, and Faith felt the full weight of the last half hour lift. It was such a relief to turn the whole thing over to him that she felt dizzy for a moment. She took a breath and started talking.

Once she'd finished, Earl said she could leave soon. He'd verify what she'd described. She showed him which were her footprints and he carefully placed his over them. He stood at the sleigh, then turned and shouted that she should go home. He'd call if he needed anything more from her. She'd slipped into the driver's seat and saw him talking into what looked like a walkie-talkie with a long antenna. She realized she'd forgotten to tell him about the photos, but she didn't want to get out of the car. In a very short time the scene would be photographed in much greater detail than she'd achieved, and right now, she had to tell her children why Earl was there.

"What's going on, Mom?" Ben's voice, which had recently started to travel up and down many octaves, sounded at the moment like a very little boy's. A very scared little boy.

She'd turned around and reached for both their hands.

"I'm sorry I had to leave you. I had to get the police to come immediately. There was a young woman in the sleigh who's had some sort of accident and is dead."

"Dead!" Amy had shrieked. "Was she all bloody?"

"No, honey," Faith said gently. "Nothing like that. I think we'll find that for whatever reason she climbed into the sleigh and—"

Ben interrupted. "Had a heart attack. I bet that's what happened. Like maybe she had this thing wrong since she was born and nobody knew it."

"Possibly." Faith could read her daughter's mind, though. "But usually people with congenital—that's what it's called if you have something from birth—conditions are aware they have them. Every year you go to Dr. Kane for your checkups. He knows what's going on in your bodies inside and out."

Faith could feel the muscles in Amy's little hand relax. Just the mention of the pediatrician's name had been enough. Amy adored him.

"But people on the island don't have good health care. You've said that yourself. Even with the Island Medical Center. Maybe she didn't get checkups. She could have had a heart condition and not known it." Ben was nothing if not stubborn. He always had been and adolescence was making it much worse. Faith feared the years to come would be a test of wills, particularly hers.

"It's possible, Ben." She turned back around and started the car. "Now what should we make Dad for dinner? Sonny told me he had brought in the shrimp and crab we bought at the market, so we know it's going to be especially tasty. Risotto? You can help me stir."

Both children were comfortable in the kitchen and catholic in their tastes. They'd gobble down a seafood risotto with as much pleasure as they'd inhaled the cupcakes. The tiny Maine shrimp and peekytoe crabmeat would make for a delicious risotto (see recipe, p. 245) and, paired with some steamed broccoli with a squeeze of Meyer lemon, would meet everyone's dietary needs. Plus risotto was comfort food for Faith; the creamy Arborio rice served the same purpose for her that mac 'n' cheese did for others.

They'd gone to bed early. This whole time on Sanpere had seen increasingly early lights-out. The kids hadn't whined once; tired from their days outdoors, they'd fallen into their parents' laid-back rhythm. Unlike in Aleford at the parsonage, the phone never rang interrupting meals—or sleep. It hadn't even rung the evening after Faith had discovered the body. She wasn't needed at present.

But the next morning there was a knock on the door.

It was Nan and Freeman Marshall, their nearest neighbors on the Point. Nan held a casserole and Freeman something wrapped in aluminum foil that looked very much like a pie. Older than the Fairchilds with children and grandchildren scattered across the island and several states, they'd nevertheless become close over the years. Refusing the job of caretaker, as he did for others, Freeman "kept his eye on things" when the Fairchilds weren't there, and they'd never had a problem with clammers tearing up the small meadow in the front of the house with their pickups or hunters breaking in looking for shelter—and a bottle or six-pack.

As she greeted them, Faith saw at once it was a more formal visit than usual. She called for Tom, who was upstairs reading. The kids were making yet another snow fort—this time back in the woods away from the shore. She knew it was a formal visit, because Freeman's hair was slicked back and he was wearing one of his Carhartt jackets that didn't smell like bait, over several flannel shirts. The top one was pressed. Nan had a bright blue fleece on that matched her eyes and the slight sheen in her white hair. Faith remembered that their daughter was working at Hair Extrordinaire across the bridge in Sedgwick and Nan had obviously been there recently—getting ready for the holidays. Faith was happy to see them. She was always happy to see them, but a little uneasy too. Freeman was one of the few fishermen who still had his boat in the water. Why wasn't he working today? It was sunny and milder than it had been the day before. The icicles hanging from the roof had been dripping steadily all morning.

Faith led the way toward the seating area, Tom came down, and everyone exchanged pleasantries. The casserole (scalloped potatoes and ham) and the pie (lemon meringue, Tom's favorite) had been handed over and Faith's thanks were genuine. Nan was one of the best cooks on Sanpere.

Then they came to the point.

"The girl you found; it was Norah Taft. Thought you might not have heard and that you'd want to know," Freeman said.

Faith realized that the girl's identity, or lack thereof, had indeed never been far from her thoughts. Taft wasn't an island name. Yet, from his tone of voice, it sounded as if Freeman had known her.

Tom reached over and took her hand.

"Her mother was a Prescott," Freeman continued. "Married someone from away and came back here after the divorce when Norah was fourteen or so. But we all knew her. She used to spend summers with her grandparents. Tiny little thing. No brothers or sisters, which is why Darlene—that's her mother—used to send her home. Plenty of cousins."

Nan's eyes were filled with tears. "She was a real favorite and the apple of her grandparents' eye. They were gone when she came back to live for good and maybe they could have helped. She wasn't the Norah we'd known. Angry at the world, especially her mom. Changed her name last year. We had to call her 'Zara.' Don't know where that came from. She started running away when she was fifteen, but she always came back. Until last summer, that is. No one's seen or heard from her since August. Never even started her senior year."

The only reference Faith knew to "Zara" was the Spanish-owned clothing outfit that had come under fire in 2007 for marketing a handbag with swastikas on it, then again several months later for a T-shirt with an update of the racist late-nineteenth-, early-twentieth-century golliwog figures. Either Norah Taft had come in contact with fashionistas or she'd simply liked the sound of the name.

"You were close to her," Tom said.

Freeman nodded, reached in his pocket for his red bandanna kerchief, and blew his nose loudly.

"As I say, we all knew her since she was born. She'd come to our house and make cookies with Nan and our grandkids. Took her out on the boat with me more than once. There wasn't an evil bone in her body. I don't know what happened between her and her dad, but she never mentioned him when she came back and we never asked."

"What were people saying? About the divorce? About why her mother came home?" Faith asked. She was sure they knew.

"The same old saw." Nan threw an apologetic look at Tom, indicating she wasn't lumping him in with this sorry group. "He'd found another woman and left them flat is what people said. To my knowledge, Norah never was in touch with him again."

A hard time to lose a parent under any circumstances, Faith thought. Norah would have been around Ben's age. With a foot in childhood and the other stepping toward adulthood, kids entering adolescence could easily slip into any number of crevasses—ones that could become permanent dwelling places.

"Where did she live?" Faith asked. "I don't remember ever running across her."

"Darlene's parents had a camp on Little Sanpere and they moved in there," Nan said. "It isn't much, but it has heat and plumbing."

Little Sanpere was a small island that was connected by a causeway to Sanpere, many times larger. The bridge that spanned Eggemoggin Reach stretched from Sedgwick to Little Sanpere, and people who lived on Sanpere, including the Fairchilds, generally thought of Little Sanpere as a place they quickly passed through on their way home. In turn, those who lived on Little Sanpere were a tight community, the same families occupying their land for generations.

"She worked at the day camp one, maybe two summers. You probably saw her there when you dropped the kids off or picked them up," Freeman continued.

Faith shook her head. "I don't remember seeing anyone that blond. She looks . . . looked Scandinavian."

"That was another new thing. 'Bout a year ago she did it herself with peroxide. Before that she was a redhead. Like a copper penny," Nan said.

A copper penny brightly shining in the morning or afternoon sun. Faith *had* seen her before. Seen her smiling face and watched the campers vie for her attention; try to stand next to her as they waited for a parent. She felt her own eyes fill with tears.

"Oh, Tom, you must remember her too. It was when Ben first started going."

"Is there anything we can do? Would it help if we went to see her mother?" Tom asked. He was squeezing Faith's hand harder now.

"Early days. Maybe in a while. Darlene's not in great shape. Blames herself," Freeman said.

Faith nodded. She'd blame herself too.

"Have the police determined the cause of death?" Tom asked.

There it was. The question that Faith had been both wanting and not wanting an answer to since she'd found the body, muffled against the cold, in the sleigh. The body, so cold that no carriage robe would ever warm it again.

Freeman stood up and walked over to the large windows.

"Been a funny winter so far. Plenty of snow, but not even the cove froze yet."

"It was drugs," Nan told them. "An overdose." She broke down completely and sobbed. "She had tracks up and down both arms. The syringe was right there in a bag. A heroin addict. That's what they're saying. Not even eighteen and hooked."

Faith got up and put her arms around her friend.

"I don't know what this world is coming to when children—she was still a child in my book—are in this much misery that they have to escape that way," Freeman said, turning away from the winter scene in front of him. "Come on now, mother, let's go home. We'll call you if there's anything new. Imagine there'll be a service. Darlene's a regular churchgoer."

At the door, Nan said, "We thought you'd want to know and better to hear it from us. You know what this island is like for gossip. But you put it out of your minds now. It was a tragedy just waiting to happen for a long time. We all knew that. You concentrate on getting better, Tom, and everybody having a good holiday. Remember, you're invited for Christmas dinner."

Faith smiled. After hearing about this festive gathering for years, being here for it was a lovely bonus. "We wouldn't miss it for the world. And you still haven't told me what to bring."

"Just yourselves is—" Nan started to speak, when Freeman interrupted.

"Some of that chocolate bread pudding stuff you gave us last summer would go down a treat," he said, rubbing his hands together and obviously picturing the groaning table. As they left, everyone brightened visibly at the prospect of being together for a happy occasion.

The empty mug in Faith's hand was stone-cold and she realized with a start that the room was cold too. Outside, the Christmas sky was still as bright as day. It was very late. Accidental death, or maybe suicide. That's what the coroner had ruled. In the end, Norah's mother had decided she couldn't take a large funeral—the entire island had been in shock at Norah's death, especially the kids her age, and they would all turn out. A fund had been established in Norah's memory for more drug abuse prevention and awareness in the schools. Darlene had been quoted in the island paper and the *Ellsworth American*—"I don't want any parent to ever go through what I am going through and will for the rest of my life. I would have traded it for my Norah's if God had let me."

God hadn't, and Faith was reminded of what the late Reverend William Sloane Coffin had said after the accidental death of his twenty-four-year-old son: "God's heart was the first of all our hearts to break." As she trudged up the stairs to bed, Faith knew that when Norah slipped away, God's was the first of all those broken hearts Daisy Sanford mentioned.

Miraculously the kids slept until six thirty before jumping on their parents' bed and urging them to wake up to see what Santa had brought. Ben had managed to keep the secret of the jolly old fellow's true identity, whether out of real regard for his sister or to save as a weapon for when she did something really outrageous such as entering his room without permission; Faith didn't care—just let Amy keep believing a while longer. Last night in a whisper before sleep, her daughter had confessed her fear that Santa might not know they were in Maine. He might think they were in their house in Aleford as usual. Faith had reassured her of Saint Nick's omniscience; he'd always find them.

They'd had juice, coffee for Tom and especially Faith, plus the cardamom raisin bread that Faith always made for Christmas morning. They were due at the Marshalls' at noon, so they skipped a big breakfast, just eating some yogurt and fruit, with a sprinkling of granola, after the stockings had been emptied and the gifts beneath the tree opened. The phone rang at nine.

"It must be Granny and Grandpa!" Ben was up like a flash. It would be Tom's parents; Faith's would be involved with church services.

"Just a minute," she heard him say. It must not be her in-laws. "I'll get her. Oh, Merry Christmas."

Ben handed her the phone and said, "It's for you, Mom." He hunched his shoulders and raised his arms. Not somebody whose voice he recognized.

"It's Mary Bethany, Faith."

CHAPTER 2

"I'm so sorry to bother you. You must be in the midst of celebrating with your family."

"With children my children's ages, the celebrating was hours ago and we're not doing anything special now, Mary."

It wasn't a bother, but as Faith spoke, she was wondering why Mary was calling—and on Christmas morning of all times. They weren't close friends. In fact, it was her impression that Mary didn't have many—or any—close friends. The woman was probably alone today, on Christmas, and Faith promptly decided to invite her to join them. There was always room for one more at the Marshalls' table.

"We're going to Nan and Freeman's for Christmas dinner. Won't you come with us? I know for a fact that there's enough food to feed the entire island and then some."

"That's very kind of you, but I'm afraid I can't get away."

"Oh, Mary, the goats will be all right for a few hours," Faith said. It suddenly seemed important that she come. Faith didn't like the idea of Mary all by herself in that isolated house on Christmas—or any day, for that matter, Mary had told Faith that Nubian goats were very needy and got upset if they were left for too long. It apparently affected their milk. "I should really have started with a Swiss breed, something like White Saanens, much more placid," she'd told Faith. "But my first two were Nubians and here I am."

"We'd be happy to come get you," Faith urged and asked about the only thing she could think of that would keep Mary away. "Is there a problem with one of the herd?"

"It's not the goats," Mary said. "It's, well, it's something else. Faith. I know this is a lot to ask, but is there any way you could come over here for a little while?"

Startled by the unusual request, Faith heard herself answer, "Of course. When would you like me?"

"As soon as possible," Mary said, hanging up.

Faith stood a moment with the receiver still in her hand, thinking about Mary. The older woman lived by herself on her family farm, raising the goats, growing some vegetables, and making superlative goat cheese. The cheese had been their initial point of contact. Tasting some at a friend's house, Faith had tracked Mary down—that in itself hadn't been easy. Then it had taken a while to exchange more than a brief hello, thank you, and good-bye with Mary. Faith had felt as if she were befriending a woodland creature, luring a doe into the open. But Mary was proud of her cheese—and her herd. That was what drew her out. Over the last few summers, Faith had helped her with some new recipes— herbed chèvre, chèvre with sundried tomatoes, and a delectable cranberry-honey mixture. Noting the state of Mary's finances— the woman had once confided she couldn't afford to keep her house as warm as the barn and might start sleeping there in the winter—Faith had encouraged her to sell her cheeses more widely than at the weekly summer farmers' markets on the island and in Blue Hill. Mary was now shipping cheese down to the Portland Public Market and a few closer to home most of the year.

When they'd arrived last week, one of the first things Faith had done was drive to the farm to get some cheese. Tom was on a low-fat diet, but Faith had gone online and discovered that there was some evidence that goat's milk actually reduced cholesterol and had all sorts of other healthy properties. Even if this wasn't true, salad with *chèvre chaud*—warm rounds of the cheese—was so tasty, his spirits would soar. Tom had confessed early on that he'd taken his health for granted and at times this betrayal by what he referred to as his "well-oiled machine" caused some depression.

Mary had been very sympathetic when she'd heard about Tom's illness—and comforting. "One of the Sanfords had the very same thing and was back fishing before the season ended." She'd also pressed various rose-hip concoctions on Faith, swearing that, in addition to any and all goat products, they could cure everything from "a sprained ankle to a broken heart." This was the way Mary spoke—slightly quirky and always direct. She was a reader. Books were stacked all over the parts of the house Faith had seen—the kitchen and a peep into the adjoining parlor. She was sure the rest looked the same. The two women often exchanged titles and sometimes the books themselves. It was another bond. Over the years, Faith had become very fond of Mary and wondered what her story was. The woman never talked about her personal life, and what little Faith knew had been gleaned from remarks others had made.

Certainly there was an underlying sadness to Mary Bethany's life. Didn't she need something, or rather someone, besides her books and her goats? Had she had it and lost it?

Faith replaced the receiver, thinking how human the goat in the background had sounded. Almost like a baby crying.

Mary Bethany had not slept since she'd found Christopher in her barn. At first, she'd determinedly blocked out all thoughts of what to do except take care of his immediate needs. She changed his wet diaper and burst out laughing as he sprayed her before she could get the new one on. His skin was softer than any kid's fleece. Soft—everything about him was soft from the top of his head to the soles of his feet. How could finger- and toenails be so small, so perfect? He curled his fist around her finger and made that soft mewling sound again. So different from her demanding nannies. So different from the cries of enraged infants she'd occasionally heard in the aisles of the Granville Market.

Lacking any alternative, she had filled one of the bottles with goat's milk, warmed it, and watched in delight as he greedily sucked it dry. Mary prided herself not only on her cheese but her milk. It was always sweet and fresh. Two lactose-intolerant cus-tomers swore they couldn't tell the difference from cow's milk, as if that were the standard. Cow's milk—Mary thought it should be the other way around. She would never have taken up with cows. Much too bovine. No personality. She'd known cows.

It was only when Christopher had once again fallen asleep—as she rocked him gently in the chair her mother may have rocked her in—that Mary began to consider her alternatives. Happily, calling the authorities was not a choice. There were no authorities to call. She doubted the Staties would be down patrolling Sanpere on Christmas Eve.

She was happy about this for several reasons, first and fore-most being an innate disinclination to "open up a can of worms." They'd bring in social workers, put Christopher in a foster home, everything his mother was clearly trying to avoid by leaving him in Mary's barn. Mary had no idea who the woman could possibly be, but she did know one thing. Christopher's mother had chosen Mary, and she had chosen her because she thought Christopher was in danger. "Keep him safe," she'd written. The baby was a trust, a sacred trust, and Mary Bethany was not going to betray that. Let it be according to her wish.

But what to do? Even though she rarely saw other people—only at the bank, the market, or if she happened to be in the shed when they came to buy cheese or milk—there was no way she could pass the baby off as her own. Besides her age and the lack of any physical evidence—Mary had always been as slender as a reed— the notion of Mary with a lover would be greeted not only with skepticism but derision. She could hear them now: "Mary Bethany pregnant? Maybe by one of the goats."

Mary was born on the island, but the Bethanys were from away. Her parents had come to Sanpere when her father got a job as a welder at the shipyard after the war. Her mother's family had come from Italy and endowed Mary with the dark hair and Mediterranean features that she shared with others on Sanpere. But their looks had come down from the Italian stonecutters who had arrived in the late nineteenth and early twentieth centuries to work in the now abandoned granite quarries. Mary's grandparents had landed in New York and worked in the garment business— the wrong kind of Italians for Sanpere. True, Mary's father's family were Mainers, but from the north, Aroostook County—potato farmers. They weren't fishermen. Her father had learned his trade in the service, met her mother, Anne, at a USO dance, and when the war was over, they'd ended up on Sanpere not for any particular reason, but because people have to end up somewhere. Without the kinship network that was as essential and basic to Sanpere as the aquifer and ledges the entire island rested on, Mary and her older sister, Martha, were always viewed as outsiders.

"If you invite her to your party, I'm not coming! She's weird and you know it. Besides, she spends so much time in that barn of theirs with the cows, we could all catch hoof and mouth."

"You stop, Patsy. I almost peed my pants last time you got me laughing about Mary. I told you I didn't want to have her any more

than you do, but Mumma says I have to. You know what she's like when she sets her mind to something."

"I'm with Patsy, Vi. It's your birthday. Can't you tell your mother that it will ruin your day if Mary comes?"

"I've told her and told her, but she just about took a switch to me. Said I was cruel and that I should think of Mary Bethany like some kind of poor little animal."

"Well, she got the animal part right."

The girls started to giggle uproariously at this last remark. Soon one grabbed at her crotch and said, "I got to go; you've done it again!" They streaked across the playground back toward the school. Recess was almost over anyway.

High up in the branches of the old oak shadowing the packed dirt and a rusted swing set that made up the playground, Mary Bethany tried to decide whether she should go back to class and finish out the day or head home. She closed the book she'd been reading—the tree was one of her favorite places for privacy—and weighed the pros and cons. If she headed for home now, she could take the long way by the shore and maybe find some sand dollars bleached by the sun or some razor clamshells. She had a whole string of them hung in garlands on a big birch in her secret place back in the woods. It was as far away from her house as she could get and still be on their land. When the wind blew, the long shells made a soft clatter that she pretended were real chimes.

But if she didn't go back, the girls would win—again. They wouldn't know they'd won. They hadn't looked up and seen her in the tree. Not that they would have cared. Not that they would have said anything different. No, they wouldn't know they'd driven her away again. But she would.

Tucking the book, one from the library, carefully under her arm, Mary climbed down with ease. She was tall for her age and athletic—another thing her fellow sixth-graders liked to mock. "If

it wasn't for those bitty titties, Mary could pass for a boy any day,"
she'd heard Patsy say more than once.

She looked out at the ocean. The school had a clear view of
Granville's bustling waterfront. The men were bringing in the day's
catch. With a sigh, she turned and trudged toward the worn stairs
that led into school. There had never really been a choice. She wasn't
about to let them control what she did.

Up in the tree listening to them, she'd had a strange feeling.
Almost like she didn't exist. They were talking about her and saying her name, but she didn't know who that person was. And it
had come to her that she didn't know who that person wasn't either.
Who was Mary Bethany anyway?

Her sister, Martha, knew who she was. Always had. She'd left
school and the whole entire island the minute she'd turned sixteen.
That had been three years ago when Mary was only nine. Martha
had been a bossy big sister, always after Mary to keep her side of
the room tidy and not bring in any of what Martha called trash and
Mary called her treasures—a nest that had fallen to the ground,
pieces of beach glass and bits of china dug from an old cellar hole.
Each week, Martha had heated water on the stove, filled the big
washbasin, and scrubbed Mary so hard, her skin turned bright red
and her scalp stung. After Martha left, Mary sometimes forgot all
about the ritual, and her mother never reminded her. It wasn't the
kind of thing she did. Mrs. Bethany put food on the table three times
a day, did her chores in the garden, and saw to her chickens. Martha
and Mary had had to keep their clothes clean for as long as Mary
could remember. After Martha was gone, this was another thing she
sometimes forgot too.

In the summer it didn't matter. Nothing mattered during the
summer—that glorious gift of total freedom. Mary swam in the
ocean and rinsed the salt off in the warm fresh-water stream that ran
beside the meadow marking the end of their property. They had a
saltwater farm, right on the sea; but nature had decided to give them

a bonus—the wide stream and the well it fed provided them with a seemingly endless supply of pure, sweet water.

Martha had come home only once, two years after she left. She'd announced she was getting married to a Mr. Hutchins and they'd be living near his people in New Hampshire. Before she left, she took Mary to Ellsworth and bought her a set of underpants with the names of the week on them, two skirts, a pair of jeans, several tops, and a beautiful white blouse with lace on the collar. Also new shoes, sneakers, and socks. Mary had been dazed by the sudden influx of garments and even more dazed by the information Martha imparted about a "friend coming to visit" each month one of these days, by and by. When the "friend" duly arrived, Mary had been profoundly grateful to bossy Martha and had thought of writing to her, but they'd been sticking to cards at their birthdays and Christmas, so she'd left it at that. Martha had also yelled at her the moment she saw her about those weekly baths, demanded she go scrub herself clean, and Mary had taken that to heart too. Vi and the others had no right to say Mary was dirty now.

She missed her sister. She missed her soft breathing in the other bed at night. The bed was still in the room, but empty and destined to stay so. Mary had heard her mother refer to Mary as a "mistake" often enough to know there wouldn't be another one to join her.

Martha would have known what to do about Vi, Patsy, and the other girls in Mary's class. The island was a pretty small place and there weren't a whole lot of choices when it came to friends, especially since each grade didn't have many students. When Mary had been little, she'd played with Doug Harvey, whose family owned the adjoining farm, but starting in first grade they'd been teased so much about being boyfriend and girlfriend that they had barely spoken to each other for years.

When Martha left, Mary had begged her father to let her have one of the barn kittens as a house cat, but he'd been firm. They were farm animals same as the rest and their sole job was to keep *the rodent population down. When the feline numbers got too big, he'd take a litter, put them in a sack with some rocks, and throw them into the cove. Mary had watched and waited. The next time she saw him head in that direction with his cargo, she'd followed, silently slipping through the pines. As soon as he'd disappeared back up the path, she'd run straight into the freezing water, dove under, and grabbed at the burlap. She sputtered to shore and cut the string with the penknife she'd brought. Miraculously, one of the tiny creatures was still alive and she'd put it under her shirt for warmth and gone straight into the woods to her fort—a deep fissure between two granite ledges that she'd roofed with blowdowns and pine boughs. She knew what to do and fed the kitten milk with an eyedropper. Later she'd taken the drowsy ball of fluff up to her room and kept him there until he was weaned. Him. The kitten turned out to be a he and she named him Pip, because she had great expectations for him. Mary was glad Pip was a he and not a she. A she would have had kittens and then what would Mary have done? She wished she could have kept Pip in her room longer, but she didn't dare— although, since her parents slept off the kitchen, there was only a slim chance they'd find out. The upstairs of the house wasn't heated. In the winter Martha and Mary had slept under a mountain of quilts, often waking to frost on the inside of the window. But a slim chance was still a chance and Mary knew what would happen to Pip if he was discovered.*

So, she'd had to move Pip outdoors, bringing milk when she could and hoping he'd survive on what he could find in the woods. He grew into a fine orange tiger and always came when she called, leaping at her and rubbing up against her leg, leaving his scent, marking her for him to find again and again. When she stroked him, he purred so loudly he sounded like her father's table saw.

Late that fall, she'd carried him to the cat lady's house. She had a name, but everybody just called her "the cat lady," because she must have had more than thirty of them. Mary had knocked on her door, opened it, and pushed Pip in. He was promptly greeted by a chorus of yowls. Then she dashed to the side of the house and stayed there, looking around the corner from behind a lilac bush, until she was sure the cat lady hadn't taken an unaccountable dislike to Pip, tossing him out the way he'd come in.

After that Mary didn't rescue another kitten, another Pip. It wasn't for lack of desire—she couldn't bear to give one up again.

The birthday party. Before Martha left home, Mary had always been invited to the parties of the girls in her class. Wonderful parties. Cakes with pink sugar roses, balloons, and always a little bag filled with candy and a prize to take home. She still had a barrette with a butterfly on it that had been in one of those bags. There had been games and she'd been good at them—three-legged races, pin the tail on the donkey. She'd never had her own party, but one year Martha and a boyfriend who had a car took her to the Tastee-Freez off-island for ice cream on her birthday. On the way back they'd stopped at a yard sale and that's where Mary got her Charles Dickens books. Martha had said she could have fifty cents to spend on anything she wanted. The set of books was a dollar, but Martha talked the woman down, pointing out nobody else but "my nutty little sister" would want the "moldy old things."

Once Martha was gone, the party invitations had stopped coming. A lot of things stopped. There was no one to watch the Fourth of July parade with or the fireworks over the harbor later that night. Mr. and Mrs. Bethany weren't interested in things like that. "A farmer can't take a day off, no matter how independent he is," her father had said, which was as close as he got to making a joke. Her mother said nothing.

So Mary was used to not being invited places. When she'd collected the mail from their box on the main road the other day on her way home from school, she'd been startled to see a small, bright purple envelope with her name on it in unfamiliar script writing. Martha always printed. When she opened it, she knew immediately

Vi's mother must have made her send it. Even before overhearing the girls talk, Mary had planned to make a polite refusal. She just hadn't been able to find a time yet when the house was empty, so she could use the phone. Most days it seemed no one was around, busy outdoors. Now when she had a call to make, either her mother or father was always in the kitchen. She was going to tell Vi's mother she was needed at the farm. That she appreciated the thought, but she was needed.

Mary had repeated the phrase to herself several times. She liked the sound of it. "I'm needed at home."

As it had turned out, Mary *was* needed at home. Her father's first heart attack came just as she'd begun to think she could move off-island, get some kind of job, and take courses at UMaine. She'd decided to be a teacher. A teacher who would treat all her students with the same kindness and respect—no favorites and no scapegoats. She wouldn't teach on the island—they wouldn't hire her anyway, not Mary Bethany, the outsider. She'd pictured a classroom of maybe third-graders up where her father was from. They'd gone there once when she had been about seven. The potato fields were in bloom and she thought the wide openness of it all was beautiful She'd miss the ocean, but it would be a change. A good change.

His second attack was much worse than the first and he'd had to have an operation in Bangor. After that, there was no question of working. He sold his cows and most of the farm equipment, and leased the fields to the Harveys. He seemed to disappear right before Mary's eyes, shrinking into his clothes until he hardly looked like a grown man. He'd never had time to get interested in any hobbies and hadn't been a reader. He sat in the parlor and watched the television Martha had brought with her when she'd come to see them after he was released from the hospital. "It's cheaper than a nursing home," she'd told Mary, who had been surprised by the gift. They'd never had a television and her mother had always made disparaging remarks about the crop of antennae that sprouted from island roofs. "Put him in front of it in the morning and turn it off when you put him to bed at night," Martha instructed.

It was a depressing notion, but Mary had found that Martha had been right and her father was content to sit and watch day in and day out. He even seemed to enjoy certain shows, occasionally shouting out answers when *Wheel of Fortune* was on.

Anne Bethany's schedule continued without the slightest variation. She rose before dawn, tended her chickens and the garden in season. She made meals her husband didn't eat. She was in bed and asleep at eight thirty. She wasn't interested in becoming a nurse and made it clear to Mary that taking care of her father was her job—a job in exchange for room and board now that she was an adult.

Mary had had no choice, and wouldn't have abandoned her parents and the farm even if she had. Martha called once in a while, but after that one trip, kept her distance.

So, Mary had stayed. Maybe if she had been more outgoing, more self-confident like Martha, she would have fit into island life better—or had the guts to leave, parents or no parents. The years went by and late one afternoon her father died quietly in front of the TV. Mary had gone in to offer him some broth. Vanna White was turning over *T*s.

The farm had been paid off a few years before Mr. Bethany's illness, so Mary and her mother had had enough to get by, especially after Mary started running a small B and B during the summer months to pay the mounting shorefront taxes. Her mother had taken her father's death as a personal affront and, after several years of intense anger, joined him, presumably to give him what for. That had been ten years ago.

Mary was alone. There was no lover past, present, or future. When she considered the complications love presented—gleaned from her reading and from observing those around her—she was usually glad to have been spared the bother. But it did mean she couldn't pass the baby off as hers.

Gradually, as the sky lightened, she had come up with a plan. Easy enough to say that Christopher was her grandnephew, that his mother couldn't take care of him. Although Martha hadn't been on the island since her mother's funeral, it was well known that she had had ten children herself and that those ten had been equally fruitful and multiplied. Mary invented a rich tale of a young niece with three children already, abandoned by her good-for-nothing cheater of a husband, driving through the night to leave the baby after calling her aunt in desperation.

"Could you take him for a while? Just till I get my feet on the ground?"

Mary had enjoyed rehearsing to herself—"She was so upset, I'm surprised she remembered to bring little Christopher."

She'd tell her neighbor Arlene and ask her to pick up some baby supplies the next time she went off-island to Ellsworth. Arlene had two grandchildren she thought hung the moon. She brought them over to play with the goats when they visited every August. Arlene would be a big help. And since she also had a big mouth, Mary wouldn't have to tell the story to anyone else.

That settled, Mary had turned her thoughts to the rest of the plan. And the rest of the plan had meant calling Faith Fairchild. She watched the sun come up, waiting for the right time.

Faith knocked on Mary's back door. Few people used their front doors on Sanpere—or anywhere else in New England to Faith's knowledge. It was a mystery why they bothered putting them on houses at all. Using Mary's front door other than during the winter months was also complicated by the tangle of lilac and rose bushes that had grown up over the granite stoop.

Mary opened the door and slipped out. Faith was puzzled. From the urgency in Mary's voice, she had expected to be ushered immediately in and told whatever Mary thought was important enough to pull someone away from hearth and home on Christmas Day. She'd said it wasn't the goats. What else could it be? Mary didn't have anything else to worry about. Or, Faith thought with sudden apprehension, it might be Mary herself. This must be it. She was ill. Cancer. She had cancer. And she'd just heard yesterday.

"Faith, I don't know how to put this any other way. I want to tell you a secret."

Mary's face, although slightly anxious, didn't look distraught. Or terminal. Faith felt anticipation begin to replace her fears. She loved secrets.

"But I have to have your absolute word that you won't tell anyone else. Not even your husband."

Husbands were exempt from the not-telling-secrets rule, but maybe Mary didn't know that, not having one herself.

"Tom's a minister. He'd keep anything you tell me totally confidential. He has to or they take away his collar or robes or something."

Mary folded her arms across her chest. She was the kind of woman who looks so ordinary that you have trouble placing her— did I go to elementary school with her? See her in the waiting room at the bus station in Bangor? Talk to her in line at Marden's, the big discount store in Ellsworth? Vague familiarity at best. Now Mary stood transformed by the determined gesture and defiant expression on her face. This woman was a woman you'd remember.

"No Tom. If you can't agree, I can't tell you." She paused. "And I'm sorry I called you out all this way for nothing." Mary's farm backed onto Eggemoggin Reach. By water, or as the gull flies, it wasn't far from the Fairchilds'. By land, it took a good fifteen minutes.

"It's not a crime or anything like that, is it? I mean, of course you haven't murdered anyone." Faith thought she'd better ask. It was no never mind to her, but Tom tended to take a dim view of her involvement in these things.

"No crime has been committed to my knowledge," Mary said firmly. "But you don't have to agree. Go into the shed. There's some fresh cheese. Take one home with you for your trouble."

"Oh, Mary, of course I agree. You have my word." Instinctively Faith put out her hand and Mary shook it, opening the door wider.

Faith stepped into the kitchen, thinking they should have mixed spit or pricked their fingers with a safety pin. But she didn't think for long; she simply reacted and was on her knees by the basket instantly. Christopher was wide awake; his dark eyes shone up at her and his mouth curved in what was definitely a smile. They weren't supposed to do this until they were older, but both of Faith's babies had smiled from birth—and recognized her face, despite what the experts said.

"Where on earth did this beautiful baby come from?"

"I found him in the barn last night when I went to do the milking. His name is Christopher."

"In the barn! Christopher! Was he in the manger? Any visits from angels lately?" It was too much.

Mary grinned. "And I'm a virgin too. You can hold him if you want. He's a hungry little fellow and I was just going to warm a bottle."

Faith was only too happy to comply. She adored babies, especially other people's at this point in her life.

"Sit down in the rocker and I'll tell you everything I know, which is not much. And I'll tell you why I wanted you to come.

"I couldn't involve anyone on the island. It would be too dangerous for the baby. His mother obviously brought him here because she knew how isolated it is—still, there is the bridge, and word could spread to the mainland easy enough."

The Sanpere Bridge across Eggemoggin Reach connecting the island to the mainland had been a WPA project, a graceful suspension bridge that looked from a distance as if a particularly talented child had constructed it from an Erector set. For many on the island, it was still a bone of contention. Joe Sanford, age ninety, had never been across. "Never had a reason. Everything I need is here." But others found it pretty handy, especially before the Island Medical Center was built and the closest health care was in Blue Hill. A new generation of bridge haters had recently grown up, as wealthy off-islanders began to build second homes similar to Newport's "cottages." These people wanted to preserve Sanpere in aspic. In other words, "the last person across always wants to pull up the bridge behind him."

Mary was right not to involve anyone on Sanpere, even with a blood oath. There were no secrets on the island, and the bridge made sure they traveled.

"But I can't find his mother by myself. Aside from taking care of him, I can't—"

Faith finished for her. "Leave the nannies. Besides needing your company, they haven't been taught to milk themselves yet. So, very fortunately I'm here for a while."

Mary looked a bit embarrassed. "I'd heard about that business with the real estate man who was found murdered by the lighthouse and how you figured out who did it." Several summers ago, Faith had found a corpse while walking along the shore near Sanpere's lighthouse. The death appeared to be accidental, then more "accidents" occurred until Faith untangled the threads leading to the killer.

"This isn't like that," Mary said, "but I thought you might be able to help me find out who his mother is and why she left him here."

Faith studied Mary's face. Her normally forgettable face—a plain, pleasant face, rather flat and with the look of one of those antique Dutch wooden dolls. But today it wasn't normal. Faith had never seen Mary look so excited. Not even when one of her does had quintuplets the spring before last.

"But why? Why do you want to find her? To give the baby back?"

Mary was horrified. "Oh, no, not to give him back."

"Then why don't you just keep him? Your little grandnephew," Faith said.

Mary had been through this the night before many times. Just as she had debated back and forth whether to call Faith. She had changed her mind about the latter so many times that she still wasn't completely sure that it was the real Faith in front of her or the one she had conjured up and talked to during the wee hours.

"I think she's in trouble. She must be in trouble; otherwise she wouldn't have left him here. And I feel that I have to find her. It's hard to explain. It just doesn't seem fair to Christopher either. To have her simply disappear. What would I tell him when he was older? I'd have to tell him. Too horrible to find out when he's grown that everything he thought was real wasn't."

Faith had thought this was what Mary would say. It was what she herself would do. Besides, Mary would be in a precarious legal position. They hadn't mentioned it, but they both knew it. There hadn't been any birth certificate in the basket—or adoption papers to sign.

What Faith didn't ask Mary—and wouldn't ask—was, "How will you feel if she wants him back?"

Faith decided to call home. She needed to stay longer. When she'd left the house, Ben had been assembling some kind of LEGO for geniuses. Amy was spreading pinecones with peanut butter and rolling them in birdseed, planning to hang them in the firs outside the cottage as a Yule treat for the birds. Tom had been dozing by the woodstove with the latest Peter Abrahams in his lap. Still, Faith thought she'd better check in and see whether anyone minded if she stayed for another thirty minutes or so. The food was ready to go to the Marshalls' and they weren't due there until noon. Tom answered. Reminding herself that she'd kept secrets from him before—and always with the best of intentions—Faith told him Mary's story. Literally Mary's story, the one fabricated for public consumption. Tom immediately said there was no need for her to come home yet. Their conversation was so brief that Faith was pretty sure he'd picked up the book and was eager to get back to the page-turner.

"Okay, what can we figure out from this stuff?" she asked, spreading the contents of the baby's basket on the enamel-topped kitchen table. Mary's circa 1949 kitchen was currently back in vogue. Unchanged—as if it had been transported intact like Julia Child's to the Smithsonian. Reproducing what Mary took completely for granted would cost more than all the goat cheese she could sell in her lifetime. Many, many more dollars than those stuck in the Hellmann's mayonnaise jar left so trustingly on top of the refrigerator in the shed.

The basket itself, although a roomy one, was unremarkable. You saw stacks of them at Pier 1—or rummage sales. Baskets and mugs—that was what future archaeologists would find in our middens, Faith had often observed as these ubiquitous items arrived for First Parish's annual May Market sale. The red bow on the handle was the kind usually found attached to wreaths and the wire was threaded through a small white cardboard tag with Mary's name written on it in block letters.

She set the basket aside. Mary had put a pillow in what Faith recognized as an antique bread trough—where dough was put to rise and definitely an item a collector would covet. The pillow was covered with a quilt and Christopher now reposed on top of that under the afghan that had accompanied him.

His mother had packed three sleepers; Faith picked each one up separately. Then she examined the snowsuit.

"Pretty generic. Not Baby Dior or Hanna Andersson—or even Baby Gap. Therefore, we're not talking money here, although . . ." Faith gestured to the stacks of bills. "There's certainly money here. The clothes are new; they haven't been washed, so that tells us she didn't buy used baby clothes at a thrift store or get them passed down to her. But they're not recognizable brands, so she could have picked them up anywhere."

Mary cocked her head to one side, looking from the baby to the clothing. "No other children and no family involved. And she wanted brand-new clothes for Christopher."

Faith nodded and said, "She does have a computer, though—or access to one."

"How can you tell?" Mary asked.

"The note's a computer printout. Not typed on a typewriter. Much smoother."

"I thought the wording of the note might mean something," Mary said, picking it up. "Not the 'Keep him safe' part, although since she wrote that first I'm sure it means she thinks or knows he's in danger—but the 'Raise him to be a good man' part. Sounds like she hasn't had much luck there—or worse."

"I'd guess worse," Faith said. "It sounds like Christopher's father is not her idea of a model father figure. Maybe not her own father either. Or it could be her father who is the ideal, but then why wouldn't she go to him for help, or her mother, for that matter?"

"Maybe both passed away?" Mary handed the note to Faith. "She didn't sign it. Just stopped writing. Do you think she was interrupted or was it that she couldn't think of any way to finish it?"

"Either or neither," said Faith. "But she has to be someone you know, Mary. Your name was on the basket and in the letter. Plus she knew you had a barn and kept goats—knew your routine, that you'd be out to milk them at six. She wasn't taking any chances that the baby wouldn't be found quickly."

"I've been going through all this since I found him, believe me. And I can't think who she could be."

"And you didn't hear a car? Or notice footprints in the snow?"

Mary shook her head. "She's a smart one. I figure she stepped in the ones I made earlier. What puzzles me, though, is that I didn't hear the nannies. They can raise quite a hubbub if a stranger comes near."

"Which further suggests it's someone you—and the blessed goats—know."

Faith put the clothes down. She had to get going soon.

"What else?" she wondered aloud. "The afghan—exquisitely handmade. But it doesn't tell us anything except she's a good crocheter or went to some kind of fair that had a handwork table."

"My neighbor Arlene could read it like a book. Tell us where the yarn came from, who does that kind of stitch—at least on the island. Maybe we can think of a way to show it to her without having her get suspicious."

"The cloth diapers suggest she's pretty green."

"You mean inexperienced?" Mary asked.

Faith laughed. "No, as in environmentally friendly, ecoaware. No disposables, but washable cloth diapers."

"A tree hugger. Well, I'm with her on that one. Easy enough to wash diapers."

"Wait and see. The jury's still out on whether you use more resources washing the cloth ones than those other diapers consume. And they do cut down on diaper rash. I know how much time you spend tending your herd, but babies are even more work than your nannies."

Mary doubted this, but she was on shaky ground here.

"Computer access, environmentalist, young—that's a logical

presumption—and can't keep her baby. This all says 'student' to me." Faith was feeling quite Holmesian and wished there had been a bit more evidence such as cigar ash or mud from a shoe, so she could say that the young woman had been in Morocco recently, purchasing smokes at a stall in the bazaar from a red-haired man with a limp named Abdul.

Hair!

"Are there any strands of hair on the blanket—or on Christopher himself?"

"How stupid. There was one and I forgot to mention it. It's dark like mine, or like mine used to be." Mary was starting to go gray. "It's not mine, though, because it's long. Not Christopher's either, but the same color." Mary's hair was sensibly short. She cut the bangs herself and exchanged cheese for a trim from one of her customers who'd worked as a beautician before moving to Sanpere. The name of her former salon was Curl Up and Dye. Mary couldn't decide whether it was funny or sad.

"Well, we've certainly narrowed it down. A young female student with long dark hair," Faith said dejectedly.

"It does seem impossible," Mary agreed.

But Faith was nowhere near giving up.

"Don't say that. We've barely scratched the surface. What about the money? Where would a student come up with this kind of money? Have you counted it?"

"There's fifty thousand dollars in one-hundred-dollar bills."

Faith's mouth dropped open.

"As soon as I leave, you have to hide it. You should have done it already."

Mary nodded in agreement. "I have the perfect place. I'm going to—"

"Don't tell me. I don't know why, but it's better if just one of us knows."

"A student," Mary mused. "Unless she comes from a very rich

family with ready access to a trust fund—and then maybe she would have bought more expensive baby clothes—there's only one thing I can think of that brings in that kind of money for someone her age."

"Drugs?" Faith had been thinking the same thing since she'd first seen the stacks of bills. And these thoughts had taken her back to last Wednesday, back to the body in the sleigh. Was Christopher's mother an addict like young Norah Taft? Another victim? The baby looked healthy—blooming with health—but what problems might await Mary further down the road?

"I heard," Mary said softly, "about your finding that girl . . ."

Faith put her hand on Mary's arm. "We have another girl to find now."

Christopher was awake. Mary realized he would want to be fed. It had amazed her to watch the way he moved from light to deep sleep to short periods of consciousness when he was hungry. She'd always thought it must be hard for her kids to leave a doe's nice warm womb and it was obviously the same for babies.

"I know you have to get going, but could you stay a few minutes more and give him a bottle while I check on the herd?"

Faith picked up the baby, softly stroking his sleek dark hair. "My pleasure."

On the way to the barn, Mary chided herself. She'd been so wrapped up in Christopher, she'd been neglecting the nannies. They were such social creatures. Her old dog had died last spring and she hadn't gotten around to getting another. The goats seemed to miss his visits—and the presence of the wild goose that had made a nest in their pen, laid her eggs, raised the goslings, and then vanished.

She wasn't worried that the herd would be cold. In their own inimitable way, they didn't mind lower temperatures or snow, but they hated rain and hated drafts even more. She'd have to make sure no wind was getting through any chinks in the boards.

When Mary returned, Faith gave Christopher's chubby little cheek a last kiss and reluctantly relinquished him.

"I wish I could stay," she said. "But I'll be back as soon as I can. And call me at the Marshalls' if you need to."

The two women looked at each other. If Mary had to call for help, Faith knew it wouldn't be for Dr. Spock–like advice. The scene in front of her could have illustrated his or any number of baby books. Mary was tightly swaddling the baby in a flannel blanket she'd made by cutting up one of her nightgowns. The rocker was waiting by the warm stove.

But the something-wrong-with-this-picture was the mound of cash on the kitchen table. Cash that Faith had a strong feeling didn't lawfully belong to Christopher's mother. And the real owner wasn't going to waste any time looking for it. Looking for it all over the great state of Maine.

CHAPTER 3

Miriam opened her eyes and promptly closed them again. The sun streaming in through the broken window shade resembled a klieg light trained on the red carpet. The simple act of opening and closing her lids set the full force of what had been a dull ache across her forehead free to pound her entire skull. She needed to get some Tylenol. Much Tylenol. And water. Her tongue somehow managed to feel smooth and sticky at the same time. It had lodged itself behind a molar, choking her slightly.

She had the mother of all hangovers.

Scenes from last night cartwheeled uneasily across her brain. Her eyes flew open. It was her room, thank God—and she was alone. Even better, fully clothed. She closed her eyes once more—in weariness now. The weariness that had been her constant companion for months. Last night all that alcohol hadn't made the slightest dent in it, despite her best efforts. She was owed, she'd told herself as she'd pushed open the door of the bar down the street from the apartment.

Someone had made a halfhearted attempt at seasonal decoration. Cardboard cutouts of wreaths and candy canes were taped to the walls; a dusty tree with a single string of blinking lights partially blocked the hallway that led to the restroom—unisex, unfortunately. The seat was always up, and worse. MERRY XMAS was sprayed on the mirror behind the bar in what appeared to be shaving cream.

Holiday cheer. What an oxymoron. She'd dredged the word—and the notion—from some long-ago cramming for an English test or maybe the SATs and felt a momentary glimmer of pride that she could still do so.

She hadn't had so much as a sip of beer since she'd discovered she was pregnant. Not that she'd ever been a big drinker, especially a beer drinker. After the repeated positives—and it had to be someone with a warped sense of humor at the "personal care" company who decided to color them blue, as in "the blues"—when people had pressed her to join in, she'd made herself a "vodka" and tonic in the kitchen, careful to pour away some alcohol from the bottle. When the bottle was empty, she bought a new one, replacing the entire contents with water, and picked up a couple of large containers of cranberry juice—might as well get some vitamin C. She wasn't worried that anyone joining her would complain about a drink without much kick. The people who passed through the apartment were usually so strung out that they wouldn't have noticed if she'd replaced the liquor with white vinegar.

Maybe Bruce would have. Bruce noticed things like this. He'd even noticed her switch to what he called a "Cape Codder."

She hadn't been drinking Cape Codders last night. No need for vitamins now. She'd opted for the house white (poured from a box). It had a witty clam-flat nose with a slightly frisky petroleum-product aftertaste. When somebody else was paying, she'd switched to tequila and, as the night wore on, the two had tasted much the same. At midnight, a guy wearing a Santa hat had appeared with buckets of chicken and got almost everybody singing Christmas carols. In the middle of "Jingle Bells" he'd started crying about his kids. They lived with his ex-wife, and the bitch had moved to Ohio. He wasn't going to see them until the summer. An older woman at the end of the bar, who had been doing shots by herself all night, got up, put her arm around him, and walked him out the door. Someone started singing again. The one about grandma getting run over by a reindeer, the mean one. Miriam was glad when they moved on to "We Three Kings," although that coincided with major breast-milk leakage and she missed most of it. She'd gone into the bathroom and used the pump, which she was carrying in her purse all the time these days. Lactation was not a problem. Getting rid of it was. She tried not to think about anything at all as she poured the fluid in the sink and watched it spiral down the drain. Tried not to think about its cause—or where it should be going. "We Three Kings." She knew all the words. They'd sung carols in school. Her town had been so Gentile, they didn't even bother to put a menorah on the bulletin board for equal time. One year her teacher had all the children take off their shoes and put them outside the classroom in the hall, just like little Dutch children did at Christmas. Kriss Kringle would leave them a surprise while they studied their multiplication tables, she'd promised. When Miriam whispered to her that she was Jewish, the teacher had patted her arm and told her not to worry, that God loved her anyway. The big surprise was a candy Kiss for each child, even the sole heathen. And Kwanzaa? If local people had heard the word at all, they'd probably thought it was one of those way-too-spicy dishes from someplace they'd never been, or want to go.

The Magi. Okay, so they brought gifts, but "frankincense"? "Myrrh"? Granted, these were precious substances back in the day, but what were Mary and Joseph supposed to do—sell them? Get someone to front for them? At least one of the kings had had the sense to bring gold. And maybe the shepherds had slaughtered a sheep, so at least there'd have been something to eat.

Back in the bar, people were drifting out and new people were taking their places. Miriam found herself trying to explain about the three kings and their stupid gifts to a group in one of the booths, but they didn't get what she meant. She was pretty sure that's when she'd decided to come back to the apartment.

She had to get out of bed. Had to do something about the pain. But she pulled the blanket up over her head and let herself sink back into oblivion. There was some pain that Tylenol couldn't touch.

It had been a good day. The teacher had divided the class into four spelling-bee teams. She read the words out loud very precisely— "occasionally," "remunerative," "deciduous"—and each team conferred quietly before writing the answers down on a sheet of paper. Miriam had known every single one and her team was the winner. Fifteen extra minutes of recess. Sheila Riley asked her to be her best friend just before they returned to the building. Of course Miriam said yes. Sheila had beautiful, long blond curls and big blue eyes. There wasn't a mean bone in her body and everyone wanted to be her best friend. Miriam couldn't believe Sheila was choosing her! They left school together, but had to get on different buses. Sheila's family lived on the water in a big house. And now Miriam was going to get to see the inside. Sheila had invited her to sleep over next weekend. They were going to have a campfire on the beach and make s'mores.

Her footsteps slowed as she walked up the driveway to the house. Her mother was home. The garage door was open and Miriam could see that the car was there. It was always there. Or her father's was. Sometimes he took her mother's to work, because he said if somebody didn't drive it, the tires would go flat.

Miriam walked around to the back of the house. They never

used the front door, which led straight into the living room. They never used the living room either. The furniture looked brand-new, even though her parents had bought it before Miriam was born. That had been over twelve years ago.

She went in through the kitchen door. It looked the way she'd left it this morning—her cereal bowl, spoon, and the glass she'd used for her orange juice were in the drying rack next to the sink. Her father's dishes were nowhere in sight. She'd heard him in the bathroom as she was leaving. The only time he ate breakfast at home was on Sundays.

Her mother would be in bed. Maybe she'd be awake enough to listen to Miriam's news—about winning the bee and going to Sheila's. Maybe she'd want Miriam to heat up some broth. That and saltines were what she mostly ate. Maybe she'd want Miriam to pour some water, so she could take one of the blue pills that were in a container tucked under her pillow. Once when her mother was in a deep sleep, Miriam had tried to slip the small container out and read what was on the label. Her mother had awakened immediately and with surprising swiftness grabbed the pills from Miriam's hand and told her to leave them alone.

"These are not for children."

Miriam had never tried again.

The house was silent. They didn't have any pets. Not even fish. Miriam walked through the dining room to the hall and up the stairs. They were carpeted, like the rest of the house. It was a place without much sound of any kind. Not even footsteps.

She turned the knob on her mother's door. The drapes were closed and only a small night-light was on. The furniture, a few pieces of artwork on the walls—everything looked gray. Her mother lay motionless under the covers, and every day Miriam had the same thought: "What if she's stopped breathing?" This was the worst part about coming home. The part where she went over and put *her hand on her mother's cheek to feel whether it was warm or not. Sometimes her mother would open her eyes and say a few words, but that had been happening less and less frequently.*

The cheek was warm. Miriam let out her breath, unaware that she had been holding it. Her mother didn't open her eyes today, but Miriam thought she saw a little smile on her lips. Her face had once been a very beautiful face, but now it looked as if the skin were too tight for the bones beneath. Miriam slipped off her shoes and gently lay down next to the still figure. "I'm here, Mom," she said softly. "It's me."

"Amen. Thank you for that nice blessing, Tom. Now let's eat." Freeman Marshall looked down the long table that had been made even longer with the addition of several card tables. His wife was at the far end, grandkids to either side. The Marshall family wanted everyone, no matter what age, around their holiday board. No children's table in the kitchen for them, and if things got a little messy, Nan was there with a roll of paper towels.

"Grandpa, could we say a special one for Norah, I mean Zara?"

"Of course, Jake. How 'bout you do it?"

The teenager shook his head, so Freeman bowed his and said, "Dear Lord, we know you are taking good care of our little girl who you chose to take from us so early. We don't always understand how your wisdom works, but we know it is here guiding us every day of our earthly lives. As we celebrate the birth of your son, we give special thanks for Norah's birth and her years with us. Help Darlene, her poor grieving mother. We'll be there for her too. Amen."

This appeared to satisfy Jake Whittaker. He nodded and almost everyone reached for a serving utensil. Faith hung back. Jake's mention of the girl—had they baked cookies with Nan together? Gone out fishing with Freeman?—pierced Faith's heart. In her mind's eye, she was seeing the picture that had accompanied the obituary in this week's *Island Crier*. It was a school picture taken junior year. Norah—Faith couldn't think of her as Zara—hadn't changed her hair color yet and although she sported numerous piercings, there was still something of the cheerful, younger girl Faith remembered in the upturn of her lips and the way she looked directly into the camera. What had happened to her when she left the island? What had happened the last time that had kept her from coming back to those who loved her and only wanted to keep her safe? People like Jake, obviously a close friend, and the rest of the Marshall clan? Her mother?

The weather had grown much colder. The icicles that had been dripping last week were rigid, glistening daggers in the weak sun, and the cove was frozen solid near the shoreline where the water wasn't deep. Too cold for burial. There would be an interment of her ashes in the spring when the ground warmed up. A spring she wouldn't see. The idea of an urn, or box, sitting on the undertaker's shelf all winter was ineffably sad. Faith hoped Norah's mother was keeping it at home, but some people found it too painful to have the tangible reminder of their loss in view.

Freeman had mentioned the brevity of Norah's life and the unknown ways of the Almighty. Reconciling faith and reason seemed almost impossible at times like this. Since finding the body, Faith had had recurring regrets—the "if only's" of life. If only she'd stopped at the historical society early in the morning, the girl might have been alive and they could have gotten her to the medical center in time. Even when Earl called and told Faith that the coroner's preliminary report indicated the time of death around two in the morning, Faith still felt there must have been something she, or someone else, could have done. The coroner was ruling it "accidental." Norah Taft had miscalculated the amount of heroin she'd injected—or calculated correctly if it had been suicide. Hers wouldn't have been a painful death, but it must have been a painful life.

Life. The white face, the white snow, the black sleigh vanished as Faith flashed back to a few hours ago and a very different face—little Christopher's. A death and a birth. There wasn't any connection, except the coincidence of her presence so close to each one—a departure and an arrival. No connection, but yet, a feeling that there should be one, if only in a sense of the mystery of existence.

"Dark or light?"

"Pardon?" Faith was startled into a sudden awareness of the scene around her.

"Dark or light meat?"

Faith passed her plate to Nan, calling cheerfully, "A little of each, thank you." The merry scene, which had been momentarily so far from her thoughts, returned and she was back. Christmas dinner. A Down East version of the Cratchits.

Years of catering all sorts of events and her own attendance at numerous family gatherings had not prepared her for the array of dishes in front of her. Turkey was the centerpiece—two of them. The birds had been carved by Freeman and his oldest son, Willie, and platters of the succulent, moist meat anchored each end of the table. The space between was covered with bowls of mashed potatoes—white and sweet—several kinds of cranberry molds and a quivering mass of something that looked like lime Jell-O and cottage cheese; dinner rolls; cornbread; biscuits; pumpkin muffins; slabs of butter; creamed spinach; pureed parsnips; candied carrots; pickled beets; Hoppin' John from the Marshalls' Southern daughter-in-law; the dilly beans and various concoctions that Nan and other women in the family had put up the previous summer; several kinds of stuffing—including Faith's favorite with oysters—plenty of giblet gravy; a platter of crab puffs; chunky applesauce made from the apples in the old orchard near the shore; and finally

Kraft macaroni and cheese, because some of the young fry were picky eaters. It wasn't haute cuisine; it was Marshall cuisine. Faith knew most of the family had gathered for thick, creamy lobster stew the night before—their Christmas Eve tradition—otherwise that would have been the first course. Nan had explained this—and that they always skipped appetizers like cheese and crackers, because nobody wanted to fill up on anything before the main event.

"Where's my chutney, Ma?" Willie asked.

Nan jumped up. "I didn't forget. Just didn't bring it in." She turned to the Fairchilds in explanation. "Willie has to have my rhubarb chutney with his turkey or it isn't Christmas."

Many of the faces around the table were ones Faith had never met, but knew from the Sears portraits crowded on the Marshalls' mantelpiece. Only Willie, his sister Debbie, and their families lived on the island. The others were scattered from New Hampshire to North Carolina. But everyone came home for Christmas.

It could have been a *Saturday Evening Post* Norman Rockwell cover. Work clothes had been exchanged for Sunday best and many of the men had indulged in *both* aftershave and hair gel. Several of the women had recent perms. Nan and Freeman beamed at their progeny. It was all very idyllic. Except it hadn't been achieved without struggle, and the idyllic part was in the moment. Willie, the oldest, was open about his drinking problem—a problem that had started when he had worked on the fishing boats that traveled out to Georges Bank for weeks at a time in search of large catches. Days of mind-numbing boredom were punctuated by short intervals of frantic, extremely dangerous activity, and the combination created an addictive thirst. Faced with the prospect of divorce and losing contact with his two children, he entered a rehab program in Ellsworth and joined AA on the island. He'd been sober for twelve years. Two more kids were born. There was nothing alcoholic being served today, not even in the hard sauce for the plum puddings.

And Faith knew that one daughter had had a messy divorce and another was on the brink of one. Her husband, a bear of a man from away—Vermont—kept leaving the table for a smoke outside.

In short, the Marshalls were just like millions of other American families sitting down to eat today—problems solved and unsolved, connections occasionally stretched thin, but a palpable sense of family. Their roots extended deep into the island's granite bedrock; their forebears lay beneath headstones from that same granite in the island's cemeteries.

Idyllic moments were all well and good, but it was the working out of life's curveballs that mattered. The "never stop talking to one another even if you are right and the rest of the family is wrong." The "dropping everything and coming home in good times and bad." Faith felt her spirits rise. The Marshalls were a powerful tonic.

Conversation was swirling around her, and those who lived away had reverted to their Sanpere cadences. This, combined with the laughter, made it hard to figure out what was being discussed, but deciphering it all was making Faith feel as happy as a clam at high tide.

On her right side, Willie was complaining about the law requiring fishermen to buy sinking instead of floating line for their traps—a major expense, even though there was a buy-back program for the old line, because the sinking line deteriorated faster. When he'd left the deep-sea boats, he'd fished with Freeman for a time, but had been on his own for years. Now that the kids were in school, his wife was his sternman. "Better than sitting home worrying and I get a workout for nothing that women pay good money for up to Ellsworth at Curves," she said.

"As I was saying before I got interrupted . . ." His sibs weren't going to let him get away with anything and there was a chorus of "Keep talking like that and you're going to catch it when you get home! Forget about any canoodlin' tonight."

He tried again. "I've been fishing in the Gulf of Maine since I was a kid and Dad since Hector was a pup. Neither of us and no one I ever heard tell of has caught a single whale in our lines. Not a tail, not a fin. So for Washington to paint us all with the same brush is not just as stupid as the bastards are usually, but a disaster. Fine. Whales get caught in line. That's not good. But, Jeez-zuz! We don't even get many whales here—and any that have been injured are because those cruise ships smack into them! They've got plenty of Mobys down on Cape Cod and Cape Ann. I can see the point there, but to apply it irregardless is number than a pounded thumb!"

"We got to do something, Willie," his father called from the head of the table, reaching for the sweet potatoes that Nan had made with plenty of butter and brown sugar—just the way he liked them. "Added to the cost of fuel and the price for lobster going straight down to hell in a handcart—well, I don't see how anybody's going to make it this year."

On Faith's other side, talk was about the economy as well.

"I'd counted on getting housecleaning jobs next summer, but folks aren't going to be renting what with this economy. They'll stay home if they've been able to hold on to them, instead of driving all the way up here."

"Wreath sales were way down too," a woman across the table said. It was Debbie, the daughter who lived on the island with her husband, an electrician, and their three kids. One of them was Jake. "At least people always need wiring installed or replaced. Maybe I should learn plumbing and we'd be sitting pretty. Cover all the bases."

"More like a throne—the porcelain kind," her brother said, and laughter broke out again.

Faith looked down to check on her kids at the far end of the table. Amy had cleaned her plate and her blond head was bent toward the brown one next to her. It belonged to the granddaughter from North Carolina, Faith thought. It looked like the two little girls were sharing secrets or more likely plotting a getaway from all the boring adult talk.

Ben was listening in rapt adoration as Jake talked about his car and how he'd tricked it out with all sorts of stuff from NAPA Auto Parts, including a gearshift that lighted up at night. "Got a vanity plate that says 'Way too cool'—I used a numeral for the 'too' and left the y off 'way,'" Faith heard him say proudly. "All cost me a pretty penny."

She helped herself to another serving of the stuffing and wondered for a moment where Jake's pretty pennies for a car were coming from. Maybe he was working with his father, learning the trade. The island could certainly use another electrician. She reminded herself to compliment the family on their holiday window. Most likely Jake rigged a dinghy with an outboard and had his own traps during the summer. He was very involved with sports during the school year, she knew from his proud grandparents, which wouldn't leave time for much more than homework after practice.

Tom's plate was empty. It had borne little resemblance to the plates of Christmas Dinners Past—mounds of comestibles that immediately were consumed by his enviably active metabolism. At this one he'd eaten lightly—the doctor had cautioned him on heavy meals, advising smaller ones spread out over the day—and Tom had avoided fats, although since the whole table was swimming in them that had been almost impossible. The turkey provided plenty of the protein he needed and, without gravy, met the low-fat requirement. Nan's biscuits and dinner rolls didn't need butter. They melted in your mouth as they were. So, he certainly hadn't starved after proclaiming on the way over that he was hungry enough to eat a boiled owl—a Maine phrase he'd picked up from their host. Now he was having an animated discussion with Freeman about a McMansion going up on the other side of the island that had "raised a ruction." It wasn't because the house was an obscene contrast to the way the majority of people on Sanpere lived—as the Fairchilds thought when they'd heard about it—but because, Freeman informed them, the owner was using an off-island crew to build it and buying all his materials off-island too. "Heard the stone for round the fireplaces is coming from Africa. Now I ask you, Tom, what is wrong with our granite? I'm sure whatever they're quarrying in Africa is finest kind, but he's setting on the stuff. Why wouldn't he use it? There's still a couple of small operations here."

"Got to have something exotic to put in the caption when the house is featured in *Architectural Digest*," Debbie said.

Faith was no longer surprised at the things people on the island knew, or underestimated their sophistication. When their Aleford neighbors the Millers had convinced them to rent a place on their beloved Sanpere Island when Ben was a toddler, she had resisted with every bone in her body. An island off the coast of Maine? Vacation had meant the Hamptons to Faith as a young twenty-something before her marriage. And afterward, as a newlywed, it had meant Provence or Portofino. The craggy, rockbound coast where dressing up meant exchanging one kind of L.L.Bean shoe for another and L.L.Bean jeans for an L.L.Bean skirt was not her idea of a getaway.

It was partly the food that hooked her that first summer—peekytoe crab, fresh halibut, all the lobster you could possibly want, mussels and clams gathered just before they went into the pot. The growing season was short, but each fruit or vegetable became that much more special. Strawberries in late June. New peas to go with salmon for the Fourth of July. Then salad greens, broccoli, blueberries, squash, and cukes until tomatoes flooded the farmer's market in August. There was a rhythm to what she put on the table over the summer months and a rhythm to their lives that she had come to treasure, watching the June lupine in the small

meadow in front of the house give way to daisies, Indian paint-
brush, Queen Anne's lace, black-eyed Susans, and finally golden-
rod and tiny purple asters in late August. A rhythm that matched
the tides she never tired of—the emptying out of the water that
left a shiny mudflat interrupted by granite ledges, and the water's
return that hid what was below, its surface ever changing, its color
reflecting the sky.

Then there had been the people. People like Nan and Freeman, and so many others. This wasn't simply a place where people
left their cars unlocked when they went to pick up their mail at
the post office or dashed into the market for milk, but the keys in
the ignition, often with the motor running.

As the summers had passed, the depth of her feeling for the
island increased—although she still made time for several visits
to her sister, who moved from her Manhattan town house to East
Hampton in the summer. Hope was a year younger than Faith.
Her determined—and always well-shod—little feet had taken her
from college to B school to Wall Street in one straight, successful
line. She'd met and married Quentin, her soul- and workmate.
They'd synchronized their BlackBerries and found time to pro-
duce Quentin III, now four years old. Nannies and advanced technology enabled Hope to shift households seasonally, for which her
sister was profoundly grateful. Faith's life had taken more zigs and
zags, none more marked than her departure from the Big Apple
for the mackintoshes of New England when she'd married Tom.
Her sojourns with Hope put her in touch with her roots—the
three Bs: Bloomies, Barneys, and Balducci's—and their Hamptons
equivalents.

She'd be calling Hope later and missed her now. When they
were little, they'd interpreted the "We like sheep" passage in Han-
del's *Messiah* literally and created their own version, adding "and
goats and chickens and cats and dogs too." Each year they sang a
few bars together over the phone or in person. Yes, it was corny—

like saying "Be an angel" when they hung up after talking for a long time. It was their mother's phrase and they'd gone from regarding it as an admonition to realizing it was an endearment.

Nan was standing up and putting on the apron she'd taken off earlier and hung on the arm of her chair. A signal understood immediately by all the women present, and they jumped to their feet like marionettes on strings.

"Time to take a breather before dessert," Nan said.

Most of the men were rising now too.

"Now, mother, we'll all pitch in and help. Once again, you've given us a dinner to remember," Freeman said.

"Freeman Marshall, you know very well that you're dying to show off that iceboat you've been working on out in the barn and all you men would just get in the way. Get your jackets and go on out. Cold will give you an appetite for the pies and the rest of the desserts."

In the kitchen as they were putting away the remarkably few leftovers, Nan told Faith, "Freeman's been iceboating with some of his friends for years now. These are the same crazy boys that used to go down to the shore, take a pole, and push themselves around on ice cakes in grade school, then take their motorcycles out on the ponds when they were in their teens. I'll never forget hearing about one time when Freeman was crossing Georges Pond and it was late in the season. The ice was okay in the middle, but as he went in close to shore, it cracked. He managed to jump off and get to dry land, but his friend Forrest on the other side didn't know that. Just saw a headlight pointed at the sky and then nothing. He thought he'd lost him and yelled several times before Freeman answered—steamed, because he thought his bike was gone for good. Next day a bunch of them managed to find it with a grappling hook and they got it to shore, except there was a lot of do-si-doing with first all of them finding the thing, then lightening the load in the rowboat to bring it in, still with one person rowing. They thought it was some funny, but Freeman's father heard about it and gave him major hell. I'm sure my boys—and girls"—her eyes swept the room and three grown women loading a dishwasher froze in their tracks—"did a lot of things I didn't know about and I'm glad I didn't."

Faith joined in the laughter, which ended abruptly when Debbie said sadly, "I wish we had known what Norah was up to. Jake has been so upset. He won't even talk about it. I was surprised he asked Dad to say a blessing for her. I haven't even heard her name cross his lips since we got the news. I'm worried about him—and all the other kids in her class." She turned to Faith. "Our grades are so small that the kids are tight. They knew Norah from summers and better once she and Darlene came back."

"Tight enough, so they cover for each other. Yes, I know I'm way far away in New Hampshire, but it's the same all over," her sister said. "I'm not saying Jake knew exactly what she was into, but some of her friends had to have. Knew where she was getting the drugs, even if it was off-island."

Nan sighed. "You're right, Connie, but it doesn't change anything. It's been such a strange fall and now this."

"What do you mean 'a strange fall'?" Faith asked. She was cutting the plum puddings and couldn't believe that her mouth was watering again so soon after the main course.

"Thirty break-ins in September alone, mostly summer places closed up for the winter. Freeman and I didn't want to worry you, since no one was going to bother your place with us keeping an eye on it. November was just as bad until the weather turned. They're pretty sure they were looking for stuff to sell for drugs. Hunters might camp out in your living room and maybe take a nip or two from what you left behind, but they don't take anything."

Debbie picked up where her mother left off. "They used a crowbar to pry open doors, stripped the places of anything of value—and summer people leave some pretty expensive things—

plus they sometimes took canned goods and clothing. The only comical thing about it all was when we heard they took an iron from one cottage. An iron!"

Faith smiled. It had made her think a woman must be involved either directly or indirectly—"Honey, could you pick up an iron; this one is shot"—or an extremely anal-retentive male.

But it was no laughing matter. She'd been on the island long enough to know that drug trafficking was a perennial problem in Maine—just as rum-running had been during Prohibition and for the same reason. With roughly 3,500 miles of coastline, it was impossible to police every harbor large or small, every inlet, every cove. Plus there were more than two thousand coastal islands where a boat from Canada could land its cargo, and another pick it up.

"I don't want to talk about this anymore," Debbie said. "It's Christmas. I feel bad for Darlene. It's hard enough raising teens with two parents and we don't know for sure why she divorced Norah's father and came home so fast, but I never heard of her trying to get help for the girl—or herself. Right now I want to sit here for a minute and have a cup of coffee before we all dive into dessert."

Her sister, Connie, gave her a hug. "I didn't mean anything about Jake."

"I know you didn't, so forget it and tell me what was different about your crab puffs this year. They're always good, but these were even better."

The secret turned out to be a dash of Old Bay seasoning and the women settled around the kitchen table with their coffee talking about recipes, diets tried and untried, husbands, and kids. The things women talk about.

"You're sitting down in this nice warm kitchen while we've been freezing our butts off!" Willie came through the back door, ice crystals on his beard. "Where's my pie! And I want some of that chocolate bread pudding Faith brought that Dad has been raving about."

And so they picked up where they left off. Pies, plum pudding, angel food cake with strawberry sauce frozen last July, Christmas cookies, and Faith's chocolate bread pudding (see recipe, p. 247). Her secret was using the chocolate bread made by When Pigs Fly, the Maine bakery company, which she could get near Aleford. They also sold the bread and a kit to make it online. Besides the bread pudding, it was delectable as French toast, warmed, with ice cream, spread with honey-sweetened chèvre, or just plain with butter.

After the last belt was loosened, the Fairchilds walked back to their house under another brilliant, starry sky. Tom carried Amy on his shoulders. She reached up and grabbed a snow-covered pine bough, sending a dusting over the four of them. Ben threw a snowball at his sister, laughing when it fell short and landed on his mother's shoulder instead. Seeing the lights they'd left on shining through the dusk, they ran toward home in one accord.

"I guess we've finished opening everything," Brenda Carpenter said wistfully. "You'd think my brother and sister-in-law could think of something else besides oranges to send every year. Rubbing it in that they're living in Florida as if I could care. And this year I sent them another one of those Towers of Treats since last year he said it was some good, even if they can't eat nuts."

Her husband shook his head. "You're just more thoughtful, honeybun. And you've really spoiled me this Christmas." He extended his arm out straight, all the better to see the Rolex watch she'd given him. They were still in their nightclothes, otherwise he'd be admiring the solid-gold cuff links with his crest engraved on them that had been in the toe of his stocking next to a dozen of his favorite candy bars—Almond Joy. Brenda had found the Carpenter crest online and although Daniel doubted he had any claim to it, he didn't mind pretending. It was all part of the game.

Clients were impressed by things like watches and cuff links, evidence that you'd been racking up some hefty commissions. A Realtor didn't just need an expensive car. Everything about him—or her, Brenda had gotten her license a number of years ago—had to spell success. This was the way you sold the best houses, and got the best houses to sell.

He looked over at his wife. There was a slight pout on her face, which he'd soon take care of. It was a face *she* took care of and you'd never guess her real age, especially right now. The sheer negligee she was wearing was trimmed with pink marabou at the neck, hiding any of the ravages of time that the surgeon hadn't been able to reverse. She wasn't wearing anything underneath and her breasts were full and firm. Damn, she could still turn him on, Daniel thought to himself, shifting slightly in his silk pajamas.

Ten years ago when she'd walked into his office to apply for the receptionist's job, he'd barely glanced at her résumé and hired her on the spot. Best decision he'd ever made. Maybe he'd gone on appearance, but she was a hard worker, pulling in a decent amount now—some people preferred looking at houses with a woman—and it all went into his account. None of that women's lib nonsense about it being "her" money. The economy was in the toilet and had been for a while, but not for Carpenter Fine Homes buyers or sellers. Upturns, downturns—the rich knew how to stay rich and get richer. He'd been observing them for his entire adult life and had picked up more than the faux patrician accent that didn't reveal a hint of his hardscrabble childhood in a trailer near the Maine–New Hampshire line. When the deal called for it, he could do an "ayuh" or two—let the suckers think they were pulling a fast one on this Down East penny-ante real estate agent. Brenda was even better at it than he was with her "some goods" and "finest kind."

They were in the great room off the kitchen, which had state-of-the-art stainless appliances and granite countertops. Part of the fun of this business was trading up yourself and he didn't see how much higher they could go. Right on the shore, a killer view, five bedrooms, five and a half baths, home theater, home gym, wine closet, three-car garage. All the bells and whistles.

Brenda had hired a decorator from Portland to do the house for the party they gave the Saturday before Christmas each year—totally tax deductible. There was a real tree in this room—so tall it almost scraped the cathedral ceiling. The theme was "The Night Before Christmas," complete with a sleigh on the lawn. Daniel had nixed putting it on the roof, which apparently was in the original verses. The decorator was good, but tended to get carried away. The tree did look pretty spectacular, though, wrapped in gold mesh with pastel "sugarplums" and ropes of shiny silver beads. Tiny lights buried deep in the branches finished the effect. Although the house had been built only ten years ago for wealthy summer people from Manhattan, it looked like one of the Victorian "cottages" in Bar Harbor, and the pine boughs on the banister, fragrant wreaths over the fireplaces, everything but the twenty-first-century kitchen, suggested a family that had been celebrating the Yuletide for generations in their own time-honored fashion.

There was a sound, not of tiny footsteps, but tiny paws on the parquet.

"Come to Mommy, sweetums," Brenda cooed at Snowball, her bichon frise—a gift last Christmas. "Let me see the pretty collar Daddy gave you."

"It ought to be pretty," Daniel said. "Those *ain't* rhinestones, you know."

Brenda put the dog down and walked over to where her husband was sitting, glanced down, and promptly sat in his lap. "I think Daddy needs a great big thank-you."

"And I intend to get one, but first let's take this wrapping paper out to the trash in the garage."

"Can't it wait? Besides, it's cold out there."

"I thought I took care of that on your birthday."

He went to the coat closet, put on his heavy shearling, and handed her the full-length sable he'd given her last month when she'd turned thirty-five again.

"As if I'd forget." She slipped into the coat, stroking the sleeves with feline grace. "All right, Mr. Clean, let's get rid of this mess."

When she stepped from the door in the kitchen that led into the garage, he took the paper from her and told her to close her eyes and reach into her right pocket.

"Now open them and tell me what's in your hand!"

"A car key! I knew there was another present! I could tell by your face! Oh, Daniel! Come on, let's get dressed and drive someplace for brunch. My other Lexus was only a year old, but this girl isn't going to complain one little bit. On second thought, let's take our time getting dressed. Brunch can wait."

He kissed her hard. "I'm so lucky. Sometimes I can't believe it. That whole other life doesn't seem real."

Brenda put her hand on his lips. "Hush now. It wasn't and I don't want to hear about it. Ever. You got a bad break and now you've got a good one. You didn't do anything wrong. Anyway, they're both gone now. You know where Rebekah is. She can't bother you. And we can handle Miriam, Daddy! So don't worry."

"I'm not. Just sometimes I think—"

"Don't think. That's when people get into trouble. It's Christmas. Let's celebrate. I want a mimosa and a whole lot more. Christmas! Guess your family tree is shaking! I can just hear what my mumma, God rest her soul, would say if she'd known I married a Jew boy. But I haven't been sorry. Not one minute. Not this girl."

It was too early to go to bed, but no one had the energy after the Christmas feast to do anything but sit by the woodstove. Faith was

reading while Tom and the kids played Boggle. Game playing—
indoor and outdoor types—was firmly embedded in the Fairchild
genetic code. It was totally lacking in Faith's and over the years
she'd managed to tactfully avoid both Tom's family's marathon
Scrabble tournaments and vigorous fall weekend touch-football
matches. It had taken some doing.

Everyone was beginning to droop in the soporific heat the
powerful little stove was putting out. Faith felt her eyelids grow
heavier and heavier. Maybe they should go to bed. The idea had
great appeal. Call it a day—a wonderful Christmas Day.

"Dad!" Amy's exclamation startled Faith. "We haven't done
'The Queens Came Late'!"

Tom always recited Norma Farber's poem out loud to his family and anyone else around on December 25. It was a tradition
they'd started when Ben was two.

"Don't worry, honey, I was just thinking it was about time.
Why don't you and Ben get all ready for bed and we'll do it here
in front of the fire?"

"With cocoa and some of that Christmas cake we made at
home?" As Ben lurched his way into full-blown adolescence, his
appetite increased in direct proportion to inches grown. Between
her husband and son, gallons of milk disappeared from the fridge
almost as soon as Faith unpacked the groceries from the market.
Even so, it was hard to believe her son was hungry again now.

"Sure, cocoa and cake," she answered. Since her friend Helen
Barer had given her the recipe (see p. 248) for this Norwegian Christmas cake—Mor Monsens Kake or Mother Monsen's
Cake—the Fairchilds had made the toothsome buttery concoction
studded with currants and almonds every year. It kept beautifully
and melted in your mouth.

Ben and Amy soon reappeared in the doorway together. No
longer in sleepers with feet, Faith thought with a pang, but still

children. She clung to the thought. The years were going by much
too fast.

Tom began:

> The Queens came late, but the Queens were there
> With gifts in their hands and crowns on their hair.
> They'd come, these three like the Kings, from far,
> following, yes, that guiding star.
> They'd left their ladles, linens, looms,
> their children playing in nursery rooms
> And told their sitters: "Take charge! For this
> Is a marvelous sight we must not miss!"
>
> The Queens came late, but not too late
> To see the animals small and great,
> Feathered and furred, domestic and wild . . .

This mention caused Faith's thoughts to drift to Mary's
goats. Mary's small, furred, domestic animals, and from there
to Christopher, the baby who had appeared so mysteriously—so
miraculously?—on Christmas Eve. In the poem the Queens bring
useful gifts—chicken soup, "a homespun gown of blue," and a
cradle song to sing. Faith would have to drop off some useful gifts
from the Granville Market tomorrow and make a trip off-island
soon for more. She had gently explained to Mary that unlike goat
kids, human babies needed more nutrients than goat's milk—
superb in every other way—could provide and Christopher would
have to have formula. And Huggies. "Just as a backup, Mary. You
can't keep washing what you have on hand."

> The Queens came late and stayed not long,
> for their thoughts already were straining far—

past manger and mother and guiding star
and child a-glow as a morning sun—
toward home and children and chores undone.

"Say it again, Daddy," Amy begged.

"Absolutely," Tom said. He usually did it at least two times, occasionally three, when they'd all be reciting it together by then.

Faith's eyes were definitely closing now. She'd been stretched out on the couch. That long-ago Mary—so young, her first baby, and all those heavenly hosts plus the Magi and shepherds. It must have been a comfort when the Queens finally arrived, Faith thought drowsily. Women who would have some idea of what she'd been through and what she needed most. Yet, she always looked quite calm and collected in all those Adoration paintings. Serene, and beatific. Much the way Mary Bethany had looked this morning when Faith had left her holding Christopher, the newborn from another manger.

She got up and moved everyone along to bed. Christmas was over; the New Year beckoning Janus-like backward and forward, past and future wrapped in one unknowable present.

CHAPTER 4

It didn't make sense. Although, Faith thought, sense was a rare commodity. She was trying to fit the square facts she had into a sensible schema—only, as usual, it was round.

Today was Boxing Day. She knew that the British tradition dated back to the Middle Ages when the lower orders received a pittance from their lord and masters for the year's arduous labor. "Box" was literally a box of goods or later a sort of piggy bank. Nowadays, Boxing Day might bring a more substantial bonus from an employer. For most, though, it meant exchanging another gift or two, eating up the Yuletide leftovers, and going to the sales. This morning the Fairchild family was observing the holiday with eggs, bacon, mouthwatering cinnamon rolls, and the Christmas crackers that Faith had brought from Aleford and forgotten to put out yesterday morning.

She looked around the table at her family wearing brightly colored tissue-paper crowns. Ben was in a fit of laughter over his riddle from the cracker—typical British humor that he read over again:

Why did the bald man paint rabbits on his head?

Because from a distance they looked like hares.

Amy still had a tentative expression on her face from the first go-round, indicating that she thought she understood the joke, but wasn't sure.

All in all, a typical meal—although the headgear was novel.

Tom and Ben were heading out with their snowshoes for a ramble in the Tennley Preserve, acres of shore and woodland donated by a doctor's family in his memory. The trails would be buried under the snow, but Tom thought they could find their way using the markers the preserve had nailed on the trees. In any case, he was so familiar with the place, he was sure he wouldn't get lost even without them. Ben had filled his knapsack with granola bars, water, extra gloves—and a compass.

"It's not that I don't trust your memory, Dad," he said, grinning.

"It's that you think I don't have one to start with," Tom finished for him, reaching across the table for the last piece of bacon.

"Hey, I wanted that!" Ben complained.

"I guess I forgot," his dad said, breaking it in half and handing it over to soften his words and deed. "Let's clean up and go. The day's almost over!"

Faith had learned early on that the Fairchild family considered the day wasted if it didn't actively start at 7 A.M.—or earlier. It was comfortably past eight now. For once, she agreed with Tom. She wanted to get going too. First she was dropping Amy off at the Marshalls'. She'd been invited to spend the day with them as company for their granddaughter on a family outing to Ellsworth. They were going to swim in the pool at the Holiday Inn, check out Marden's, and go to the movies. Amy had been anticipating December 26 even more than December 25.

As for Faith, she was eager to get back to Mary's. A brief conversation last night revealed that Mary was literally getting the hang of baby care. "I've rigged up an old tablecloth as a sling and I'm carrying him around on my chest when he's not in his basket or being fed. I saw a young mother with something similar at the farmers' market last summer and her baby looked pretty content. This way I can milk too. The nannies are always so happy when I start to pull their teats that they'd never kick. Real cooperative," she'd told Faith. Faith had answered that Mary had probably seen a Maya Wrap, a cotton baby sling with adjustable rings that made a pouch. She wished it had been around when her children were infants. It was apparently a lot easier on the back than the baby carriers of yore. Mary had invented it on her own and Faith was impressed once again by the woman's intelligence and ingenuity. Finding Christopher's mother was a far greater challenge, however. Women had been coming up with ways to carry infants close to their bodies, leaving their hands free for work, since humankind first walked the earth. Something like locating a young woman, who'd recently given birth, with only a hair to go on, was like searching for the proverbial needle.

She sighed. Tom, scraping plates, heard her.

"What's up, honey? Why don't you come with us? Or," he added, correctly interpreting his wife's level of enthusiasm for hours of snowshoeing and eating granola bars in the wild, "we can do something else. The three of us."

"No, go." Faith was very happy that Tom's energy was returning. And the last thing she wanted to do was go snowshoeing. She didn't mind cross-country skiing. She loved the soft swishing sound the skis made through the silent forest. Snowshoeing was less aesthetic—and harder work.

"I was just thinking about Mary." This was true, but the woman herself was occupying only a portion of Faith's thoughts.

"I'm sure her niece won't leave the baby with her for too long."

"That's not it. Mary would keep the baby forever, I'm sure." And I hope she will, Faith said to herself. "I guess I wish she weren't so isolated. So much on her own."

Tom gave her a kiss. "You're a very good person, but no, we can't adopt Mary and her entourage. The parsonage is barely large enough for us. Have fun playing with the baby—and the goats."

Faith kissed him back and hastened Amy along. As soon as she dropped her daughter off at the Marshalls', Faith had two stops to make before going to Mary's.

It was only when Amy had been delivered and Faith had refused coffee and pie from Nan—they were having a second breakfast before setting off for Ellsworth—that the thought nagging at her since the previous day pushed everything else she'd been dealing with aside. The thought that had evoked her earlier sigh.

Could Norah Taft have been Christopher's mother?

This was the square peg she was trying to fit into the round hole. The facts that fit: Norah was involved with drugs and therefore could have been around the amount of money in the paper bag; also, like everyone else her age, she would have known how to use a computer to type the letter; plus the pointed directive to "raise him to be a good man"—perhaps a reference to her father? Not a good man? The facts that didn't: Norah had short, blond hair, so where did the long dark strand come from; Mary hadn't seemed to know Norah, so why did the girl choose to leave the baby with her; and most glaring of all—how could Norah have put Christopher in Mary's barn on Christmas Eve? At that point the girl had been dead for six days.

But maybe her newborn son was why the girl had come back to the island. She could have been bringing her baby to someone to take care of and that someone decided afterward that she, or he, couldn't handle the responsibility. Again, though, why Mary? Her reputation on the island so far as nurturing went only applied to goats. And if Norah had brought the baby to her mother, which would have been the likeliest course of action, Darlene would never have given him up. Or let Norah out of her sight.

The proximity of the two events—Norah's death and Christopher's birth—was haunting Faith. She grasped at what was admittedly a tenuous thread and knew she *had* to find out whether Norah had given birth to the baby in Mary's barn. And Faith knew there was only one place to go for the answer.

Two stops. She had to pick up supplies for Mary at the market —Huggies and formula. Mary had told her not to bother with baby wipes—she bought them by the carton to keep the nannies' udders clean, and as for Vaseline, Bag Balm, also for her cosseted herd, would do the job better. Mary's hands were as soft as the finest French leather gloves. Faith had never milked Mary's goats, but she imagined their udders felt the same. Christopher's pelt would never suffer.

But the market could wait. Her first stop was Maine State Police Sergeant Earl Dickinson's house in Sanpere Village. A basket with some more of Faith's cinnamon rolls, wild strawberry jam put up last summer, and a spread she'd made with some of Mary's fresh chèvre, dill, and a touch of dry mustard, was resting on the back seat. She'd called before leaving the house to ask whether this was a convenient time to drop off a little Christmas cheer. The cheer part nestled next to the basket in the form of a bottle of Shiraz from a South Australian winery. It was called "The Victor" and whether that referred to a person or event, Faith didn't know, but she enjoyed the name as much as the wine itself—mildly spicy and very good with lamb dishes. The case in the cottage's basement left from the summer had gone untouched since the Fairchilds were members of the Cold Water Army these days while Tom was on the mend.

She'd intended to bring some of her jam to Jill and Earl last fall, Faith reminded herself to alleviate the slight twinge of guilt she was feeling. The old gift-basket ploy. Ah, what a tangled web we weave . . .

After their marriage several summers ago, Jill and Earl had moved into Jill's apartment above her store, the Blueberry Patch, knowing they would have to find another place to live—quickly. It wasn't just that Jill was tiny and Earl a six-footer, but the living quarters, which had been the loft of what was once Jill's great-grandfather's cobbler shop, tended to let in refreshing breezes in summer and arctic ones in winter. Before her marriage, Jill had lived in Portland during the school year, where she was a speech therapist, a fact that never failed to amuse Faith since Jill was the quietest person she knew. And one of the prettiest. In another day, she'd have been known as a pocket Venus, perfectly proportioned with shoulder-length rich brown hair, smooth bisquelike skin, and large, dark brown eyes. These eyes were sparkling now as she opened the front door before Faith had a chance to knock.

"Come see the dining room. I just finished painting it yesterday!"

The Dickinsons' house was one of those on the island where visitors *did* use the front door, first climbing up some wide granite steps that led to a porch that stretched grandly across the front of the Victorian house. Captain Ellis Reed, who owned a fishing fleet and the shipyard, had built it. In his day, he was the wealthiest man on Sanpere and constructed a dwelling to flaunt this in a discreet New England manner, but flaunt it still. The original house had two wings topped by turrets and enough gingerbread for several Hansel and Gretel witch cottages. It stood on a high knoll overlooking the harbor. The barn and outbuildings stood on one side, set far back from the road. There had been an orchard and well-kept gardens behind the house, sloping down to the mill-pond. Reed owned the mill too. A fire in the 1960s had destroyed the barn, sheds, and one of the wings. It devoured most of the orchard too and for years a blaze of bright pink fireweed growing in the ash-laden soil was the only clue that anything else had ever occupied the spot. Various owners made attempts to repair and restore the Reed house, but when Jill and Earl went house hunting, it had been empty for some years. Water had seeped in through the roof and broken windowpanes; several feral cats were living in the kitchen. The newlyweds made a ridiculously low offer and were surprised and—Jill later told Faith—a little scared when the owner, eager to set out for his trailer in St. Pete, accepted it. Since then, they had brought the house back, if not to its former glory, to something very close. The gardens and replanted orchard were their particular pride and joy.

Faith entered and hung her parka on an elaborately carved hall-stand, complete with beveled mirror. Her cheeks were red with the cold, and next to her, Jill looked like an ice maiden.

"This is for you and Earl," Faith said, handing over the basket.

"Oh, thank you! I've been so busy trying to finish the house for New Year's that I'm afraid we've been living on frozen dinners and pb and j's."

Faith winced. Nothing wrong with the occasional peanut butter and jelly sandwich, especially with the right peanut butter and jelly, the bread lightly toasted, but frozen dinners! Later she'd drop off some of the Portuguese sausage and kale soup she'd made. There were some sacrifices that even home décor—besides the Food Channel, Faith was devoted to HGTV—did not justify. Admittedly, they had a time limit. The Dickinsons were giving an old-fashioned New Year's Eve party for all ages. The Fairchilds planned to be there, then take off for the five-hour drive to Aleford the next day.

"Come see. Earl's on the phone. He'll be with us in a moment. You'll have coffee. We have that. Also some of Kyra Alex's scones. I ran up to Lily's early this morning. Thank goodness Kyra doesn't close when we need her most—these dark winter days! There are maple walnut and raspberry lemon, just out of the oven. Maybe a blueberry left. Earl has already started in on them." In her enthusiasm, Jill was practically a chatterbox. She tugged at Faith's hand, pulling her in the direction of the dining room. Coffee and scones sounded good. More to the point, while Jill was getting things ready, Faith could talk to Earl alone. She followed her into the next room and stopped in the doorway.

"It's perfect!" Faith said. "I never would have thought to paint the walls this color, but it works. And I love the trim."

The dining room was substantial, with a three-sided bay window overlooking Sanpere Village and the harbor beyond. There was a fireplace on one wall. The Dickinsons had refinished the mahogany mantel and the oak floors. They gleamed in the pale sunlight streaming in through the windows, over which Jill had hung simple deep rose damask valences. What made the room especially striking now was the color on the walls—a dark teal that popped in contrast to the cream baseboards and other trim.

"Instead of a mirror over the fireplace—everybody does that—I'm going to put one we bought at an auction up in Bar Harbor last summer at the end of the room between the doors, so the table, and the view out front, will be reflected. The mirror goes almost from the floor to the ceiling. I have a great still life of gold chrysanthemums in a Chinese vase with a porcelain figurine on a surface draped with one of those paisley shawls ship captains used to bring their wives from India that will just fit above the mantel. It picks up all the colors in the room, almost as if it were painted for it."

Once again, Faith marveled at how the do-it-yourself button had unglued Jill's tongue.

Earl walked in and greeted her. Putting an arm around his wife, he asked Faith, "So, what do you think?"

"I think she's pretty terrific and the room isn't bad either," she said.

The Dickinsons laughed.

"When Jill showed me the paint in the can, I thought she was crazy. It looked dark as pitch, but she was right, as usual." He gave her a squeeze.

"What am I thinking!" Jill said. "I promised you coffee and scones ages ago. It won't take a minute. Why don't you sit in the living room?"

Since the only object resembling furniture where they were was a ladder, Faith followed Earl across the hall to the living room. Originally it had been the parlor and some sort of office for Captain Reed. One of the first things the Dickinsons had done was to remove the wall between the two. The end result was a large, airy open space with another, more ornate fireplace—this one with a marble mantel—and parquet floors that had been restored to the same luster as the dining room's. Faith had seen both rooms, and others, in various stages, and PBS's *This Old House* had nothing on the Dickinsons'. Fortunately they had eschewed authenticity when it came to furnishing this room, avoiding the uncomfortable, slippery horsehair furniture of the period. Instead they'd opted for large overstuffed sofas and chairs upholstered in velvety olive green. The walls were the color of buttermilk and Jill had covered pillows with a purple and gold fabric that looked as if it had been cut from a tapestry. An enormous Oriental rug picked up the colors. The carpet hearkened back to more of those spoils from the Far East, but Faith knew Jill had found it, and the pillow fabric, at Marden's—that Down East Aladdin's cave, overflowing with overstocks and slightly damaged goods. Maybe Aladdin's brother's cave. The one who knew a bargain when he saw it?

Faith came straight to the point once she and Earl had sat down, aware that it wouldn't take long to heat up some scones and make coffee.

"Do you have any more leads on what happened to Norah Taft?"

Earl frowned. "You need to put her out of your head, Faith.

I wish to God I'd have found her. Or somebody else. Somebody who wouldn't keep thinking about the whole thing so much. I know that's what you've been doing. Could see it right away."

Faith started to protest, but before she could get a word out, Earl stopped her, raising his hand.

"Now, hear me out. Norah Taft OD'd, pure and simple. Those might not be the right words. Nothing pure, or even simple, about the situation, but that's what happened. Why she picked that spot we'll never know, but the works were all right there in the sleigh with her. She'd had time to put them all in the bag and I'm willing to bet her last thoughts weren't unhappy. Not with the amount she shot up. But don't even go there. It was bad luck that you happened along and you have to let the whole thing go."

Faith had stopped listening in the middle. "You mean everything was in the paper bag? She wasn't holding the syringe? Nothing tied around her arm? That sounds like she might have taken the heroin someplace else and somebody put her in the sleigh with everything in the bag all neat and tidy. There were a lot of footprints in the snow. Could have been more than one person."

"You've been watching too much TV. She wouldn't have blacked out immediately. As for the footprints, people have been taking pictures there all week, just like you wanted to. Why she picked the sleigh, we'll never know. I agree she may have been with people, but the tracks on her arms and other parts of her body indicated that she was no stranger to knowing how to get high. She may have told someone or more than one person where to drop her off, I'll admit. She had to have come to the island by car. No bus or train that I know of. But she ended her own life."

Faith's mind was racing. Earl's words had raised all sorts of possibilities. She'd think about them later. Now she had to ask her main question—the reason for her visit. She could smell the coffee. Jill would be in with a tray any minute.

"Did the autopsy show that she'd been pregnant? That she'd given birth recently?"

"What!" Earl stood up and walked over to the window, his back to Faith. The gesture was clearly meant to indicate that Faith had crossed some sort of line with her question, but what kind of line was it? Had she stumbled upon the truth and he didn't want to corroborate it—or did Earl think she was inappropriately nosy?

"Did Norah have a baby in the last week or so?" She *had* to find out.

He turned around. "I'm not going to ask why you want to know this, but here it is. That poor girl had plenty of problems; being pregnant wasn't one of them."

Jill walked into the room carrying a large tray.

"At last! Everything's piping hot and I opened your jam, Faith."

"More like a kettle of fish," Earl said dryly. "Now, let it go once and for all." He was looking straight at Faith. She had the feeling he'd like to make her sign something, or at least swear an oath.

"What on earth are you talking about, Earl?" Jill asked, her face deflating like a day-old birthday-party balloon.

"Nothing, honey," he said, reaching for a plate. "I'm having one of each of these scones, so I don't have to choose, *and* I need more than one of these fancy little cups of coffee to wash them down."

"The cups are beautiful," Faith said, picking hers up. Above the dark liquid, the Limoges porcelain was so thin you could almost see through it. "I was just giving Earl a hard time, as usual," she reassured her hostess, stopping short of what she was saying to herself—*something I plan to continue to do if necessary.*

Jill smiled in relief. "Oh, you two. You'd think I'd know the way you tease each other by now. You'll be the death of me yet."

❄   ❄   ❄

Miriam Carpenter sat staring at the blue book in front of her. Her professor had offered her the chance to come in and take the exam today, the day after Christmas, when Miriam had called her office last week and told her she was too sick to take it during the regular schedule. Having a baby was not an illness, but Miriam's labor pains had coincided with Anthropology 106's final exam. As she looked at the questions again, she wondered if Professor Patel had suspected anything. Miriam was tall and big boned. It had not been hard to conceal her condition under the many layers of clothing necessary in Maine, as the days grew shorter—and colder. Yet, during the last few classes, the professor seemed to be eyeing Miriam in a speculative manner and twice she had asked her how she was doing in what Miriam thought was a pointed way. But then, she had always been a little paranoid. Or maybe it was only lately. But she was definitely a little, make that more than a little, paranoid now.

Miriam herself hadn't known she was pregnant for quite a while. She'd always had irregular periods and hadn't had any symptoms like morning sickness. Her breasts were tender and seemed larger, but Miriam hadn't realized what that, plus her skipped menses, meant for a number of weeks.

"You can take a makeup exam. I always keep one in reserve for situations I think merit it," Professor Patel had said. "You've done so well this semester. It would be a shame to skip the exam and lower your grade. And if you could possibly do it before the first of the year, I won't even have to give you an incomplete. But you must be going away for the break, home for Christmas."

"No, I'm not going home for Christmas. I'm Jewish and, well, I'm not going home. I live off campus, so I'll be around," Miriam had told her.

No, Miriam wasn't going home for the holidays, or any other days.

The professor had suggested the twenty-sixth and here she was.

She'd stayed in bed most of yesterday nursing her hangover and still felt tired, but her head was clear.

She stared at the first essay question.

Discuss the roots and implications of gender-motivated infanticide past and present. You may select one society or several upon which to focus.

Infanticide. That had never been an option. Whether male or female. As soon as Miriam did know she was pregnant, she also knew she would have the baby. Knew she would have it, because she was going to stop thinking about it. It wasn't that she was in denial so much as she was simply on a kind of all-encompassing autopilot.

Bruce hadn't found out until early last week. They'd stopped having sex in August when he'd started bringing Tammy around. He was so high most of the time that even before, sex hadn't played a big part in their relationship. What had? The drugs, mostly marijuana to start with. She'd never felt so free, so happy. Even coming down, she'd never gotten blue or angry the way Bruce did.

Gradually, it was enough just to be around drugs and the people doing them. Mellow folks, good folks. Folks who smiled when they saw her. Folks who cared about her—at least when they were using. She found she didn't need to get high, which was a good thing, because somebody had to keep house—and keep the money straight. Somebody had to let kids on campus know where they could go. Somebody had to deal with the suppliers when Bruce was too wasted. She had been the responsible one. "Baby, I don't know what I'd do without you." She hadn't needed drugs, just Bruce.

She'd come to a party at his apartment and stayed. He looked like Kurt Cobain, or that's what the girl next to her had said when he walked into the living room, leaving the group shooting up in the kitchen. He'd grinned that big, lazy grin and walked straight up to her—her, Miriam, not the other girl. He'd chosen her.

"Hey, pretty lady, where have you been all my life?"

It had been good. She was sure it had been good. Then one night he walked out of the kitchen into the living room and Tammy was there. Miriam heard him say the same words. She'd learned Bruce relied on a few stock phrases in life and this was one. Another was "Laws are for other people—dumb-ass people." But she still couldn't leave him.

Tammy took over the sex part—the girlfriend part—and Miriam was left to do everything else, which was mainly cleaning the apartment after the parties, because Bruce was trying to get straight and mostly succeeding. He didn't need her to keep track of the business anymore. He was straight when she'd told him about the baby.

"I should have known. You look like a cow. I thought it was all those chips you've been scarfing down."

The only food craving Miriam had had was for Humpty Dumpty salt and vinegar potato chips and she had been consuming a fair number of bags.

Bruce had stopped talking at that point.

Her hand automatically went to her neck. She'd wound a long scarf over a turtleneck and would have added a cowl if she'd had one to be sure the necklace of bruise marks his fingers had left stayed hidden. She had thought he would choke her to death and struggled desperately, pulling at his hands, fighting for breath. They'd crashed to the floor, knocking over a lamp. The bulb had exploded and Tammy had come in. Would he have killed her if Tammy hadn't been there? She'd taken in the scene dreamily—she was always pretty far gone—and said, "Leave her alone, Brucie. She's not worth getting upset about."

They'd left her on the floor. She hadn't moved from the protective fetal position she'd rolled into once he'd stood up. He would kick her. She'd assumed he would kick her, but he didn't.

"Get rid of it. If it's here when I get back, I'll get rid of both of you. Permanently."

He was leaving for Canada, picking up a major score of prescription drugs, and Tammy was going with him. They were going to spend Christmas there and stay through New Year's Eve. When she'd overheard their plans, Miriam had been so relieved at having the place to herself—she was sure the baby was going to pop any day—that she didn't feel hurt at being so obviously excluded. Last year Bruce had taken her to New York City, her first time in the Big Apple. Where did that name come from anyway? It *was* like a big red perfect Delicious apple. Just waiting for her to take a bite.

She hadn't wanted to sleep, exploring every inch of Manhattan and some of Brooklyn—walking across the bridge was amazing —while Bruce did whatever it was that he'd come to the city to do. He had laughed at her enthusiasm and taken her to the Rainbow Room on the sixty-fifth floor of Rockefeller Plaza one night, first showing her the biggest Christmas tree she had ever seen. They'd sipped Bellinis, which Miriam had read about, and between courses, danced. Bruce had told her to go out and buy a fancy dress. She'd found the perfect one in a funky store on Prince Street. It looked like the one Marilyn Monroe was wearing in the famous photo where she's standing on a grate in the sidewalk and the subway passing underneath blows her skirt up, revealing those million-dollar legs. Miriam didn't have legs like that, but the white chiffon bodice clung tightly, revealing plenty of cleavage. The skirt was full and as she danced it swirled about. She wore her hair loose and knew that for once she really did look beautiful. They made a handsome couple—Bruce with his fair, almost Nordic looks, slightly taller than Miriam. She basked in his gaze. He'd told her over and over how "hot" the dress made her look. They were young, in love, and had plenty of money. She didn't even look at the prices, but ordered shrimp cocktail, veal scallopine, and tiramisu for dessert. Something else she had only read about. The first bite was heaven—mascarpone cheese, custard, ladyfingers soaked in coffee and some sort of liqueur. The last bite, even more memorable because it was the end. The waiter told her the literal translation of tiramisu was "pick me up," that in Italian it meant "make me happier." Miriam didn't think she could be any happier. It was the best night of her life. And it had been just a year ago.

Looking at the clock in the classroom, Miriam pulled her thoughts from the past to the present and started writing. Gender-motivated infanticide. China was the obvious choice, but she didn't want to be obvious.

> The cruel Arctic climate of the aboriginal Inuit reduced
> the male population significantly as they pursued their
> traditional hunting and fishing roles, forcing the . . .

She wrote furiously for a while, and then paused. What if her parents had known the sex of the child they were going to have before she'd been born?

She wouldn't be here.

How old was she when she'd first heard her father say to her mother, "You're worthless. Completely worthless. You couldn't even give me a son," in that flat, cold voice he used before he would start the rest? Not caring that Miriam was in the doorway —was she six? Or seven?—and could see it all. Could hear it all— her mother's cries.

Miriam shook her head to force the thought to the back of her mind with the rest of the things she didn't want to think about. It was getting pretty crowded.

But the image persisted. She had a vague memory of her mother happy. Sewing clothes for Miriam's dolls. Baking pies. The scenes were so out of focus that Miriam wasn't sure they had ever been sharp. Maybe they were from a movie she'd seen, a book she'd read, and wished she'd been in.

She didn't remember when her mother—Rebekah—had stopped getting out of bed. Oddly enough, what she could remember was when Rebekah stopped leaving the house. Miriam had been invited to someone's birthday party and her mother had started through the door to the garage to drive her. She had paused, turned around without a word, and left Miriam sitting in the car. She was nine.

Neither parent ever came to any school functions. Her father was too busy and her mother just didn't. Was it acute depression, agoraphobia, anorexia nervosa? Miriam had been transfixed by the descriptions of these mental illnesses in the psych class she took last semester. She'd jotted her mother's symptoms in the margins of her class notes and it was all she could do to keep from cornering the professor after class to ask more questions. But he wouldn't have had any answers. Not to the big question. Not to the why. The why it started, why it worsened, and finally why she left her little girl alone for so many years. The one thing Miriam did know was that her mother had really died when Miriam was nine. The subsequent years were simply marking time until it was official.

Whatever was wrong mentally with her mother, it began to eat away at her body during those years until at the end she really was physically ill. Was it cancer? Could chemo or radiation, maybe both, have saved her? And what were those pills? The ones she wouldn't let Miriam look at? Where did they come from? Miriam never saw a doctor at the house, and doubted that her mother would have left the house for an appointment.

By the time the ambulance took her away to Maine Medical, Rebekah was so thin she barely raised the covers on the bed. She'd been refusing food for a long time and, at the end, water. There was no question of treatment. Even had it been possible, Rebekah Carpenter was making it clear that she wanted to leave her life forever.

Which is what she did. She never came home again.

Why had she refused to get help? Or was it Miriam's father who refused to recognize that his wife's illness was real—always had been.

And the drugs. Supplied by . . . ?

Miriam was in ninth grade when her mother died—two short days after being hospitalized. But she died free of pain. Miriam blessed the morphine—the drug that gave her her mother's smiles back, smiles that the pills hadn't produced. That last day, Miriam slipped away from school at lunch. She was holding her mother's hand at the end and didn't shed a tear—not even when one of the nurses pulled her gently away and took her to a room where she sat with her as she waited for her father to come. Miriam had been grateful for the company, couldn't swallow the juice the young woman kept pressing upon her, and when it became apparent that her father wasn't going to come, the nurse had driven her home, walking her to the house. Miriam still had a card with her name and phone number on it. When she'd first discovered she was pregnant she'd thought about calling this Diana Taylor, but she wanted to keep the memory of her separate. Separate and unsullied by what happened afterward to Miriam. There had been that brief moment when she'd been totally cared for and she had often hugged it close in the years since, especially at night, trying to fall asleep. If she'd had a girl, she would have named her Diana. Not Rebekah.

Her father married Brenda a month later—why wait? When Miriam met her and realized who she was, she knew they'd been together for years. All those essential training conferences in Miami and Vegas. All those long weekends in Boston.

Of course her father would marry Brenda, petite, a perfect size four, but really stacked. Even at age thirteen, Miriam had felt like one of Swift's Brobdingnagias whenever they were in the same room, which wasn't often.

Miriam's friends tried to be supportive, but she couldn't stand to be with them. After a while they stopped calling, continuing to greet her in the hall, but leaving her alone. That's what she'd wanted, right?

Just as she had been the spelling champ, Miriam led her class in every other subject. Junior year the guidance counselor called her into her office and asked Miriam where she thought she'd like to go to college.

"With your grades and test scores, you should be able to get in any place you want, possibly one of the Ivies. True, you're lacking in extracurricular activities, but I think our geographic will make up for that. Not too many students here of your caliber. I'm sure your parents will be taking you to visit places in the spring."

The counselor was new—fresh from college herself. Miriam told her she'd let her know.

"Work on your essay now. So many students put it off. I'm sure you'll be eloquent."

She'd beamed at the prospect of having one of her advisees at an elite school, shaken Miriam's hand, and checked her name off a list.

Miriam never went back, and when the counselor cornered her in the hallway, Miriam told her the family was taking care of things themselves.

Or not. Miriam *had* broached the subject with her father, waiting to catch him alone. He had expressed surprise.

"Any responsibility I have for you ends on your eighteenth birthday, which is, I recall, virtually coincidental with your high school graduation date. If you want to go to college, that's your business. Nothing to do with me."

She should have been angry, but it was what she had expected, and she'd doubted that she would fit in at college any better than high school. Her life would take a different course. Since she was sixteen, she'd been waitressing at various places in nearby Portland. It kept her out of the house, and she'd put all her earnings in a savings account. She liked the atmosphere in the various kitchens and mostly liked serving her customers. Sure, there were the occasional jerks who sent stuff back or stiffed her tip, but mostly they were just people happy to be out eating for a change.

Miriam was first in her class, but she told the principal she didn't want to be valedictorian. What would she say to her fellow classmates? Who was she to give any kind of advice?

Needless to say, her father and Brenda were not at the graduation ceremonies, and when she arrived home afterward, she'd found a note on the floor of the front hall telling her to pack her things and be gone by the time they came back from work. That was all that had been in the envelope. No keys to a new car—the school parking lot had been filled with these traditional graduation gifts for weeks now. No savings bond. No card. She'd packed quickly. She didn't take much. Then she'd added some of Brenda's jewelry, especially the pieces that had belonged to Miriam's mother. Miriam didn't consider herself a thief, but thought of it as making up for a lot of years of gifts like tube socks. And Brenda could get them back. Miriam pawned her stepmother's trinkets after withdrawing her savings from the bank. When she returned to the house to pick up her bag, she put the pawn tickets in Brenda's jewelry box—and left for good.

That summer she waitressed in Bar Harbor, the only recent high school graduate not college-bound. When the restaurant closed at the end of the season, she got a job at an Applebee's in Bangor and rented a room nearby that she'd found on Craigslist, using the library's computer. The room was small, but cheap and clean, and nobody bothered her.

By the middle of the fall, she was bored out of her mind, and with her savings and current earnings, she began to think college might not be out of the question—or a bad idea. The admissions counselor at the University of Maine thought so too. Miriam lied and said that her father was dead as well as her mother—not a stretch, considering. He wouldn't be providing financial aid in any case.

When she'd left home, Miriam had taken her birth certificate, high school transcript, and the one picture she had of her mother. There weren't any of the two of them together. Baby pictures of Miriam, with either or both parents, had been destroyed or never taken. When she was about eleven, she had come across her mother's high school graduation photo in a book of Robert Frost's poetry—a graduation gift? She looked beautiful, self-confident. The kind of girl most likely to succeed.

UMaine didn't need a photo of her mother, treasured though it might be, but they needed everything else and she was accepted. Miriam moved the short distance from Bangor to Orono and her days were soon filled with classes, schoolwork, and two jobs. Going to the party at Bruce's apartment had been a last-minute decision. She'd given in to the entreaties of a girl in her dorm—entreaties, Miriam later realized, fueled by the girl's desire to have someone straight to drive her and her car back to campus and put her to bed.

Professor Patel moved, scraping her chair on the floor. It occurred to Miriam that the professor must like her. She could have had a graduate student proctor the exam, or not have offered the opportunity at all. It made Miriam want to do her best. She glanced at the clock on the wall. There wasn't much time left. For the exam. She had all the time in the world for everything else. No responsibilities now—to anyone.

It had been an easy delivery. She could have done it herself, she realized afterward, but she had been frightened at the thought of being alone and had gotten a name from a bulletin board at a coffeehouse. The card was a little circumspect—"Looking for someone to talk to about alternatives to hospital birthing?" When Miriam called, the woman said she was a licensed midwife, and maybe she was. They met that same day later in the afternoon at the coffeehouse. Miriam had told the woman about when she thought she'd deliver and also that she couldn't have the baby where she was currently living. The woman hadn't seemed surprised and told her Miriam could come to her place.

It had turned out all right. Miriam called the woman's cell when her contractions started and went to her house soon after. By the time she got there, the contractions were so close together that Miriam never had a chance to feel afraid. The woman knew what she was doing and even insisted on keeping Miriam overnight after the delivery, bringing her cups of strong green tea. During labor, she kept lighting fragrant candles and playing that waterfall kind of New Age music that Miriam's yoga teacher in high school had liked so much. It was something they were trying that year, letting students take yoga instead of field hockey or soccer. There were only three kids in the class. Three kids who didn't have to worry about peer pressure, because they didn't have any peers.

The pain hadn't been too bad. Not what Miriam had expected after eavesdropping on women talking about childbirth while she'd waited on their tables. "With your pelvis, you were born to have babies," the midwife had said admiringly.

Then she gave Miriam a beautiful handmade baby blanket and Miriam gave her one thousand dollars.

Time was almost up. She scribbled the last few sentences and put her pen down.

December 26. The day after Christmas. The English called it "Boxing Day." She'd have to look up why. A box, a Pandora's box.

That was what her life had been like. Except for him. Except for Christopher.

In the end she'd had to act fast—with Bruce and Tammy in Canada and far away from the apartment, she'd hoped to have more time with her child—but, in the end, the only thing that mattered was that he was safe, in a place no one would ever find him.

CHAPTER 5

Pulling up to Mary's house was a relief. Instead of all the speculating Faith had been doing, there would be something concrete in front of her.

Yesterday she had asked Mary if she thought she could construct a list of possible mothers from memory. Knowing Mary's trusting ways—the mayonnaise-jar honor system for cheese and the bouquets of flowers she also put out in the summer—Faith had not imagined Mary would have something as businesslike as a guest register. Her B and B was only marked by a small sign at the turnoff from Route 17; advertising was by word of mouth and an index card pinned to the bulletin board in the Granville Market, where it often got buried under flyers for septic systems, yard sales, crab pickers, and all kinds of boats from skiffs to schooners.

Faith knocked at the back door and went into the kitchen. Christopher was asleep in his makeshift crib; he looked so darling it was all she could do to keep herself from stroking his soft hair. "Never wake a sleeping baby." That and "Don't eat cucumbers with milk" were the only two pieces of advice she had ever received from her mother-in-law. The cucumber lore dated back to an unpleasant gastric episode in Marian's childhood; the baby wisdom had come later. With Ben's arrival, Faith understood what Marian, the mother of four, had been driving at. Sleep was a precious commodity, especially during the never-to-be-forgotten weeks of colic.

"I only started asking for a name, address, and phone last summer," Mary told her. "Before, I'd left something people could sign if they wanted to—I introduce myself when they arrive and they tell me who they are and usually where they're from. Nobody's ever left without paying, but my cousin Elizabeth told me I should be keeping a better record and sent me this book—I'd just put out a pad, nothing fancy. She said that you never knew—and she was right, as usual. See? Hers has a place for all sorts of information we can use."

"Elizabeth? This is the one who lives out West? And gave you her goats when she moved?" It was easy to keep track of Mary's relatives, since she had so few. Faith had heard about only this cousin and Mary's older sister, Martha, who had flown the coop as soon as possible many years ago. She'd settled in New Hampshire, not far away in terms of miles, but light-years away in terms of contact.

"That's Elizabeth. She grew up in the north—potato country —and moved out West to Arizona when I was about twenty. My sister was long gone and I was here alone with my parents. Elizabeth thought her two nannies would be company for me. Where she was going wasn't goat country."

Mary shook her head, apparently in astonishment that such places existed.

"I'll never forget the day they arrived. She found someone with a truck who was coming this way. All goats have personality, but these two were loaded with it. I know I sound crazy, but I swear they were smiling at me when I took them off the truck. Goats do smile, you know. Or at least that's what I call it. The larger doe was Dora the First; the Dora I have now is Dora the Second. The other Dora lived to be twenty, but I lost the other one, Cora, when she was only twelve."

Filing away the interesting notion of two Nubian goats as a substitute for human contact for further thought, Faith mentally thanked Elizabeth for the easier-to-grasp idea of a guest register and sat down to work after refusing Mary's offer of some rose-hip tea. Jill's cups were small but the coffee strong, and after two Faith didn't want any more liquid refreshment, however therapeutic.

Mary was explaining the list she'd made.

"I went through the book last night when he was asleep—he's a good little sleeper. Are all babies this way or is he special?"

"Definitely special," Faith said.

"I have a lot of repeat customers. The Bradys come every year for two weeks in August. He grew up on a farm in New York State and likes to do the milking. They're great birders and go up to Grand Manaan to see the puffins, or the gulls at Schoodic, which is closer, but they still throw their tent in the car in case they decide to stay overnight. I don't like to charge them when they're gone, but they insist and I guess since they leave their things, it's fair. But I take something off for the breakfasts."

Faith didn't want to push Mary. It was rare to hear her this loquacious—the goat soliloquy had been very touching—but there were a lot of names in the book and if every one evoked a lengthy reminiscence or Capricornian tangents, they'd be lucky to locate Christopher's mother by the time he was old enough to drive.

Mary seemed to arrive at the same conclusion.

"But you don't need to hear this. Right off the bat I eliminated the women who are over a certain age. He's a miracle all right, but we have to be realistic."

Faith nodded in agreement. In the Bible, Sarah had been ninety years old when she brought forth Isaac—Abraham was one hundred, not much of an age difference when you get up to that point in life. As for their son, there would have had to have been yet another miracle if they were going to make it to Isaac's high school graduation—or even his bar mitzvah.

"I wasn't going to include the people who have been here before. These are people I know pretty well and I can't imagine any of them abandoning a baby, but then I remembered what you said—that the mother had to have known my routine. So, I decided it made sense to look at them first. Here's that column. Three names."

"What can you tell me about them?" Faith asked.

"The first two come with their families and I've watched the children grow up. Both women are in their thirties, I'd say, and judging from the kind of attention they pay these children, I think it's unlikely they'd drop a new addition off here."

"Unless it was an extremely unwanted addition," Faith said, imagining scenarios ranging from the result of an illicit affair to an overwhelmed mother teetering on the brink of despair. But still, Mary was right; it seemed unlikely. For one thing, the woman's husband, if not the other children, would certainly have noticed the change in her appearance. "I think we can skip them for now. Who else?" she asked.

"Elaine Reynolds fills the bill—right age, unmarried—at least, no ring and she never mentioned a husband but did talk about a boyfriend this summer. Seemed real happy about the whole thing and said she was going to bring him next year. Maybe the boyfriend wasn't ready for fatherhood."

Faith circled the name.

"Only problem is, Elaine lives out in California. North of San Francisco where they make the wine."

"Napa?"

"That's it."

"So, she'd have to either have taken a newborn on the plane across country, probably to Portland or Bangor, then rented a car and driven up here, or she delivered someplace nearby. Did she have family in Maine? How did she find Sanpere?"

The influx of summer people doubled the island's population from roughly June through August and there were always day-trippers coming to Granville to visit a working fishing village—a dying phenomenon—but Sanpere was not a well-known tourist destination. Someone from so far away would most likely have had some kind of connection.

"She went to Bowdoin, and a bunch of students used to come here with one of the professors to gather specimens for a marine biology class. She fell in love with the island and her dream is to move here for good someday. I know she doesn't know anybody, because she specifically said it would be hard to leave friends and family in California to come to a place where she would be a complete stranger, but she didn't care. Sanpere was where she was 'meant to be.'"

Faith reluctantly erased the circle around Elaine's name. The logistics of the cross-country trip ruled her out—and with friends and family, surely there would have been someone closer to Napa with whom she could have left the baby. Plus the lack of current connections in Maine made that scenario a dimly lit one. Could the young woman have been so taken with Mary that she went to extraordinary lengths to have the baby here? Faith looked at her, bent over her list, her faced screwed up in determination to do the right thing. Mary was special, but would this Elaine have developed such a strong affection for her after a few brief summer stays? It sounded as if what the woman was most attached to was Sanpere itself. And wanted her child raised here? And Mary was the person she trusted to do it well?

Faith drew the circle around Elaine's name again.

"Now here," Mary said with the air of a magician pulling a rabbit from a silk hat, "we have the column with the names of women I knew were pregnant for sure. There were two of them."

"Great!" Finally, they were getting someplace, Faith thought.

"A first child for each. The Warrens live in Bolton, Vermont—not that close, but still a doable drive, especially because the weather was good Christmas Eve. The Tuttles were from Saco—south of Portland. Even though I know both women are possibilities, I can't see either of them giving their child up. They were so happy to be pregnant. Normally I don't chat that much with new guests, but these two told me they were having a baby just about the moment they walked in. Both couples were looking forward to coming back next summer and every summer after that to watch little whoever play with the goats. The nannies are very sweet playmates, you know."

Faith did know. And now she also knew they smiled. Once again, she thought that someone looking for strong maternal instincts would only have had to watch Mary with her herd and listen to her talk about them to conclude she was a natural-born nurturer. Granted, her charges were ruminants, but if you were looking for Mother of the Year, Mary was a contender.

Not only did Mary keep her goat house clean and dry—it looked like something from Carl Larsson's *The Farm*—but she also religiously tended to the nannies' every need from physical to psychological. All her goats had had their horn buds removed and Mary gently but firmly discouraged butting from the moment they were born. She greeted each one by name starting with the queen, stroking and petting them several times a day. After the stress of breeding—and delivering—she read to them and even sang to them, as Faith discovered one day, hearing a stirring rendition of "Seventy-six Trombones" with accompanying bleats issuing from the barn. Their play yard was just that, with several cable spools courtesy of Bangor Hydro for the nannies to climb on. The pasture had a high electric fence and Faith was pretty sure the Nubians were better fed than Mary, who seemed to exist on whey sweetened with honey (bartered for cheese), rose-hips in various forms, and whatever vegetables, fresh or put up, the garden yielded. Maybe it wasn't such a bad diet; rather, it was the thought of it that repelled Faith. Yes, she knew people—including some near and dear—thought she was a food snob, but it came with the territory and she considered the label a badge of honor.

"Okay, so those are definites. What about women of child-bearing age, either part of a couple or single, who hadn't been here before? First-timers?"

Mary beamed. "That's this third column. In June I had a young woman from Norway for three nights who was 'seeing America' for the summer, starting up here and working her way to San Diego. She had some sort of bus pass and rented cars when she wanted to go someplace out of the way. She said my cheese wasn't like the real goat cheese from Norway. *Gjetost*. She was correct about that! I've tried it. The Bradys brought me some. I think you can even get it at Hannaford. Brown. Kind of sticks to the roof of your mouth and sweet. The Norwegians must have very different taste buds."

Faith had tried the cheese also. Once. She didn't think it was a taste bud problem, though. Think of gravlax—that heavenly dill-cured salmon served with mustard sauce. She thought *gjetost* was one of those cultural things. Like the Swiss and muesli or all those countries where the sheep's eyeballs were the pièce de résistance of the meal. Of course the Norwegians, and Swedes, ate lutefisk, cod soaked in lye for something like several years, and the smell alone could clear out the sinuses of a small country. Maybe it *was* the taste buds.

"How about if she didn't go back to Norway?" Faith said. "How about if she met a sailor in San Diego, they fell in love, but since the baby obviously couldn't be his, when she began to look pregnant, she came back to Maine, remembering the goats and thinking it was like home. Dropping Christopher off on a cold winter's night would be nothing for a Viking."

"She had graduated from the university in Oslo shortly before her trip," Mary said. "And was looking forward to the job waiting for her, plus she had just purchased an apartment with her boyfriend. She was traveling light, but one section of her backpack was reserved for those plastic snow globes with the names of the states she'd visited. I gather they were to be a surprise for him," Mary said.

"This doesn't sound like someone who would get swept off her feet and change her plans. Do Norwegians get swept off their feet?" Faith's friend and neighbor Pix Miller had spent time in Norway and had familiarized Faith with the Nordic temperament. Faith recalled Pix also mentioned the high out-of-wedlock birthrate and lack of any stigma. It would probably have been of little concern to this girl to add to the statistic.

"Besides," Faith continued, "it would have been complicated staying here past the time she'd declared to the immigration official upon entering—and then there were all those ties back home," Faith said. "Especially those snow globes to give her honey— interesting focal point for the apartment's décor. I think we can eliminate our Norwegian, but not entirely."

Mary moved to the next name on the list. "Around the Fourth, a cousin of the Harveys they didn't have room for stayed for a week, but I never saw her but once briefly. She took all her meals, even breakfast, over there, came in at night and went straight to the room. She was alone, so either she was here without her husband or not married. I doubt she'd leave her baby this close to kin if she wanted the whole thing to be a secret."

Faith nodded in agreement. "Anyone else?"

"A woman from New York City, but she had to leave after one night. Something about her husband's allergies. Goodness knows he was sneezing enough. Whoever heard of being allergic to goats?" Mary said scornfully.

Faith kept her mouth shut.

Mary pointed to the next name. "Amanda Truman. Her parents were staying over to the Lodge, and since they brought her with them at the last minute, there wasn't room there and she slept here, but they picked her up after breakfast every morning."

No room at the inn, Faith thought. There weren't many places to stay on Sanpere unless you owned or rented. Besides Mary's B and B, there was a larger one as you came off the bridge. The owners advertised in the local paper *and* boasted a big sign you couldn't miss. In Granville, there was a motel that had been there forever and was open year-round, as well as two other seasonal ones. Then there was the Lodge. Originally built and run by a professor of botany from the University of Maine as a place for naturalists to gather in the summer—it offered three squares, plenty of hikes, and an abundance of field guides—it had undergone several transformations over the years. Currently it had had a facelift and was geared toward families with hefty disposable incomes.

"Amanda's a college student. About to be a sophomore. Goes to that place Hillary Clinton went to."

"Wellesley College. You know the Millers over by me. Their daughter, Samantha, graduated from there."

Mary nodded. "Ursula's granddaughter." It didn't surprise Faith that Mary knew Pix's octogenarian mother, whose family were original rusticators on Sanpere. The trick on the island would be finding someone who *didn't* know the redoubtable lady.

"Amanda didn't look pregnant, but still it would have been early. Let's see. If Christopher was born a few days before he arrived here—that's what it looks like to me—he'd have been started in March."

Faith liked Mary's choice of word—"started." It suggested sowing seeds in little peat pots under Gro lights. Things Mary did. Not other things that Mary did not.

"Kind of mopey, though. She would have been happy to stay here with me and the goats all day. Near the end of the week she

told me her parents had made her come because they didn't ap-
prove of her new boyfriend and had nixed her plans to go with
him to South America—Colombia—for the summer. I gather he
was older than she was."

"South America! Colombia! Where did her family live?"

"Brunswick."

"Bingo!" Faith stood up and stretched. "Relatively close by,
about two hours away. She would have been heading home for
the break. Easy enough to drive here before doubling back to
the blazing Yule log or whatever the Trumans had waiting. If
she'd been having what so euphemistically are called 'issues'
with her parents, she could have used the situation to explain
why she wasn't arriving for the holidays until the last moment—
Christmas Eve. The money comes from a drug connection
through the boyfriend, or rather manfriend—and maybe that's
who soured her on men." Faith could hardly contain her excite-
ment. "He dumped her when she didn't go with him or when he
found out she was pregnant." By the end of the sentence, Faith
had sketched out an entire portrait in her mind, visualizing the
young, pregnant student. Not so young as the Virgin, of course,
and not a virgin, but the faces in Faith's mind were similar—
beautiful Botticelli-like ovals. Amanda Truman was definitely
Christopher's mother. Maybe Samantha Miller knew her. They
would have overlapped by a year. But how to bring up the question of *enceinte*? She couldn't tell Samantha what was going on.
Faith couldn't even tell her own husband. But there were other
ways to check out the girl.

"Let's quickly take a look at anyone else, then start making
calls, beginning with Miss Amanda."

"Here's the last one. Miriam Singer. She was here with her
husband, but they weren't wearing rings. Or at least he wasn't and
her ring didn't look like a wedding ring. It was silver with a dark
green stone—not an emerald, maybe malachite."

Mary certainly noticed people's hands, Faith thought, but then, she would—all that milking. A kind of occupational quirk, much the way a manicurist would notice nails.

"They were young and I started thinking about them right away last night when you said Christopher's mother might be a student. I'd kind of forgotten about Amanda.

"There was a University of Maine Black Bears bumper sticker on their truck—a new one and the sticker was too. They stayed a week, and he was gone almost all the time. Said he was helping a friend, whose sternman was sick, but he didn't get up early enough for fishing and he came back late. Seven o'clock he'd show up, then take her off to get something to eat. Where at that time of night I don't know."

Even in the summer, Sanpere's culinary offerings were sparse. The best place to eat, Lily's, only offered dinner on Friday nights and even then stopped serving at eight. The Granville Market made pizza and Italian sandwiches, a surprisingly good combination of cold cuts, pickles, and mayo on an oversized hot dog bun. They were open until nine, but the food ran out well before then. There were several restaurants overlooking the harbor in Granville, which served reliably good chowder, lobster rolls, and deep-fried haddock, but people ate even earlier here than in Aleford, and the Singers seemed to be keeping city hours—or something else.

"She spent the day helping me with the goats and the garden," Mary was recalling, her voice filled with fondness. She had obviously liked Miriam. Miriam must have been very nice to the goats.

"So much that I didn't want to charge them full price, but she insisted she'd just been having fun. That it was a vacation for her. We kind of suited each other. She wasn't much of a talker and that was fine with me. She ran out of the books she'd brought to read and I told her to borrow something from my shelves. She picked *Great Expectations,* which could have been a hint, I suppose.

But she didn't look or seem pregnant. The opposite. Ate as much breakfast as I cooked and then we'd stop for lunch. She liked making it and a few times did that thing with the warm goat cheese and salad you're always talking about."

Miriam Singer sounded like another possibility. Possibilities. How many times had this word coursed through her mind in the last hour? Faith wondered. The pregnant couples from Vermont and southern Maine. This Miriam. And Amanda Truman. Possibilities.

Christopher chose the moment to wake up and show Mary what a more typical infant could be like. She dashed over to him in alarm and picked him up. His lusty cries continued, his face was bright red, and his eyes scrunched shut with the effort.

"Hungry? Needs changing? Rocking? What?" Mary asked Faith.

"All of the above, and while you're doing it, I'll think what to say to Amanda Truman." She also made a note to herself to get Mary one of the new swings that were safe for infants; the motion would both soothe and entertain little Christopher. She'd noticed that Mary always put him down to sleep on his back and supported his head when she picked him up. She seemed to know instinctively how to keep him safe, as his mother had written.

A few minutes later Mary returned with the baby and settled into the rocker to feed him. His face was back to normal and his eyes wide open as he sucked at the bottle in blissful content.

"When you finish feeding him, we'll call Amanda. If she answers, that's perfect—and kids of any age in a family usually get to the phone first." Ben went for the Gold every time the phone rang in the Fairchild household. "If someone else does, you say who you are and why you're calling, then ask to speak to her. The story is that you moved the bed in the room where she stayed and found a bracelet that you recalled seeing her wear, but you wanted to make sure before you mailed it to her. A pretty gold bangle."

Mary looked up, horrified. "I couldn't possibly tell so many lies!"

Faith sighed. She had been afraid of this, but she couldn't very well call and say she was Mary. It would be all right if one of the parents answered, but not if Amanda did. And what would she do once Amanda herself got on the line?

"We'll write it down. It will be like reading from a script." Faith paused to let the idea sink in. "If you want to find out whether she's Christopher's mother, you have to do this, Mary. You *have* to get Amanda on the phone and ask her if she perhaps left something other than a bracelet here."

Fifteen minutes later, Faith was engrossed in rocking Christopher, and Mary was waiting for someone in the Truman household down in Brunswick to answer the phone.

"Hello, is this Mrs. Truman?" Mary said, and did her number, only faltering slightly when she described moving the bed.

"Perhaps I should speak to her," Mary said.

Faith wished Mary had an extension. It was maddening not hearing the other side of the conversation.

Mary gave Faith a thumbs-up and began an improvisational performance that would have done any Barrymore proud.

"The hospital! Oh, dear. I hope it was nothing serious. There's that dreadful flu going round. And pneumonia."

The next minute Mary turned her thumb down and the corners of her mouth joined it.

"Please tell her I hope she feels better and, if it is her bracelet, to let me know and I'll mail it to her. Good-bye."

"Tonsils," she told Faith mournfully. "They thought the vacation would be a good time for her to have them out. She's needed the surgery for a while, but didn't want to miss any school. Turned out the adenoids had to go too and she had a reaction to the anesthesia. They actually had to keep her two nights and she almost missed Christmas!"

"All right. No, not all right. Darn! I was sure it was Amanda." Faith knew this wasn't going to be easy, but she always tended to hope.

"She said Amanda enjoyed staying with me and 'my little goats.'"

Faith had to hide her smile. She gave Mary a moment to mutter, "Little goats, the idea," a few times, then nudged her attention back to the list.

"Let's look at the two couples you knew were going to be parents," she suggested, "starting with the Tuttles from Saco. What could be more natural than for you to call and say you'd like to send some of that jelly of yours or whatever to congratulate them on the new baby? You know what I mean. Say how much you're looking forward to seeing them next summer."

"What if something went wrong with the pregnancy? I had a toxemic doe once. Oh, Faith, I don't think I can keep calling up strangers, even strangers who have stayed here."

Mary was tough, but she was also shy. Apparently she'd reached her limit with Amanda's mother. Faith sighed, stood up, and handed Christopher over to Mary. "Okay, I'll phone."

She dialed the number and a woman answered.

"Hello, may I speak to Mrs. Tuttle, please?"

"Speaking."

"I'm a supporter of the Sanpere Chamber of Commerce and over the holidays we're trying to reach people who visited our island last summer to plan for next summer. Would you mind answering two quick questions?"

"Not at all. We had a lovely time and will be returning next summer."

"Well, that answers my first question, which was whether you had had a positive experience, and my second as well, would you come again?"

Mrs. Tuttle laughed. "This is the easiest survey I've ever done."

"Could you tell me if you plan to return to the same accommodations as last year?"

"Why, of course. It was ideal. Bethany Farm Bed and Breakfast. I really should have written to Mary. I'm glad you called. It's reminded me to get to it. We had a baby last month and she said to let her know. Little Cecilia will adore Mary's goats next summer."

"I'm sure she will. Thank you for your time."

Faith hung up. "Cross out the Tuttles. Little Cecilia will be here with them next summer toddling around with Dora Two and the rest of the gang."

"I don't know how you do it," Mary said.

After a brief time-out for baby worship—he was getting more adorable by the minute—Faith called the couple from Vermont just to be sure and reported that the Warren family now numbered four. Twins. She decided it wasn't necessary to call Norway and reassured Mary that since she hadn't actually said she was from the chamber of commerce, only a "supporter" of it, which she was—the Fairchilds contributed every year—no lies had been told or laws broken.

"I'll phone Miriam Singer and call it a day for now. I have to get home."

"I've taken too much of your time already," Mary apologized.

"Nonsense, I'm enjoying myself."

And she was. It was keeping her mind off Norah Taft, plus Faith was beginning to regard the whole thing as a kind of scavenger hunt.

The number listed in the register for the Singers turned out to belong to a Mr. Ballou in Sebago and when Faith tried information for Calais, the town they listed in the register, there was no Miriam or Bruce Singer. She tried the one Singer the operator gave her, but the woman who answered had never heard of them. She was positive their street address wasn't in Calais either.

Faith felt her spirits rise. A fake register listing. The Singers had something to hide.

"How about we try Orono? Because of the UMaine bumper sticker," Faith suggested.

But that was a dry well too. The only Singer had never heard of any others in town.

"I've been so stupid!" Faith jumped up from the table where she had been studying the list. "The bag. The bag the money was in. It had the name of a store on it. It wasn't from a Hannaford or any other chain. Must be a pretty small mom-and-pop operation. The name looked hand-stamped. 'Sammy's Twenty-four Hour Store'—wasn't that it?"

"I think so," Mary said. "The baby's asleep again. I'll go check."

Mary had hidden the money somewhere outside her house, Faith noted. Somewhere that required boots and a jacket. But, since Mary returned shortly, somewhere not too far away.

"'Sammy's Twenty-four Hour Store.' Just the name. No address." She took off her things and joined Faith at the table. "Are you sure you don't want a cup of tea now?"

Faith thought it was time for whatever rose hips did for little gray cells, and while Mary filled two mugs, she put her wits to work. First she ruled out Hancock County by looking in Mary's Yellow Pages. The store wasn't listed, although an amazing number of twenty-four-hour stores were. Maybe Mainers did keep late hours—although more likely very early ones. The busiest store on the island was a small one that opened at 3 A.M. It was where the fishermen stopped to get their coffee and doughnuts. Also lunch for many. A lot of them hit it again for a six-pack on the way home. At those times, it was hard to find a place to park.

"If the Singers wrote down a phony address and number," Faith said, "they probably didn't give their real names either. At least their last names. They were calling each other 'Miriam' and 'Bruce' right?"

Mary nodded.

"I think we should keep looking for her in Orono. Everything about this says 'student.' I'll call information," Faith said.

"And I'll check the goats. I didn't have time before."

When Mary returned, Faith was putting on her own jacket and boots. She was smiling.

"The store is in Orono, all right. I was even able to get the operator to give me the address. When I go to pick up the baby things, I'll check it out."

Faith planned to make a quick trip to the Bangor malls tomorrow—Orono wasn't much farther. She needed to get formula and diapers in bulk, besides onesies, sleepers, and hats. The fact that Christopher didn't have a hat led Faith to believe he'd been a home birth. If he'd been born in a hospital, he'd have had one of those little pixie numbers perched on his head to keep him warm.

At the moment he was certainly warm and content, hat or no hat, sleeping soundly after his last feeding. Mary was looking as if she could use some sleep too.

"Curl up in your chair and close your eyes," Faith suggested. "You'll hear him, don't worry."

"I think I just might."

As Faith was starting the car, she was startled to see Mary come flying around the corner of her house, waving at her to stop. Faith turned off the ignition and stepped out.

"What is it? What's wrong?"

"I knew I was leaving something out!" Mary said. "Miriam Singer had lovely, long dark hair, just like the strand on Christopher's blanket. She wore it in a braid down her back, but one day she washed it and sat out in the sun to let it dry. She looked, well, she looked like the Madonna."

❄   ❄   ❄

Miriam's father had answered the phone when she'd called the day after the baby was born.

She'd been feeling very blue. Postpartum depression. The midwife had warned her she'd have her ups and downs—and that the downs could be pretty deep.

Miriam debated with herself and finally called him. He was the only person she could think of to call. She'd just had a baby. Shouldn't she call someone? She'd tell him she wasn't keeping it. No need for her father to jump to the conclusion that she was calling for money. It was just, well, she'd had a *baby*. A major life event, and during one of the downs she'd decided somebody needed to know besides herself and the midwife, whose name was Vita—no last name, at least not one she was willing to share. Miriam's involvement with Bruce had kept her from making any other friends—female or male. She had plenty of acquaintances. The apartment was always full of people when Bruce was there. But none of them were what she'd call friends. She almost called Sheila Riley, her long-ago, and short-term, best friend.

Sheila would be home for the holidays. The high school graduation program had listed everyone's future plans. Next to Sheila's name was "Boston College"; next to Miriam's "Undecided." It would be too weird to call her. Weird to call her father as well. And totally irrational. She hadn't spoken to him since she'd phoned last year to tell him she was in school. She didn't get a chance to say where before he'd told her not to come to him to pay her tuition. That wasn't why she was calling—for help. She'd just wanted him to know that she was making it on her own. Without him. It had been a pretty short conversation. She'd heard her stepmother in the background talking rapidly, as usual. Miriam had caught "You don't owe her one red cent." Brenda was a very high-maintenance lady and went through money almost as fast as she talked. She'd want to keep a tight hold on all the red cents in the current Carpenter household.

But she had to tell someone and the one person she wanted to confide in, the one person who would lovingly take her in her arms, was dead.

"Hi, Dad, it's Miriam."

"Yes?"

"Well, I just, I guess I just wanted to say hi and . . ."

Brenda was there again in the background. "Who is it, Dan?"

"It's Miriam." Her father hadn't bothered to turn away from the receiver and the words went directly into Miriam's ear.

"What does she want?"

"I don't know yet. What do you want, Miriam?"

What she wanted at that moment was to hang up, but she didn't. She got mad. Damn it. She'd had a baby. All alone.

"I don't want anything. I called to tell you you're a grandfather—a bouncing baby boy—and you can tell Brenda she's a grandmother." Miriam had added the last bit with calculated cruelty. Brenda would not like to be a grandmother.

"I assume your child is a bastard; like mother, like daughter," her father said.

Then Miriam heard Brenda's voice coming closer to the phone. "Child, what child? Miriam's had a baby? Boy or girl? Find out where she is."

It had been those last words that caused a prickle of fear to run down Miriam's spine. Not the ones about her mother. She knew she was the reason for the marriage or, as her father called it, the entrapment. No, it was Brenda's words, not her father's. It was her stepmother's sudden interest in Miriam's whereabouts and the sex of the baby that had produced a rapidly escalating panic.

"Well, good-bye, then. I've got to go."

"Wait. I need to know where—"

Miriam had hung up before he finished the sentence. She'd planned to keep Christopher with her until New Year's, which was when Bruce had said he'd be back. But as fright began to overwhelm her, she realized that anything from mundane boredom to a serious fight with his Canadian connections could change his mind, and he'd split. She had been foolhardy to even bring the baby back to the apartment.

It hadn't taken long to leave; she'd had everything ready. From the beginning, she'd known what she would do. Didn't know that it would be this soon, though. Christmas Eve. Ironic. With her father's words echoing in her ears and Bruce's angry face in her eyes, she'd decided to head for the coast right then. Christopher's father didn't want him, but for some reason Brenda, his grand-mother, might. Her father and stepmother had never had one of their own—was it because they couldn't? Miriam had always as-sumed they didn't want a child—Brenda with stretch marks, no way—but maybe they did. Or Brenda did. The ultimate soccer mom. And a little one as the ultimate accessory, a step beyond a fancy lapdog and her Louis Vuitton purses? If Brenda wanted something, Miriam knew, Daniel would get it for her, no matter what it took. In a weird turn of events, she had to keep Christo-pher safe from both his grandfather and his father—one because he wanted the baby, one because he didn't. And in his own way, each would murder the child.

Faith knew that Amy wouldn't be home until suppertime. The all-girl trip to Ellsworth the day after Christmas was a long-standing Marshall tradition, originally to purchase next year's wrapping paper and ribbon, plus any other bargains on items Santa might have overlooked. Last year Nan had scored a kayak with only a slight scratch at the L.L.Bean outlet store for a fraction of the original price. It had been on her grandson's wish list, but Santa couldn't afford it. It would be fun to see what the ladies turned up this year. The movie had been a standard component, as was eat-ing lunch at China Hill. Nan was partial to their egg foo young, and since it was the holidays, they always went for a couple of pu pu platters. Faith had long thought that someone wanting to make a fortune on the island—and yes, in a cookie—should set up a Chinese takeout. Sanpere natives thought nothing of driving the forty minutes to Ellsworth for moo goo gai pan and egg rolls—some good! China Hill and a nearby Mexican restaurant were special-occasion destinations.

She walked in the door and was surprised that the house was so quiet. Surely Tom and Ben were back by now. She walked into the living room. The woodstove was crackling and she smelled cocoa. A saucepan was soaking in the sink.

Somebody had turned the tree lights on and they twinkled softly. It was a beautiful tree. She turned her head and saw husband and son on the couch fast asleep, curled up against each other like part of a litter of kittens. The empty cocoa mugs were on the table in front of them and a plate showed cookie crumbs. They'd obviously had a good day. Never wake a sleeping baby—no matter what age.

The phone rang. In a move worthy of Jesse Owens or one of Pavlov's dogs, Ben sprinted for it.

"Hello?"

"Oh, hi. Sure. He's here. I'll get him."

He put the phone down on the counter.

"It's for you, Dad. Mr. Marshall." He caught sight of his mother as she moved back into the room.

"Hi, Mom. We had an awesome time. I bet we snowshoed ten miles. We saw a mouse skeleton. It was just perfect. Those bones are really tiny. We buried it under the snow."

"That was a good thought. Let's let Dad talk to Freeman and I'll make you a snack if you like."

"I'm pretty full right now, thanks. Would it be okay if I just went to my room and worked on my LEGO Technic?"

The stay in Maine seemed to have restored Ben's manners, as

if he'd drunk from the etiquette equivalent of Ponce de León's fabled fountain of youth.

"Sure—and if you change your mind, I'm making a sandwich for myself and would be happy to make one for you too."

Faith realized she was ravenous. The coffee and scones at the Dickinsons' had been ages ago. Mary's tea was tasty, but hadn't filled Faith up. She'd brought some rosemary foccacia and Mary had pressed more goat cheese on her—so fresh Faith was tempted to eat it with a spoon. In the background she could hear Tom's voice, but was too busy thinking of what to put with the cheese to pay close attention. With many of his friends home for the holidays on the island, maybe Freeman wanted to organize a checkers tournament—or poker. He was a legendary player in these parts.

Chèvre and fig conserve. Perfect. The conserve wasn't too sweet and very figgy. Like a figgy pudding. She felt a rush of pleasure. Faith loved Christmas.

She pressed the top slice of bread down on the filling and her hand picked up some of the foccacia's rosemary. As she brushed her hands off into the sink, the sweet smell reached her nose and she sniffed appreciatively. Rosemary. Mary. Legend had it that when the holy family was fleeing to Egypt, they stopped to wash out a few things. No Huggies in those days. Cloth diapers—and maybe Mary's linen shift and Joseph's cloak were in need of scrubbing too. Mary spread the wet garments on a dull, colorless bush to dry. When she took them off, the bush was a glorious green with tiny blue flowers and a pleasantly pungent smell. Rosemary. *Romarin* in French. *Rosmarino* in Italian. Faith took a bite of her sandwich. The taste was heavenly.

Tom hung up and came over to his wife. He pulled her into his arms, holding her tight. Tighter than usual.

"I have to go up to Ellsworth with Freeman. The state police are bringing Jake in for questioning. They found one of Norah Taft's shoes in his car."

CHAPTER 6

He had been in love with her his whole life—or at least as much of his life as he could recall. At first she was a summer girl—although her mother was from the island. Maybe that was part of what had made Norah so different, so special. He was used to seeing the other kids all year round and they never seemed to change much. His best friend, Davey, got taller but stayed skinny and was in as much trouble for not being able to sit still in high school as he had been in kindergarten. It was the same with the girls. They did stuff to their hair, and their chests began altering in an alarming and exciting way, but they were still the same girls he'd been teasing on the playground forever.

But Norah was different. Each summer she'd come back to stay with her grandparents and there would have been a complete metamorphosis. Her curly carrot-colored hair—pigtails in his earliest memory—changed each year until it hung straight to her shoulders, a sheet of burnished copper. She freckled something fierce, but didn't start caring about it until she got older. One summer, besides slathering herself with sunscreen, she carried a parasol she'd found in the attic that had belonged to her great-great-grandmother.

Logically he knew the changes were because he didn't see her day in, day out, and guessed it would be the same if, say, Davey had gone to live off-island from Labor Day until June. Still, his mind placed her in a different category from everyone else. A unique one—at once familiar yet exotic. She was from home *and* away.

Her grandparents were old friends of his grandparents'. They were all active in the grange. Norah's mother, an only child, was like another sister to Jake's dad and the rest of the family. Norah naturally ended up with the Marshalls too.

The summers her school let out before his and he was stuck in a classroom while she was out with his grandfather in the boat, baking cookies with his grandmother, or taking her canoe to one of the islands in the thoroughfare; he knew what prisoners felt like.

One June—before he shot up in mid-August—she came back taller than he was and lorded it over him until he complained to his grandmother, who told him to stop whining and wait. She'd been right, as usual. She'd also slipped him extra cookies and always made sure his milk glass was full that summer.

Together they got to know every inch of the island—the old granite quarries and the even older serpentine one on Little Sanpere. It was so hidden by alders that when they happened upon it, he'd felt as if they had stumbled on an enchanted castle in a fairy tale—the green rock jutting out in steps only a giant could scale.

She taught him how to swim in the lily pond. She'd had lessons at some Y near where she lived in the winter. She told him she didn't want him to be like all those fishermen who drowned because they couldn't even do a dog paddle. He didn't tell her they mostly drowned because the water was so damn cold it froze them before they could take a stroke. He didn't tell her, because he wanted her to teach him. Liked the way she held him up in the water and told him not to be afraid. He told her most everything else, though; especially that he wasn't going to be a fisherman. Or an electrician like his dad. Not that these would have been a bad way to make a living. It was that Jake wanted to build boats. Big boats. She laughed at him often, but she never laughed at his dream. She was the one who got him started—a dinghy. He sold it to a summer person for $400. A fortune. And she was the one who hauled them over to the historical society to find out everything they could about the America's Cup Boys and Nathaniel Herreshoff, the man who built the two yachts the all-island crew sailed to victories in 1895 and 1899. Afterward, Herreshoff became his hero and he read everything he could find about the man and the incredible boats he built. What had been a dream fast became an obsession. He made friends with people over at the Wooden Boat School in Brooklin. And that year at Christmas he got a gift subscription to their magazine from "Anonymous," but he knew who it was. He sent her a book reproducing old postcards of Sanpere that the historical society had just published, with a three-word note, "Come back soon."

She was a year ahead of him in school, but they were the same age. Something to do with when you turned five and could start kindergarten where she was. His birthday was in October, hers in August. She teased him about it the summer she turned fourteen—telling him she was robbing the cradle.

That summer. He was happier than he had ever been—and didn't know he would never be that happy again. The first summer he knew she felt about him the way he did about her. It was like they invented kissing. And it was only kissing—well, maybe a little bit more. She was working at the island day camp and he and Davey had traps out. He'd scrub himself with his mother's fancy soap to try to get rid of the smell. Norah never complained. He was going into eighth grade; she was going into ninth.

Then the next summer she wasn't on the island. School let out and there was no knock on the kitchen door. No "Come on, lazybones, let's do something." Her grandfather had passed several years ago; her grandmother last fall. She'd come with her mother for the funeral. Jake was there too. They'd sneaked off together into the woods behind the church after the service while everyone was busy eating little egg salad and tuna fish sandwiches and drinking punch in the parish hall. She had been wearing a black dress and looked more beautiful than he had ever seen her. The swamp maples had turned and some of the scarlet leaves had fallen. She stretched out on the moss and her hair mixed with the leaves. He lay beside her, at first just holding her hand. "I can't stand being away from you for so long. Can't you get your parents to move here? Your mom is always saying how much she misses the island," Jake had said. She'd shaken her head. "I don't want to talk about it. I'd come if I could. I hate being apart too. Summer will be here before you know it," she'd said, and he'd hugged her words close all winter like a warm jacket.

When she hadn't turned up by the Fourth of July, he'd sent her a postcard asking her where she was and when she was coming. It was the second time he'd written to her, if you counted the sentence with the Christmas book. He wasn't much good at writing, but it was more that he liked keeping the distance between them total and she seemed to want the same thing. "What would I tell you?" she'd said once when the question of writing came up. "'I went to school, was bored out of my gourd, came home, did homework, blah, blah.'" So they didn't write.

And she didn't write back this time either. By now the island grapevine had picked up the news and he knew where she was. Her mother had to take care of an elderly cousin who now lived in Virginia and was dying of cancer. Norah had to stay home and take care of her father.

Jake had fumed. "Take care of him? Can't the man microwave

a frozen dinner? It's the stupidest thing I've ever heard."

Then there was a postcard in early August. A covered bridge someplace in Vermont. "Tell Grandma Nan to bake a cake. I'll be in Sanpere for my birthday."

His grandmother had Norah's favorite coconut layer cake ready, but she didn't show up. They waited two days and ate it. Jake couldn't finish his piece and his grandparents had looked at him sympathetically. "Must be because the sick woman took a turn for the worse. Probably Norah's in Virginia for the funeral. You'll hear from her."

But he saw her before hearing from her.

The first day of school. He couldn't believe his eyes. He was getting a ride that year with Davey's older brother, Larry. Jake jumped down from the pickup and she was standing with a bunch of girls outside the main entrance. With so few kids on the island, grades 7 through 12 were in the same building. It was all he could do to keep himself from running over and grabbing her. Instead, he walked next to Davey, who'd conveniently said, "Hey, it's Norah. Let's go say hi. What do you think's going on? She's carrying a backpack. She must be living here." The bell rang before they got to her and Jake had had to wait until lunch to speak with her. The anticipation had made him feel giddy. At lunch he took his tray and sat down next to her.

"Are you here for good? What happened this summer? I can't believe your dad. My dad is a great cook, and could take care of himself, although he'd bitch about it. Did the cousin die? Were you close?" The questions poured out of him like a mackerel run.

"I can't talk now. But yes, I'm here for good. My mom and me."

"What about your dad?"

"I have to go. I'm going to be late for class."

He looked for her after school and saw her get on the bus. He called her name, but she didn't turn around.

Later he'd heard his mother on the phone talking about it with someone. "Poor Darlene. Well, better to divorce than try to make something broken work. Good thing she held on to her parents' Little Sanpere place."

He kept watching for her, but didn't get a chance to talk to her for a few days. He'd grabbed her and pulled her into an empty classroom. She'd screamed at him not to touch her. Not to ever touch her again. He'd backed away, stunned at her vehemence and scared that someone would hear her. She took off and he called after her, "I'll be waiting, Norah. I love you, and whatever's wrong, I don't care. I'll be here. No matter how long it takes."

This time her metamorphosis was one he watched take place, although he could hardly bear to. First she cut her hair in jagged lengths—some so short you could see her scalp—then bleached it. She began hanging out with the Goth and punk kids, loser kids. Come spring, she wore crop tops and really low-rider jeans. Everyone could see her tramp stamp just above her ass. It wasn't anything bad—a big butterfly with long curling wings that ended in vines. She had another tattoo, a chain link, around her ankle. Maybe there were others on the few parts of her body not showing. The tramp stamp started the talk that she was a slut. Talk that had begun in the winter when she'd disappear off-island and skip school. Someone had seen her in Ellsworth with a bunch of bikers—older guys. Her mother couldn't control her, he heard his mother tell someone on the phone, and he wanted to slam the receiver down. Didn't they have better things to do with their time than talk about Norah Taft? Nan and Freeman never said a word to him about Norah—or Zara, as she had renamed herself.

Just before she ran away for good, the summer she would turn seventeen, he saw her sitting on the wall on Main Street in Granville one night. She was alone. Davey had gotten his license before Jake had and they were riding around as usual. When Jake saw Norah, he told Davey to keep driving. He didn't want her to bolt. Then he said to stop at the town pier and wait. He'd been pretty sure he wouldn't be long, despite his hopes. He'd doubled back on the hill overlooking the harbor and come up behind her, calling her name softly so as not to startle her. He felt like he was out hunting with his dad, but he'd never stalked such precious prey. As soon as she heard him, she'd begun to run, but it was nothing to catch her. He'd been the star of both the varsity baseball and basketball teams for a year and before that the JV. He held her wrist gently. Her pupils were big. He knew she was on something.

"I just want to remind you that what I said when you came back still goes. I'll never stop loving you."

She leaned her head against his chest and he thought it was over. He thought she really had come back. It had all been like a bad dream. She'd relaxed against him, then stiffened up and shaken her hand free.

He called after her. "I'll be waiting."

He was still waiting when the state police came to his house with a warrant to search his car and found her red high-heeled shoe wedged under the driver's seat.

"Oh, Tom! There must be some mistake," Faith said. "Jake couldn't have had anything to do with Norah's death. If nothing else, the way he asked us to remember her at Christmas dinner proves it. Murderers don't do things like that." Or, she couldn't help thinking, unless they were very clever—and very evil.

"I have to go. Freeman is picking me up right away. Earl is one of the cops at the house and he said they'd wait. They're letting us take him in, but they'll be following. Jake hasn't exactly been cooperating. At first he ran out the back door, but changed his mind and came back. Said he'd go with them, but didn't want his father to come. Art suggested Freeman, and Jake agreed, but said he wanted me too." As he spoke, Tom was putting on his coat, a wool one he'd brought to wear to church. The words kept tumbling out. "Call Sam Miller right away and get the name of the lawyer he got for Bill Fox."

"That was a long time ago, darling, and besides, that lawyer only lived in Blue Hill in the summer."

"Then maybe he's retired up here. All I know is that he was good and we need somebody good in a hurry for this kid."

Faith tied a wool scarf around Tom's neck. He'd buttoned his coat up wrong. She didn't think anyone would notice.

"Sam will be able to find someone," she said. "I'll have him call you—and call me when you can. Your cell will work in Ellsworth. I love you."

Tom hugged his wife tight against his chest. "I love you too. Some Christmas, I'm afraid." He let her go reluctantly.

"Yes," Faith whispered aloud. "Some Christmas."

After Tom left, and after making her hurried call to the Millers, Faith was at loose ends. Ben was totally absorbed in his intricate LEGO building. She'd told him Tom had to go help Freeman with something and might be a while. Did he want something to eat? He didn't, and deprived of the modest activity of making a peanut butter and jelly sandwich, Faith felt even more restless. She knew she wouldn't be able to read. Finally, she stood at the window and looked out at the waning daylight slanting across the cove. She hated the early dark of winter. They'd passed the shortest day, and each was getting longer, but it didn't feel that way to her. It would be pitch-dark when Amy came home. Faith drew a breath sharply. Jake's mother, Debbie, was on the Marshall Ladies' Day Out. They would have reached the final phase up in Ellsworth—the movies. Faith pictured her sitting in the darkened theater with her popcorn, unaware that her son was passing by outside, escorted by the police and about to be questioned in a murder investigation.

Murder! What had changed their minds? How had they known to search Jake's car?

Murder. On some level, she'd thought it all along—and she did not flatter herself that she was any smarter than the police. What didn't fit with an overdose? What had made her instantly suspicious? Suddenly she was so tired, all she could think of was stretching out.

"Ben, I'm going to lie down for a little while. Let me know when your sister comes home and I'll make supper."

"Sure." He looked up at her in the doorway. "Are you okay, Mom?"

Faith forced a big smile and reassured her son, "I'm fine. Just need a nap."

He looked skeptical. "You never take naps. Must be the holidays."

At that she had to smile for real. Was Ben watching Oprah? Or maybe they actually weren't doing too bad a job of raising him.

Ben was right about the nap part too. She didn't take naps. Yet. And sleep wouldn't come. Instead she turned her thoughts to Christopher and Mary. Having eliminated all the other possibilities—especially the poor Wellesley girl who was probably wishing that she'd never heard the words "tonsils and adenoids"—Miriam Singer with her long dark hair was number one. Faith had planned to go up to Orono and check out the twenty-four-hour store with the hope of finding Miriam, but doubted she'd be able to get away tomorrow. She rubbed her eyes, as if that would erase all her troubling thoughts.

One of Norah Taft's shoes in Jake's car? If he had had something to do with her death, he certainly wouldn't have left a piece of evidence like her shoe in plain sight. Except it must not have been in plain sight. He would have noticed it, or someone he'd given a lift would have.

Today was Wednesday. Exactly one week ago, Faith had discovered the body in the sleigh. Only one week. But in that week, surely Jake had given rides to friends, or if not, would have seen the shoe himself. Was it placed in his car more recently? The coroner put Norah's time of death in the early morning hours. It had been a school night; Jake would have been sound asleep in his own wee bed. Not driving around.

Some teenage boys' cars resembled a mound with layers chockfull of artifacts from which future archaeologists could construct a picture of life on earth for a sixteen-year-old in the early twenty-first century—empty soda cans, fast-food wrappers, half-eaten beef jerky sticks, WD-40, forgotten outerwear, single gloves, and an illicit beer can or two. But Jake's car was his pride and joy. She doubted he would let his friends use the backseat as a Dumpster, burying the shoe out of sight.

Faith wished Tom would call. She was tempted to call him, but knew she shouldn't. Nan was the obvious source of information, but she was still in Ellsworth. Which left Faith where? Waiting for the other shoe to drop. She sat up and got out of bed. Time to do some cooking and put on some music—Motown, something with a beat. Anything to take her mind off what was or wasn't happening in Ellsworth.

Tom called at 7 P.M. to say that he and Freeman would be leaving soon. Sam Miller had reached him on his cell and given him the name of a lawyer. She'd come right away and was with Jake now. Art had appeared shortly after they'd arrived and told his son in no uncertain terms that he didn't care what he wanted, that he loved him and he wasn't going to sit down on the island twiddling his thumbs while he was in this mess. Jake hadn't said anything, but didn't tell him to leave. Faith had a million questions, but they had to keep—all except one.

"How did the police know to search his car?"

"An anonymous tip. They traced it to a phone outside a gas station in Belfast. Could have been anyone."

But it had to be someone who knew more than they did, Faith thought as she reluctantly hung up the phone.

Amy was home and she and Ben were eating some of the lasagna Faith had made, one of three pans. Now that she'd heard from Tom, she'd run one pan over to Debbie and another to Nan. Ben could look after Amy for the short time she'd be gone. Debbie wouldn't feel like cooking, or eating, but there was the rest of the family—except for Jake and Art. Nan would have plenty of Christmas dinner leftovers, but they'd look too festive. The memory of all of them sitting around the table so happily was too fresh. No, lasagna was the food of choice in times of trouble.

An anonymous tip. Jake had turned seventeen this fall. How could someone his age have an enemy? Or enemies? The shoe had to have been planted. It wasn't just that he was the Marshalls' grandson. Faith prided herself on her ability to judge human nature and her snap judgments were more often right than wrong. From the moment she'd met Jake, many years ago, she had liked him. He'd always been kind to her kids, tolerating Ben's hero worship. She didn't know him well, but she knew enough to believe that whatever had happened to Norah Taft didn't have anything to do with Jake.

By the time she'd returned from delivering the food, she wasn't so sure.

Debbie's sister-in-law had thanked her for the casserole, but hadn't invited her in, nor had Faith taken a step inside. She could hear sobs and a soft voice. Debbie was obviously upset and being comforted by another relative. At Nan's, her daughter-in-law from North Carolina led Faith into the kitchen straightaway.

"She'll want to see you."

Nan wasn't crying. She looked angry, and when she saw Faith, she hugged her hard. "Thank the Lord, Tom is with them. Freeman says Jake's talked to him, but nobody else until the lawyer

came. It *has* to be a mistake. All of this. The shoe could have been
under the seat for years. From when they were together."

"Together?"

Nan nodded. "Jake has always been crazy for Norah. Since
they were both barely out of the cradle, he only wanted to be with
her and she with him. Until she came back to the island, that is.
Then she broke his heart."

"Now, Mumma, we don't know what went on. Could be that
Jake wasn't interested in her anymore. Not after she changed so
much." Mark put an arm around his mother's shoulders and led
her to a well-worn couch next to the woodstove.

"Debbie's been worried about Jake for a long time," Nan's
daughter Connie said. "When I was here at Thanksgiving she told
me he was moving heaven and earth trying to find where Norah'd
gone. He wanted to have it out with her once and for all. That's
what he said."

Nan flared up. "Now, don't you repeat that to another living
soul! Things are bad enough. Kids say all sorts of things when
they're upset and we know he was upset at the way she'd changed.
We all were."

Connie opened her mouth to say something more, then closed
it in response to a look from her brother.

"Don't worry. Nobody's going to be talking about any of this."

Or talking about the impossibility of Norah's shoe being left
in Jake's car for a long time. He'd only had his license for about a
year and bought the car last summer from someone in Sedgwick
after seeing the ad in *Uncle Henry's Swap or Sell It Guide*—the bible
for every male over the age of eight in the state of Maine and far
beyond its borders. Both Tom and Sam Miller had subscriptions,
and when it arrived each week, Tom would start fantasizing about
driving to Lubec to pick up a dirt-cheap rototiller or Sebago for an
outboard that needed only a few parts and some TLC.

It was time to leave. Faith told them to call if they needed anything and promised to take Amy's new friend, the granddaughter from the South, the following day. She offered to have her stay overnight immediately, but her mother said she was half asleep in front of the TV and didn't know what was going on. She would be grateful if Faith would take her tomorrow, though.

"Who knows what's going to happen?"

Her words echoed in Faith's mind as she cleaned up the kitchen after returning home. The kids were watching a DVD. Amy's lids were drooping and she was soon fast asleep in front of the adventures of the Avatar, Ben's new favorite. Faith settled down next to Ben and pulled Amy onto her lap. Her daughter was still small enough to curl up there. The lingering smell of egg rolls, popcorn, and Johnson's baby shampoo from the bath Amy had taken that morning was very comforting. While the Avatar battled the Fire Nation, Faith wondered what demons Norah had been battling. What had caused her to change so drastically, always a sign of trouble, as well as a call for help, in teens? And Jake. He was searching for Norah and wanted to "have it out with her once and for all." Did he find her—and what form did "once and for all" take? A rejected lover, one who had loved for a lifetime. Nan was clinging to the belief that the shoe was an old one and could have been in Jake's car for many months, but, aside from the other issues such as a license and Norah's taking off before he'd bought the car, Faith was sure the police would not have pulled him in if the shoe hadn't matched the one left on her other foot, or found in the sleigh if it too had slipped off. Yet, if she were Nan, she'd be grasping for any straws that came her way—and at the moment this seemed to be the only one.

"Another episode, Mom?" Ben's eyes were bright. Aang, the Avatar, traveled the globe on a giant, flying Sky Bison named Appa. A handy thing to have at one's disposal. The mission was to defeat the forces of evil without bloodshed and bring peace to every continent. A tall order, but the Avatar was doing a good job.

"Sure. Yip, yip," Faith said. "Yip, yip" was the command that made the bison take to the skies.

"Yip, yip," she said again softly to herself and wished Tom were home.

"Daniel, this is our chance! You've always said you didn't want to adopt, because it wouldn't really be your baby. Well, this is your own grandson—he has *your* genes—and what will happen to him if he's left with Miriam? She's probably somewhere in some kind of hippie commune." Brenda started to raise the notion of drugs, but stopped short. She didn't want Daniel to think the baby might have something wrong with him. That Miriam had been doing drugs during the pregnancy.

The moment Daniel had put down the phone, Brenda had started in, climbing into his lap and begging him to get this baby for her. Her eyes had filled with tears with very little effort.

"It's the only thing we don't have. Look at this big house! We always said we wanted a baby and I know it's my fault, not yours. There's nothing wrong with your swimmers."

As soon as Daniel had put a ring on her finger, Brenda had gone off the pill. She figured, when it happened it would happen, and she'd tell him then. Only it didn't happen, and after several years, she raised the issue, only to find that her husband was very happy with the way things were and didn't want another child. He was, in fact, counting the days until he could get Miriam off his hands. But gradually Brenda convinced him that their child would be different—always a boy in both their minds. Someone to carry on the Carpenter name and give them something to boast about—my son the athlete, smart but not a nerd, handsome, of course. She went through the charade of "trying" for a few months and then went to see a specialist. She knew Daniel would never get checked, and besides, he'd proved his virility. The news was not good—and definitive. The drug, DES, that Brenda's mother had taken to prevent a miscarriage had effectively made Brenda herself sterile. The doctor suggested adoption. "Many of my patients have been successful in adopting from overseas."

Brenda had left in a huff. As if she'd raise some foreign child. No, they'd find a healthy white American infant somehow. Except Daniel put his foot down on this one. She could have a dog, even two, but he wasn't bringing bad blood into his house. She knew he'd never change his mind and contented herself with as many material possessions as she could amass. They had been a fine substitute until she'd heard him on the phone just now.

"We're too old, Brenda. At our age we should be having grandchildren."

"I'm only in my thirties. Plenty of women my age are having babies. And you're in your forties, the prime of life. Think of all those men who have babies in their sixties—all those stars. Michael Douglas. Fred Thompson. They're way older than you. And Chris Noth, that guy you like on *Law & Order.* He's in his fifties." Brenda had subscriptions to both *Entertainment* and *People.* "And"—she lowered her voice reverentially—"what about Donald Trump?"

In addition to "The Donald," Daniel's Realtor role model, she'd found the right words, "prime of life." Daniel suddenly saw himself taking his son down the ski slopes at Sunday River and heading into Portland to catch a Sea Dogs game. Brenda could be president of the PTA. The whole thing would be good for business. He could never even get Rebekah to go to a parents' night, let alone pass the word around the neighborhood about her husband the savvy Realtor. Brenda would be totally different. Maybe a den mother too. And then there was old age to think of. Miriam would never take care of them. He wouldn't want her to, but his son and the woman he'd marry would. Mr. and Mrs. Daniel Carpenter Junior. Plus, Brenda wouldn't get those disgusting stretch marks and sagging breasts like Rebekah had. After Miriam was born, making love to his wife—who'd insisted on breast-feeding, which only made things worse—was like making love to a lump of dough.

"Okay, we'll do it," he said. They'd spent less time on this decision than on selecting the color for the exterior of the house. It had been an agonizing choice between Silver Screen and Dappled Sunlight. Brenda had had the painters do a sample of each before going for Silver Screen. She liked the name better.

"Oh, Daddy, you're wonderful!" Brenda kissed him hard and, when she came up for air, asked, "But how?"

"You leave it to me," Daniel said.

Freeman dropped Tom off just after nine. Faith had helped a drowsy Amy to bed and left Ben watching more Avatar episodes. He was now sound asleep in front of the TV and she left him there while she heated up some of the lasagna for Tom—she'd made the one for her family with spinach, mushrooms, and a low-fat ricotta.

Ben was long past the age where they could talk about anything serious in front of him. They'd rouse him after they'd finished talking. It could be a while.

"He's not being charged with anything. They don't have anything to charge him with. He has no idea how her shoe got in his car. She's never been in it to his knowledge. They'll go over the vehicle with a fine-tooth comb—the police took it up to Ellsworth on a flatbed. Jake was pretty upset about something happening to the paint job."

Faith poured herself some brandy. Tom couldn't drink, but she wanted some now that he was home.

"Start at the beginning."

"Earl's known Jake and all the Marshalls all his life, of course.

Can't imagine how this would have been handled in Aleford. Although the town is a lot like Sanpere when you come right down to it."

Tom was rambling, exhausted. Faith let him talk. She knew what he was getting at. The fact that Earl lived on the island and knew the family meant that Jake wasn't treated like a criminal. They didn't put him in the squad car, but let him ride to Ellsworth with Tom and Freeman. It wasn't just a matter of trust, it made sense. Handcuffing the boy, putting him in the backseat behind a barrier, or anything else official, would have made him less cooperative—and from the sound of things, Jake was already very upset. They would have started in a minus column before they'd even had a chance to talk to him.

But Nan had said Jake talked to Tom.

"Jake talked to you? When was that?"

Tom was scraping his plate. She stood up and took it from him for more.

"We'd crossed the bridge and were driving up Caterpillar Hill. Jake hadn't said a word to us and we weren't pressing him. He'd been crying. Scared and angry. Suddenly he told Freeman to pull over—at that scenic-view turnout overlooking Walker Pond. The police pulled over behind us. 'I want to talk to Reverend Fairchild alone, Grandpa,' he says to Freeman. Freeman just nodded and went back to tell Earl. They must have agreed, because he got into the police car and they waved to us to get going. 'Anything I tell you, you can't tell anyone else, right?' he said, and I told him that was right, but if he was concealing a crime, I'd try to convince him to tell the police."

"Oh, Tom, I've been afraid of this. He *did* have something to do with her death!"

"That's not clear."

What was clear, Faith thought despondently, was that whatever Jake Whittaker had told her husband would stay between the two of them. This was one of the major drawbacks to being married to a man of the cloth. Tom was a repository of all sorts of secrets that Faith was dying to know, and if he told her, he wouldn't only be in trouble with the confidant, but his boss—and that could lead to such unpleasantness as eternal damnation. Not that Faith was altogether sure this existed; still, one couldn't take chances.

"What happens now?" she asked.

"He'll have a long night. He and his lawyer had only just started talking with the police when we left. Before that he'd been meeting with her. Smart boy. Very polite, but firm. Told them he wouldn't say anything until she got there. Freeman was sitting on one side of him; his dad on the other. Kind of like palace guards. Mainers are good at holding their tongues. They never said a word to him, or much to anyone else. I was kind of superfluous at that point, but I knew Freeman wouldn't want to leave until the lawyer came. I found a vending machine and got some coffee. They had whoopie pies too. Had one. It wasn't bad."

A whoopie pie that probably dated back to the Making Whoopee Roaring Twenties. Faith shuddered. A homemade whoopie pie, or one from a good old-fashioned Maine bakery, was a treat. A whoopie pie from a vending machine was an affront.

"He'll continue to be 'a person of interest' until they solve this thing." Tom suddenly sat up straight. "I can't believe I almost forgot this!" He reached out and took Faith's hand as she was clearing his plate. "Earl wants to talk to you first thing in the morning. Why would that be?"

Faith looked her tired, beloved husband straight in the eye. "I suppose because I found the body," she said. This was no time to complicate everything with her questions to Earl and the tale of a baby found in a modern-day manger.

❄   ❄   ❄

Jake wasn't that much older than his own son. Ben's cheeks hadn't known a razor, but they would soon. Already his voice was changing. He was at one end of adolescence; Jake was at the other. The thought crowded in with all the others keeping Tom awake. He finally gave up trying to get some sleep, slipped out of bed, and sat in a chair by the window looking out at the cove. He'd thought the summer skies were the starry ones until he'd seen these December nights where the firmament above was one shining arc.

It was pleasant sitting in the overstuffed armchair Faith had placed in the alcove, conveniently close to the bookshelves that lined it. "Nothing spindly, or mid-century modern, thank you. A chair where we can curl up. Together if possible," she'd declared when they were furnishing the house.

Tom stared at the cove for answers that weren't there—and knew that sleep wouldn't come either. Normally he could close his eyes and instantly be in the arms of Morpheous—anywhere, anytime. It was a trick he'd learned early in his career. That and eating whenever he could grab a bite, since he never knew when he'd be called away from a meal. Called. Calling. Jake had turned to Tom because of his calling. He was glad he had been there for the boy. He thought again of Ben. It was terrifying to realize that something like this could happen to one of his own children. Yet, things like this happened to people's own children all the time.

He believed Jake. Not because of his family, or what he'd observed of Jake himself over the years, but because what he said had had the ring of truth. Tom didn't fancy himself an expert, but he'd found that liars tended to elaborate. Their stories—and they always looked you in the eye—were detailed. Overly plausible. No holes. Jake's story was told haltingly. Bare-bones.

When he had finished, Tom had advised him to repeat everything to his lawyer, but no one else unless the lawyer said it was all right. Jake had been relieved. He hadn't wanted to tell anyone, especially his parents—or his coach. Knowing that he shouldn't, because in the worst-case scenario they could be called to testify, oddly gave him breathing room.

The coach. His team. That was the big thing and that was where Jake had started.

"The thing is, I'm kind of important to the team," he'd said. "The basketball team. We have a good chance of taking our division championship and maybe even the state. Whip those kids down in Falmouth and thereabouts."

Tom had nodded and kept his eyes on the road. He had the feeling that even a short reply on his part would have caused Jake to clam up.

"I broke training. Kids do. Like they'll have a beer and if Coach knows, he's not a hard-ass about it. But I went to a party off-island, and on a school night, plus I must have had more than a pop, although it's weird—I don't remember drinking anything except a few Cokes. Anyway, it's enough to definitely get me kicked off—and someone else from the team was at the party too. I can't tell you his name. He left early, but he was there and I'm not going to tell the cops about him no matter what."

Jake had leaned back in the seat and closed his eyes. He didn't move anything except his lips, and the rest of what he said seemed to have been dragged from someplace deep inside him, someplace he didn't want to go. Each syllable was uttered more wearily than the last.

"Maybe I've been a little crazy. No, a lot crazy. I had to find her. Norah. I heard she was at this party. Not on the island—near Belfast. It had been going on since Sunday. Somebody's house in Temple Heights. I think they were planning to party straight through Christmas. It was the week before. I climbed out of my window, let the car roll down the yard onto the road, and went to pick up the other person. My mom and dad don't know anything about this. Norah was there, we talked, and the next thing I remember is waking up behind my house in my car. Not driving it home or anything. But I must have. I was in the driver's seat. I'm no saint, but I'd never drive drunk. Except I must have. There's no other way I could have gotten home. It was about four thirty. I felt like I couldn't move. Just wanted to sleep, but I knew my parents would be up soon, so I made myself get out of the car and go in the house. I got into bed. Didn't even take off my clothes. For some reason I was freezing cold. I fell asleep and didn't hear my alarm go off. Mom was shaking me and asking me if I was sick. Then I don't remember anything except waking up in the afternoon, still feeling weird. Like I couldn't move, but I didn't want anyone to think something was wrong, so I managed to take a shower, change, and eat some supper. The next day I went to school like nothing happened. And nothing did, Reverend Fairchild. Norah was as alive as you or me when I last saw her."

Jake's choked-up voice was still echoing in Tom's ears. He stood up and once more his gaze was drawn to the scene out the window. The cove looked like a Christmas card. He loved this season—a time of hope and belief. Tonight, more than anything, he wanted to believe.

On the other side of the island—the side facing the Camden Hills far across Penobscot Bay, Jake Whittaker lay in his bed wide awake. He'd be off the team. There was no way this could be hushed up. No one had asked if anyone else went with him to the party, so he hadn't had to refuse to answer. He'd screwed up, but he wasn't going to involve Davey too. None of it mattered anyway. What this might do to his chances for a UMaine scholarship. The only thing that mattered was gone. Gone for good. He squeezed his eyes shut, trying to keep the tears from dripping out. The tears that came whenever he thought about never seeing Norah again. He wished he could have seen her body. Seen her one last time and then possibly he'd believe she was dead. He remembered that Mrs.

Fairchild had been the one to find her. Maybe someday he'd talk to her about how Norah had looked. In his mind, the clock was turned back and her hair the way it had been at her grandmother's funeral. The way it had looked with the red swamp-maple leaves tangled up in it after they'd made love for the first, and only, time. If they hadn't would things have turned out differently? The hot tears spilled down the side of his head.

It was all going to be okay. Like it had been before. That's what she'd said at the party. He hadn't told anyone what they'd talked about. Not Reverend Fairchild, not the lawyer, and definitely not the cops. It wasn't his secret; it was hers. His head ached. It had been aching since he heard the news. He was so confused. Who did this to her? It had to have been someone who was there that night. He'd tell the cops anything that would help find her murderer, but he couldn't remember past the end of the conversation he and Norah had been having when they'd returned to the house. Names. He tried to recall the names he'd overheard. Overheard. Had they been overheard? Was there someone near the shore where they'd talked? The person immediately responsible for her death was faceless. But there was someone who wasn't. Someone who had driven her from Jake and the person she had been. Someone who had made her look for a way to end the pain she was in; the pain that that person had caused. As soon as this was over and he was free, Jake had only one plan in mind: find Norah's father and make him pay for what he'd done to his daughter.

CHAPTER 7

When Mary heard that Faith wasn't going to be able to get to Orono until tomorrow, she stoked the fire, checked the baby, and sat down to think. She didn't sit in the rocker but in a big armchair her father had moved into the kitchen one day, taking the door off to do so. Some summer person was getting rid of it. A few years ago, Mary had slipcovered it with a bright floral chintz that she'd found at the Take It Or Leave It at the dump. There wasn't quite enough, so she'd used some plain blue cotton from the Island Variety Store for the back. The chair had down cushions and originally must have been an expensive piece of furniture. Over time it had proved a fine place to read, seek comfort, and above all, think things over.

She had to be honest with herself. Knowing that Faith wouldn't be able to locate Christopher's mother for another day—at least— did not make Mary unhappy. Yes, she wanted to find the woman and be sure she knew what she was doing, yet at the same time, once she was identified, no matter what the outcome, Mary was afraid she would always feel that Christopher belonged to someone else. At the moment, this figure was faceless, an apparition that would disappear in time, and she could give full range to her fantasy—that somehow she herself had given birth to the infant sleeping so soundly by her side.

"You're a fool, Mary Bethany," she chided herself out loud—and wished she meant it. There was nothing foolish about the way she felt. In a little more than forty-eight hours, Christopher had become the most important thing in her life. She understood now what all the fuss was about—people saying they'd die for their children. And what the loss of a child could mean. She wasn't a conventionally religious woman, but she was suddenly struck by the enormity of that other Mary's grief when she saw her child crucified. It was, at heart, a mother and son. As simple—and complicated—as that.

What if Christopher's mother changed her mind once Faith confronted her? Although, if she *had* changed her mind, wouldn't she have been here by now? Or called? What if she'd been away, though? Visiting with her family for Christmas? Did seeing all of them make her want her own child back? Perhaps she had been able to tell them about the pregnancy and birth. She could be on her way here right now, saying to herself she must have been crazy to leave her precious boy with an old-maid goatherd on an isolated island that boasted a total year-round population of three thousand, give or take.

Christopher was stirring. Mary got up to prepare a bottle for him. When it was ready, she picked him up and settled into the rocker. He seemed to like the motion while he drank. His dark eyes stared straight at her and one little hand was curled tightly around her finger. Every once in a while, he'd give it an extra little squeeze—as if he were telling her everything was going to be all right. Mary held him close and kept rocking long after the bottle was empty.

❄   ❄   ❄

Missy Marshall, Nan and Freeman's granddaughter—the daughter
of their youngest son, Mark—was a pistol. Amy Fairchild was an
active little girl, but an observer, a listener. The two were perfect
together and Faith was delighted to hear her daughter's laughter as they rearranged Amy's room—Missy's idea. "Can we do
something about this boodwhar? Like put the bed so she can look
out the window?" Missy's best friend at home—"You're my BF
here, Amy"—was a certain Delilah Ogletree, daughter to Lavinia
Ogletree, interior decorator extraordinaire for the entire Triangle
region. "That's Raleigh, Durham, and Chapel Hill," Missy had
explained to the uninitiated. Amy had nodded solemnly. This was
not something she was going to forget now or ever. Missy was
taking Faith's mind off both young Christopher and older Jake.
Especially Jake. When Missy's mother had dropped her off, she'd
told Faith that Art had driven Jake back to Ellsworth for more
questioning. "The phone's been ringing off the hook. This place
is exactly like home. Everybody wants to help—and not a soul
believes he had anything to do with that girl's death. From what I
understand, she was an accident waiting to happen. I'll pick Missy
up at three, if that's okay. We'll all be at Debbie's if you need us.
And don't let her sass you. She's a good kid, but her mouth has a
mind of its own."

Faith had told her Missy could stay even longer, and meant it.
As for her mouth, well, they could use one like hers today. After
the boudoir had been completed almost to Missy's satisfaction—
"I'd like for Amy to have a canopy bed, Mrs. Fairchild. Do you
think you could get one?"—they went outside to "hunt down
treasures on the shore." Both girls were in agreement on what
constituted a treasure and Faith knew they'd be back with parts of
pot buoys, line, driftwood, and anything else poking up through
the snow—not so deep on the sandy beach. Ben went along, os-
tensibly to keep on eye on them, but Faith could tell he was enjoy-

ing their visitor as much as the rest of them were. Missy was a long string bean, with a mop of brown curls, but Faith had taken one look at Missy's mother on Christmas and realized the little girl was going to be a stunner one of these days.

After the children left, Faith turned to Tom and suggested a walk.

"They're going to be a while, don't you think?" he remarked.

"It's not cold, so I'm pretty sure they'll be an hour or so. I gave Ben a thermos of cocoa and some molasses cookies."

"Are you thinking what I'm thinking?"

"Not walking?"

"Definitely not walking."

Forty minutes later the phone rang.

"Let the machine pick it up," Faith said. She felt as drowsy now as her beloved looked and a short nap would be an extra dividend.

"We can't," Tom said sorrowfully.

"I know. I'll get it."

The moment Faith heard the voice on the other end of the line, she was sorry she hadn't given in to her initial impulse. It was Sergeant Earl Dickinson, although he hadn't used his full moniker, simply saying, "Faith? It's Earl."

"Oh, hi," she said.

"Tom must have told you I wanted to talk to you. Are you busy now? I'm down on the island for a couple of hours. I don't want you to have to drive to Ellsworth."

She wasn't busy—not now. And there was no way she wanted to meet at the state police office. She thought quickly. The kids would be back soon, so she couldn't have him come by the house. The kids. Maybe she could postpone the encounter.

"Actually, I *am* kind of busy. I'm taking care of one of the Marshall granddaughters for the day."

"Mark's Missy?"

"Well, yes." While it was helpful to have a law enforcement officer who was so embedded in the island—like yesterday with Jake—at times, it was a drawback. She knew what Earl was going to say before the words were out of his mouth.

"She could take care of half the island without turning a hair. Tom's there, anyway, right?"

She was stuck.

"Well, yes." She also seemed to be stuck to this particular speech pattern.

"Meet me at Lily's in fifteen minutes. The breakfast rush is long over, but Kyra's still serving it and I haven't had mine. Lily's is pretty quiet these days anyway. I haven't seen many cars outside. Not like August."

Faith sighed. "See you there."

She hung up the phone. Tom's eyes were closed, but she could tell he wasn't asleep. His mouth wasn't relaxed, and as soon as she walked toward the bed, his eyelids flew open.

"Who wants you to do what? Mary?"

"No, it was Earl. I forgot you mentioned he wanted to speak with me."

"I forgot too. I'm sure he won't keep you long and I can make my famous toasted cheesers for the kids if they're hungry."

Tom's culinary skills—minimal before his marriage—had atrophied to the point of said sandwiches and decent coffee. His version of a classic toasted-cheese sandwich, learned from his mother, involved lashings of butter, many slices of Kraft cheddar, an iron skillet, and a lid, which he used to initially cover the skillet.

"He wants me to meet him at Lily's."

Tom got out of bed and reached for his clothes. His face brightened. "Maybe Kyra made doughnut muffins this morning and has some left."

Faith was pulling an Icelandic wool sweater over her head. She felt chilled. Emerging, she reassured her husband that even if

doughnut muffins were not on the menu, she'd bring back something delectable for him, and reminded him that she'd made a big
batch of nonmuffin doughnuts that he could have.

Earl was sitting on a stool at the counter, drinking a mug of
coffee.

"Hi, Faith. There's no one upstairs, why don't I grab us a table
while you order. I'm all set."

His geniality was puzzling. It was almost as if he had merely
asked her to meet him for a chat about what to get Jill for her
birthday, or some other prosaic topic. A topic far removed from
murder.

"What'll it be, Faith? Good to see you," Kyra said. She wore
the kind of vintage bib aprons that her great-aunt Lily might have
worn, but the young, attractive brunette gave them a style all her
own—a sense of style evident in every corner of the café.

Ordinarily, Faith would have had a hard time deciding. At the
moment, she had no appetite even for Kyra's food. A mug of coffee
would be enough. But Earl had probably ordered a full breakfast
and Faith would be sitting there with nothing to occupy her hands
except the mug.

"I've already eaten, but a toasted bagel with cream cheese and
some of your jam would be nice—the cheese and jam on the side,
please. And could you put aside two of whatever muffins you have
today for Tom?"

Kyra nodded and disappeared into the kitchen at the rear.

Faith slowly climbed the stairs to the second floor. Lily's was
located in a late-nineteenth-century gambrel-roofed house on
Route 17 that Kyra and her partner, Renée, had beautifully restored and converted into the café-restaurant. Open year-round,
it was flooded with off-islanders during the short summer season.
The rest of the year, it belonged to Sanpere. It wasn't a place for a
tryst—might as well put it in the *Bangor Daily News,* since someone you knew was bound to be there and that someone really

knew you. It was the spot for meetings of other kinds, though—from friends who hadn't seen each other in a while, caught up in the hectic everyday, to groups trying to start new island businesses and projects or help out existing ones.

Earl was at one of the round tables in what had been a bedroom. He had taken the chair that faced out the window at the road and passing traffic. It was the equivalent of facing the door in a bar.

He'd stopped at home long enough to shower. Faith could smell the citrusy shampoo Jill favored that they both used. His face was smoothly shaven; his uniform was freshly creased. The sergeant was ready for work.

"Thanks for coming," Earl said.

The food arrived and Faith saw that Earl had ordered her favorite breakfast—a sandwich called the Annie, oozing with a mix of spinach, feta, scrambled eggs, and a slice of tomato (see recipe, p. 246).

As soon as the server left, Earl took a big bite, swallowed, and got down to business.

"Why did you think Norah Taft might be pregnant?"

Faith applied a layer of cream cheese to her bagel and reached for the jam. She had been expecting this question and was prepared.

"Finding her was a shock and I keep trying to make sense of her death, although I know that's probably impossible. But for someone to overdose deliberately, there has to be some sort of reason. I thought she might have been overwhelmed by something like an unwanted child—and the effect her drug problem was having on the fetus."

She'd rehearsed her statement over and over. It was mostly true.

Earl nodded and finished half his sandwich.

"You also said you thought it was strange that the works would be in a bag."

This was easier ground.

"You must have thought so too. I know you said she would have had time to tidy everything away, but why? If she shot up in the sleigh, the syringe would have dropped to her side along with whatever she used to tie herself off with—a belt maybe."

"So, I guess what I'm asking is, did you think she was murdered when you found her?"

Faith put her bagel down. She'd done a fine job spreading the homemade strawberry jam, but couldn't manage even one bite.

"When I saw her, all I could think of was getting someone there as fast as possible, so I could get my kids away. But yes, as I waited I did think it was an unnatural death. When I heard about the overdose and the fact that everything was tucked neatly in the sleigh, I *did* think she'd been murdered. Given an overdose someplace else and moved to the sleigh. By someone with a sick sense of humor."

"Or very smart. In this weather, with the way the display was set up, it could have been a while until she was found. People were stopping by on the weekend to take a look, not weekdays. And the only house with a clear view is Daisy Sanford's across the road. Even if she did look out the front window, her eyes aren't what they used to be."

Faith drank some coffee. The warm liquid felt good and she drank some more. "Why the sleigh?" was the place to start. She doubted it was from any feeling for island history. As Earl had just said, it was a place she'd be noticed, but not immediately. Not only were Daisy's eyes cloudy, but that front room wouldn't be used much at any time of year except for company and definitely not in the winter with the cost of oil. Was the sleigh simply convenient? She pictured a car traveling down Route 17 in the early hours of the morning with its terrible burden. There were no streetlights on the island except in Sanpere Village and Granville. Whoever placed the body in the sleigh had to have been familiar with it, passing it in daylight—or living nearby? She gagged slightly on the mouthful of coffee she had just taken. The Whittakers lived only a few houses away, next to Art's business.

"Jake didn't kill her," she said. "You haven't arrested him, have you?"

"Not yet. We're waiting for more results from the lab. Things got slowed down when it looked like an overdose, accidental or intentional."

Faith knew all about probable cause and the way law enforcement worked, but she still blurted out, "You can't be serious! Constructing a case against Jake Whittaker is a waste of time!"

"Now, Faith, calm down. You have to admit it looks pretty bad for him—and we wouldn't be doing our jobs if we just said good-bye to him—but I don't think he did it either. The problem is, he's not telling us everything he knows. Maybe he opened up more to Tom. But I doubt it. Jake's still sitting sick with secrets. Yeah, he's worried about the team, but that's not all."

Faith looked confused. "What team?"

"Didn't Tom tell you—oh, wait, I almost forgot. It's like me and Jill—he can't or he'd lose his job and the guy he reports to is even stricter than my boss." Earl smiled at his own joke. "Anyway, it's all over the island, so I don't have to worry that telling you will jeopardize my job. Jake, who is normally a pretty straight kid, was at a party off-island on a school night where there was plenty of alcohol and any drug you want to name. Major no-nos when you're in training, and for an underage kid, even if you're not. Jake is one of the finest athletes we've ever had, and without him, there's no way that the basketball team will make it to the district finals—plus this was the year we were hoping to make it all the way to the state finals. Team sports—and don't forget to include our nationally ranked chess teams—are big here. Everybody from nine to ninety goes to the games to cheer the kids on. I'd hate to

be the coach at this moment. We haven't released anything offi-
cially, so he can claim ignorance. Otherwise if he kicks Jake off,
he'll have flat tires on his pickup for the rest of his life."

"Where was the party?"

"In the Belfast area."

"Which is where the call about the shoe in Jake's car came
from."

Earl nodded and finished his sandwich, using the crust to scrape
up the bits of melted feta and egg from the plate.

He pointed to her untouched bagel.

"You going to eat that?"

She shook her head and pushed the plate toward him

"I had a big breakfast before I came," she lied. "It's all yours."

She was feeling more, not less, nervous. He'd asked what
she thought he would ask, but was clearly in no rush. Little
Christopher's arrival on Sanpere had nothing to do with Norah
Taft's death. Mary and she were doing all they could to locate the
baby's mother. There was no need to involve the authorities. To
Faith's knowledge, they weren't breaking any laws. The baby had
been left at Mary's with clear instructions. And a wad of cash.

"You helped me out with Harold Hapswell's death and I know
you can keep your mouth shut. Besides where Norah was found
and this business with Jake, there are a whole lot of other things
that don't add up. Maybe you can give it a try."

"What kind of things?"

"For a start, someone had slipped her a roofie—Rohypnol, the
date-rape drug."

Faith knew all about it—and the others in the category. Roof-
ies, especially in the generic form, which did not change color
when added to liquid, were tasteless and odorless. If it was dropped
into a drink, the effect was fast acting and could last up to thirty-
six hours. If Norah had survived, she wouldn't have been able to

remember what had happened to her—and more to the point, she certainly wouldn't have been able to shoot up while under the effects of the drug.

"So that's why you think she was killed."

Earl's face was somber. "It looks like someone doctored her drink—there was a small amount of alcohol in her blood. She wasn't drinking a lot that night. Or doing other drugs. At some point, the individual—or individuals—gave her a speedball when she was unconscious is what we think happened. On top of the Rohypnol, the combination of cocaine and heroin was sure to put her permanently out of the picture."

"But why?" Faith realized how futile the question was even as she spoke. "I mean, she was just a seventeen-year-old user. What kind of threat could she have been to anyone? Unless she saw something or someone she wasn't supposed to see. Wrong place, wrong time."

"That's the assumption we're making at the moment, trying to trace her movements over the last weeks and months. We found the house where the party was from Jake's description. Clean as a whistle. Anything in the way of furniture or personal effects is long gone. It's out of sight from the road or any other houses and they must have moved a van in right away. Lots of tire tracks—cars and bikes. Oh, and a pair of sneakers over the telephone wires." His voice took on an even grimmer tone as he noted the signal for a spot where drugs were available.

Faith's mind was whirling. She knew now why Jake had gone to the party. Somehow he must have heard Norah was there and, white knight that he was, planned to rescue his fair lady. Could Jake have been the one to slip her a roofie? She knew that even on Sanpere kids could get just about any illegal substance they wanted, although marijuana and alcohol still remained the drugs of choice. But if he had, something had gone horribly wrong. She recalled what Connie Marshall had said. That Jake wanted to have it out with Norah "once and for all." Maybe Norah hadn't wanted to listen. And maybe Jake had blown up.

She tried to phrase the question in her mind as delicately as possible.

"Were there any signs that she'd had intercourse recently?"

Earl shook his head.

"That's what we expected. And what's even more interesting is that she hadn't been sexually active at all. Word on the island was the opposite, but the coroner said he'd be willing to bet she hadn't had intercourse in a year, maybe two."

"But she wasn't a virgin?"

"No."

The word hung in the air, mixing with the dust motes in the shaft of winter sunlight piercing the curtains.

Earl stood up. "You'll call me if you have any ideas about this? I realize it's not normal procedure, but this isn't a normal case."

Murder never is, Faith thought.

"Of course," she said. "Although at the moment the only thing that makes sense is that she was killed by one or more of the individuals at that party after she witnessed something she shouldn't. I don't suppose any other bodies have turned up?"

"Not yet, but I agree with you. Heroin and cocaine come in from South America through Mexico and up I-95—'the New England Pipeline'—hidden in passenger cars. Prescription drugs, some potent marijuana comes from Canada—a lot of marijuana right here in the state too. It's impossible to police given the size of our interior and the length of our shoreline. The motorcycle gangs are the main distributors. The people Norah was encountering were not the kind to bring home to the folks. Her life would have meant nothing to them."

"And everything to Jake."

"Yup," said Earl, reaching for his jacket, "back to Jake."

Davey sauntered into the classroom a few seconds after the bell had rung and headed for his desk, dropping a piece of paper on Jake's.

"Nice of you to join us, David," Mr. Trask said. "We're starting the Industrial Revolution unit today and I'm sure you wouldn't have wanted to miss it."

"No, sir. I have some Front Line Assembly CDs myself. You know, electroindustrial tunes. Very cool."

He was a wiseass for sure, Jake thought as he slid the note into his lap and opened it. A smart wiseass.

"I know where Norah is." Just the one sentence. Jake caught Davey's eye. Davey nodded and mouthed, "Later."

"Would you care to share your communication with the rest of us, Jacob?"

Mr. Trask thought he was very cool. He always used his students' full names, like he was some kind of teacher in a movie, one of those British ones. He was standing next to Jake's desk, holding his hand out. Jake popped the piece of paper into his mouth, chewed furiously, and swallowed.

"Communication? What communication, sir?"

"I'll see both of you gentlemen after school. Now, turning to today's topic: the Industrial Revolution. Who can tell me from the reading what it meant for the average person—the change from agrarian work to a factory-based economy?"

Davey knew where Norah was. How had he found out? Mr. Trask's voice seemed to be coming from the end of a tunnel. Jake had read the chapter—spinning jennys and little kids working twelve-hour days in the mills. It would be like being buried alive. He couldn't imagine not working outdoors. Even his father's job kept him inside too much. Sure, Jake would have to be in a boatshed when he was building his boats, but the rest of the time he'd be on the water. His grandfather said it was in your blood or not. Fishing was the only thing Freeman had ever wanted to do, like his father and so on all the way back to the first Marshalls to come to the island around the time of the French and Indian War. Mr. Trask was managing to pound some U.S. history into his head, Jake thought, especially when he related it to what was going on in Sanpere at the time. The detention would make them late for practice and Coach would ream them out, but there was no way Jake would have handed over the note.

I know where Norah is. Jake had found her at last.

As soon as the bell rang, he jumped up and practically dragged Davey into the hall.

"My brother saw her at a party in Temple Heights and it's still going on. He wouldn't tell me where. Just that she was there."

"Did he talk to her?"

"He tried, but she ducked out the back."

"Temple Heights is pretty small. It shouldn't be hard to find the place. Must be a helluva one if they're still partying."

"Larry said they plan to go straight to Christmas."

"I'll drive over tonight as soon as my parents are asleep."

"You mean we'll drive over."

Jake looked at his friend and saw the determination in his face. Davey was very stubborn.

"Okay, we'll go. I'll park in the road and flash my lights. Wait inside until then. My parents are usually dead to the world before ten, and if the kids are still awake, they won't say anything. I'll go out the window, anyway. There's no snow on that part of the roof." Jake's mind was spinning fast.

Then it settled into resolve—and more so as he moved through the rest of the very long day. Davey's coming wasn't such a bad idea,

Jake decided. He could wait at the back door in case Norah bolted while Jake went in the front. It was almost Christmas, and like it or not, she was going to be his present.

"Jeez-zus! It's colder than a witch's tit out there. Can't you crank up some more heat?" Davey said.

"Stop moaning—and when's the last time you sucked a witch's tit? I thought you were trying to get a pull on Lindsay Todd's." Jake hit the gas. Davey's house was set far back from the road with a large meadow in front. Nobody would hear the car pull away. It was a little over fifty miles to Belfast and wouldn't take long. No need to watch for cops until they were off-island, and even then he doubted they'd be out on a night like this. Besides, the closest Dunkin' Donuts was in Bucksport. There wouldn't be any traffic—no stupid summer flatlander going forty miles an hour and riding the brake in front of him with no way to pass. They should give tickets for going too slow. He'd have to watch it in Searsport, though—a cop car was always out no matter what the weather or time of night. When you crossed into town, the limit suddenly dropped down to twenty-five and they meant it. If you didn't crawl through, you'd get pulled over. Jake had seen four or more cars lined up in the summer, waiting for the tickets, drivers red-faced, when even the slowpokes weren't going slow enough. Made a nice profit for the town.

Davey was snoozing, but Jake had never felt more awake in his life—and happier than he'd been in so many months. It was going to be over. He could feel it in his bones. The sky was filled with stars and someday he'd get Norah a diamond that sparkled as brightly as the one straight ahead of him. It reminded him of the time of year. "Following yonder star." He went to church only when his mother insisted, but he believed in God, although his belief had been sorely tested. Since Norah had come back and left him, his whole life had been like a test. He'd passed so far and tonight he'd get his reward.

Here on earth where he could enjoy it, although if his mother was right, heaven wasn't going to be too bad. Maybe a little boring. He laughed to himself and was tempted to wake Davey up to share this ecclesiastical insight. "Ecclesiastical." Nice word. Norah liked words. She was a reader. If it was printed on a page, she'd read it. As for Jake, he stuck to his nautical biographies and boatbuilding manuals, although she'd gotten him onto Patrick O'Brian and the dude wasn't bad. They were through Searsport. It wouldn't be long now. He remembered one of his grandfather's favorite sayings: "Tickled as a cat with two tails." That about summed it up.

The house hadn't been hard to find. The convenience store in Belfast was still open and the kid behind the counter knew where the party was.

"Must all be soused to the gills. Been cleaning us out of beer for days."

The house was at the end of a long dirt drive. There had been a pair of sneakers thrown over the utility wires on the main road, so they knew it was the place even before they drove in and saw what seemed like a hundred other cars and just as many bikes. Jake had heard the sneakers were a signal for drugs—"flying high," something like that—but he'd seen so many all over Maine that he thought a lot of them had to be kids just fooling around. He and Davey had tried slinging a pair up around a cable on the Sanpere bridge a few years ago, but one of the Prescotts had driven by and given them what for before they were successful.

"Damn!" Davey said. They were walking toward the front porch. "Damn and double damn!"

"What's wrong?" Jake said from behind him. He'd been locking his car. He didn't want any couples using it as a love nest.

Before Davey could answer, the reason for the expletive blocked their path.

"What the hell are you two kindergarteners doing here?"

Davey's brother Larry was not only a few years older than he

*was but also a few sizes larger. Maybe many sizes larger. He grabbed
the back of his brother's collar and frog-marched him back toward
Jake's car. "You come too, buddy, and turn this thing around."*

Jake didn't move.

*"I said to get going!" Larry held his brother with one hand and
reached for Jake with the other. Jake dodged away from him and ran
toward the house.*

"Sonofabitch! This is no place for you. Now get back here!"

Jake stopped. "I'm not leaving until I speak to Norah."

*"Your Norah—or Zara, which is what all her lowlife friends call
her—isn't here."*

"Then I'll wait."

*Larry looked from his brother, who was keeping his mouth shut,
to Jake. "I can't do anything about you, but I'm taking Davey
home. There's some heavy shit going down in there."*

"Well, you're here," Jake said defensively.

*"I'm buying a bike off one of them. Thought I'd get a deal with
him nice and lubricated, but he's too wasted. Shoulda gotten it last
night. Now I don't care to come back. Look," he pleaded, "Norah's
not here. When I saw her yesterday, she took off. She's probably
not going to come back. She knows I'd tell Davey and Davey would
tell you."*

*"I don't care," Jake said, his earlier euphoria gone. "I'll wait all
night if I have to."*

*"Suit yourself," Larry said, and shoved his brother in the direc-
tion of his pickup. Davey made a halfhearted attempt to break free,
but in truth he was glad to be on his way home. If the scene was too
heavy for his brother, it must be pretty bad.*

"Jake, maybe he's right," Davey said. "Come on."

*In answer his friend gave him a wave, turned, and walked
quickly up the front porch into the house. The warm temperatures of
the last few days had turned the snow to slush. The crowd's comings
and goings had further churned things up. He'd leave muddy foot-*

prints since he didn't see a doormat, but he was certain the carousers wouldn't care.

A thorough search of the rooms upstairs and down plus out in the backyard and behind a decrepit shed revealed that Larry had been correct. Norah wasn't there. Jake found a Coke, popped it open, and sat on the arm of a ratty old couch. Nobody took any notice of him. He wasn't the only one sitting alone, but the others were in a world of their own, a world they'd constructed from a pipe or a syringe.

Someone had made a fire in the old fireplace. The chimney smoked, or maybe the flue hadn't been opened all the way. A girl was trying to toast marshmallows on the end of a coat hanger. They kept burning up and she'd laugh like crazy and try again. The room was a fug of smoke—the wood, cigarettes, and pot. Opened pizza boxes were strewn around, and half-eaten slices decorated what little furniture there was. Someone had once cared about this place. The walls had been covered with floral striped wallpaper that was now peeling off. There were large holes in the plaster and most of the baseboards were missing. It occurred to Jake that this might be what was burning in the fireplace.

In contrast to the temperature outdoors, the room was like an oven. People had peeled off their outer garments—and in some cases, a lot of their inner ones—piling them in the corners of the room. He inched over and opened the window a crack. The last thing he wanted was a contact high. He wasn't about to leave, though, and the spot he'd chosen gave him a view of the stairs to the second floor, the front door, and the door to the kitchen, which he'd noted had a back door when he went to get his Coke. The kitchen was where the action was taking place. As Jake watched, people flowed steadily from one room to the other. There was nothing beautiful about them. He figured he could outrun anybody there—both sexes were seriously overweight with the exception of a few girls who looked like skeletons. Bodies were pierced wherever holes could be made, including ear gauging—stretching the holes to grotesque proportions to ac-

commodate what looked like bolts or tire lugs. And everybody had tatties. He'd thought about getting one—just Norah's name—but he hated needles, and besides, the guys in the locker room would see it. How he felt was none of their business.

The music—Nine Inch Nails—which had been blaring from somebody's boom box since he arrived, was giving him a headache and his body was starting to get cramped from sitting in one position. He got up and went into the kitchen for another Coke. He was hungry but didn't want to chance the 'shrooms on the pizza. On the way back to his spot, he passed a couple of older guys from the island coming in the front door. They headed straight for the kitchen.

She walked in at midnight.

Jake jumped from the couch and stood in front of her. She looked beautiful. Her hair was white and she had on a white parka with fur trim. It was unzipped. Underneath he could see she was wearing jeans and a silky-looking flowered blouse. She wasn't wearing boots, but shiny red leather high heels. She'd always loved shoes—the more outrageous the better. It had been one of their jokes.

"Oh, Jake, what are you doing here? No, don't say anything, and get away from me quick. There's a path behind a shed in the backyard that leads to the shore. Go down and wait for me there."

The happy glow returned. She wasn't running away; her speech and eyes were clear. His Norah was back.

He gave a slight nod and headed for the front door, making it seem like he was leaving. He even took his keys from his pocket and jiggled them up and down. Norah's words, and tone of voice, had made him cautious about his movements. Clearly there was some need for secrecy—and he didn't want to be followed. Didn't want anything, or anyone, to mess things up now when the prize was so close at hand.

The path wasn't hard to find, and just when Jake was starting to think he might have to return to the house and see if Norah had pulled a fast one, she slipped from behind the trees lining the shore, one of the white birches come to life. He waited, and when she was a few steps away, he walked over and gently took her in his arms. She didn't struggle and they stood there in the starlight like survivors of a shipwreck who have found dry land at last.

"Norah," he said, kissing her hair, her face, finding her mouth.

She pulled slightly away. "We can't stay here out in the open. Someone might see us. Come back by the trees."

He followed her and said, "I have my own car now. I can take you home or someplace else. Anywhere you want. Let's go."

He wanted to get away fast—but also wanted to stay under the sheltering boughs forever, just the two of them in the cold winter night, clinging together for warmth and much, much more. It was like a dream. A dream he'd been having over and over again since she'd left him.

"I can't leave yet. I'm waiting for someone." Seeing the expression on his face, she quickly added, "Nothing like that. There's never been anybody"—her voice caught in a sob—"never anybody but you." She took a deep breath. "I've done some things I'm ashamed of, but not that."

"I can wait."

She nodded. "It's too cold to stay here or in your car, but you have to pretend not to know me at the house. You don't know what these people are like. If they think I've told you anything, there's no telling what they'd do to you."

"Norah!" Jake cried in alarm. "Let's get out of here now! What's so important about this guy?"

She didn't answer right away, but seemed to be trying to figure out what she wanted to say, and how she could say it.

"When things were really bad. When I left for good and was really into the stuff, I started dealing in exchange for what I needed. I've been clean for a while and it was rough. Why I decided to stop is complicated." She paused, and when she started to speak again, the words came out in a rush. "You have to believe me! I never stopped *thinking about you—and Grandpa Freeman and Grandma Nan. Even my mother. What happened wasn't her fault, although I believed it was for a long time. That's why I kept leaving. Whenever I saw her, it all came back and I couldn't stand to be with her."*

"When all what happened?" Jake was cradling Norah against his chest. She'd tucked her bare hands into his jacket pockets.

Her voice sank to almost a whisper. "You can't tell anybody. Promise. Promise you'll never say a word! Ever!"

"I promise," Jake said—and braced himself for what was to come. He knew it was going to be bad. Had always known whatever had happened to drive her from him had to have been bad.

"That summer. That summer Cousin Florence was dying, I was alone with my father. He was drinking a lot after work and one night he got crazy, told me I wasn't his kid. That my mother had been pregnant by somebody else when he'd married her. That she'd tricked him. I didn't know what to believe. He said since I wasn't his daughter, what he was going to do wasn't breaking any of God's laws."

Jake felt bile rise in his throat. He clutched her tightly and waited for the words he now expected.

"When he did it to me, he laughed and said he knew I was a whore just like my mother. 'You're no virgin,' he said. 'Who was it? Your little friend Jake up on Sanpere?'"

"You should have gotten away. Come up here," Jake said.

"I couldn't. When he started in on me, he told me if I tried to run off or told anybody, my mother would have an accident. A serious accident. And he would have done it, Jake. I always thought he hated me. That's partly why my summers away were so special—I didn't have to see the way he looked at me. But that summer—the summer with him—he took his hate out almost every night, even when he was sober. Every morning he left for work just like nothing had happened, getting me up to make his breakfast, as usual. I started sneaking his booze to try to forget, but he found out

and made me pay. Nothing where anybody could see, but he'd take off his belt and not stop until there was blood."

They stood in silence for a moment.

"When Mom called to say Florence had passed, she said we could get up to Sanpere for the rest of the summer. That's when I sent you the postcard. I didn't tell him that Mom had called, and when she got home later that week, he was on me and didn't hear her car. She must have thought something was going on, because she didn't call out, but came right upstairs to my bedroom and saw him."

Jake watched Norah squeeze her eyes shut tight, trying to obliterate the memory of the scene.

"That's enough," he said. "You can tell me all you want later. We have forever together, but no more tonight. I want to get you home."

"Yeah. Home. Mom called the police and had him arrested. It was horrible. I had to keep talking to people and pretty soon I was sneaking booze again, just to zone out. When I got back here to Sanpere I realized I couldn't go back to the way things had been. I wanted to be a little girl again, but that wasn't going to happen, so I decided to be Zara. But I want to be Norah now."

"You've always been Norah, my Norah. Now let's go," Jake begged. He pulled her arm through his and started up the path. She stumbled and one of her shoes came off. He grabbed it and put it back on her foot.

"I can't leave yet. You don't understand and I can't tell you. They don't know I'm clean. They think I'm the wasted chick I was and I've seen stuff straight I shouldn't have. One thing in particular when I was sleeping and they thought I was passed out. Oh, Jake, it was terrible. You can't believe what they did to this person, but I don't want you to know. Know anything at all. Ever. Tonight I'm supposed to meet this guy—he's been supplying me—and give him the money I scored from a deal I did last week. My last deal, but

they don't know that. I have the money on me. He said he was going away until New Year's, so I'd better be here. I'll tell him I'm going back to Sanpere and back to school. That I'm going to try to get my act together, because the last high scared me. That I was wicked afraid I was ODing. That part is true enough. Anyway, if I don't give him the money and just take off, he or some of the rest of them will come looking for me. And there's no place I can hide where they won't find me, even on Sanpere."

Jake had a sudden vision of driving to the Bangor airport and taking the next flight to someplace far away. They could change their names. He'd get word to his parents somehow that he was okay. He almost suggested it when she kissed him hard and began to walk quickly toward the house.

"When you see me with a can of tonic in my hand, leave and wait in your car. You can show me where it is on the way back. Then I'll go in first."

"I don't want to do it this way; I don't want to split up. Isn't there someone else you can give the money to? Someone who's here?"

Norah shook her head. "No, it has to be—wait, I don't want you to know any names. Trust me, this is the only way I can get out of this and be safe. People are always coming and going in this business. They don't care, but if they don't get their money, that's different. If I give it to one of these guys, they can say I never did."

"No honor among thieves," Jake said ruefully. Mr. Trask was given to proverbs and this one had stuck in Jake's mind. This and "Give the Devil his due." He tried to block the image of Mr. Trask from his mind or he'd go nuts and concentrated instead on the people in the house, especially the person Norah was waiting for—and prayed that they would all be denied eternal rest. All get their due.

"He could be there by now. And we can leave soon. Just think, Jake. We'll be together for Christmas."

"You and your mother can come to my grandparents' for Christmas dinner. There's always plenty of room."

"I love you."

"I love you too."

They hurried back through the yard and returned to the house separately. There were even more vehicles than before and Jake hoped the person Norah needed to see had arrived. He grabbed another soda, took a sip, and then left it on the sill while he ducked outside to take a leak. He returned and sat down in a sagging cane rocker near the front door. He knew where Norah was now. All he had to do was wait. He looked at his watch. Funny. It was kind of hard to read in this light. The music—Marilyn Manson now—was louder than before and it seemed as if someone was turning the volume up even higher. The noise was hurting his ears. But he was also getting very tired. He willed his eyes to stay open. He had to be alert for the drive down to Sanpere. He gulped more Coke, eager for the caffeine rush.

And then he saw her. Norah came into the room carrying a can of Sprite. She was smiling. He got to his feet and went out the door.

It was the last thing he remembered.

CHAPTER 8

As Faith crunched across the snow toward the house, she saw that the two little girls had been busy. A snow maiden now stood in front of the house with her back to the sea. Her face sported various shells with the exception of her mouth—a bright red, slightly lopsided grin drawn with a marker. Her earrings were unique—doughnuts, the kind floating from one end of the pot buoy line that sometimes washed up on the shore from lobster traps. Amy and Missy had skewered them to the sides of Ms. Frosty's head with wire borrowed from Tom's workbench. Around her neck a bright pink scarf was fluttering in the breeze. The sight brought a smile to Faith's face. She hurried in to get her camera and congratulate the sculptors.

"Mom!" Ben came running from his room. "You've been gone forever!"

While touched at being missed, Faith had been a mother long enough to know that the sentiment probably meant he was waiting to ask her to do something or go somewhere. It was the latter.

"We've been invited to go over to Walker Pond and watch the

iceboating. Maybe even ride on one! They've all been there for ages already."

Tom got up from the couch where he'd been reading *The New Yorker*. It always amused Faith that someone who had such mixed feelings about the land of her birth—"Where did you play?"— could be devoted to a magazine so named.

"Hi, honey." He gave her a kiss. "Freeman called right after you left. He, Willie, and Mark are taking the new boat over. He thought the kids might like to watch. Us too."

"Sounds like fun. Ben, why don't you go ask your sister and Missy to get ready? Tell them plenty of warm clothing—even though the sun is out, it's very cold. You get yourself set too."

He raced off and Tom pulled Faith over to where he'd been sitting.

"What did Earl want?"

"Just what I thought. Any first impressions I'd had when I realized it was a body in the sleigh. He mentioned how I'd helped before—"

Tom cut her off, sitting up straight.

"Helped and almost got yourself killed! What can Earl be thinking of?"

Faith put a hand on either side of her husband's face, kissed him, and said emphatically, "I'm not getting involved in the investigation. There's nothing I could do, in any case. He just wanted to use me as a sounding board. They found traces of that date-rape drug Rohypnol during the autopsy. We talked about what that could mean."

"What else other than rape?"

"No, I should have explained more. She wasn't raped and— despite the rumors flying around about her—she wasn't sexually active. The drug was used to knock her out before she was given a very potent heroin-cocaine combination."

Tom drew a deep breath.

"So it's definitely murder. She couldn't have done it herself. It's hard to conceive of someone doing this kind of thing. She was just a child."

Faith sighed. Norah wasn't a child, but she had been one very recently. It had been tough for the island to cope with her death; now they would have to deal with its new face—and that face, or faces, could be living among them.

She continued to think. From the sound of the circle Norah was traveling in, any drug from A to Z would have been close to hand, so it was hard to say whether her death was premeditated. Bringing the instruments of her death to the party for that express purpose couldn't be ruled out, however.

What did she know? What had she seen?

Faith suddenly wanted to change the subject.

"Since he's iceboating, I'm assuming Freeman either isn't worried about Jake or wants everybody to think he isn't worried about Jake."

Tom nodded and said, "Most likely both. He told me Jake's back up in Ellsworth with both his parents and his lawyer for more questioning—stress on 'questioning.' The police are taking his car apart—they have a warrant—and on the advice of counsel, Jake's voluntarily been fingerprinted and everything else they do these days. Nan, Connie, and Dottie are staying put at the house. Before all this, the guys had arranged to meet some other iceboaters today, and in any case, if they didn't get outdoors, I think they'd have exploded."

"Mom! Dad!" Ben was dressed for a polar expedition. "We're going to miss everything!" His tone of voice suggested he was about to explode himself—from the warmth of the layers and irritation with his parents. "You haven't moved an inch!"

Faith had been more exhausted by her chat with Earl in the cozy ambience of Lily's than she imagined she would have been being grilled under a bright light in an airless, windowless room at headquarters. Something about the disconnect between the topic at hand and the place. Lily's was for food and friendship, not cat and mouse. While the notion of standing around a frozen pond watching iceboats would not have been appealing ordinarily—a spa massage and facial, maybe followed by some time in a sauna, was more Faith's speed as a way to relax—she decided that the outing was just what she needed today.

"I have to make a quick call, then we'll go. We won't even take time to make coffee and cocoa. Get the empty thermoses out and we'll fill them at The Galley. Pack all those molasses doughnuts too and some apples." Last summer Faith, swearing secrecy, had convinced Marie McHenan, who had supplied the island with her delectable doughnuts for thirty years, to part with her recipe for the molasses ones, Tom's favorite. They were a toothsome blend of spices and dark molasses. She knew once they appeared, the iceboaters would pause to raise a mug. She'd made a big batch.

She went upstairs and, after dialing, crooked the phone in her neck as she pulled out the European thermolactyl moifroids she'd bought for a Fairchild family ski vacation celebrating Tom's father's birthday a few years ago. The garments' French slogan was *"Moi froid? Jamais!"*—"Me cold? Never!"—hence the name she invariably called them.

Mary answered on the fifth ring.

"Mary? It's Faith. How is everything?"

"Fine. The nannies seem to have taken to little Christopher like a charm. They're producing more milk than usual, and Faith, I think I heard him laughing when I was milking. Do babies do this? He definitely likes to be in that sling I rigged up."

"If you think he's laughing, he's laughing." Faith belonged to the maternal school of thought that believed whatever you perceived your baby to do, he or she was doing, no matter what the authorities said about developmental timing.

"It's a beautiful day, isn't it? The sky is so blue. I hope you're enjoying yourself with your family," Mary said.

Not yet, Faith thought, but soon. "We're going over to watch Freeman and some others iceboat on Walker Pond."

"Oh, those men are still little boys at heart. Have fun and I'll talk to you tomorrow."

"I'm planning on going to Orono. Are you all right for diapers until then? I know there's plenty of formula."

"Yes—and I can always wash some if need be."

"Good-bye for now."

"Good-bye."

Mary hung up the phone and started to unwrap the baby from the cloth sling. They'd been on their way into the house from the barn when she'd heard the phone and quickened her steps. Faith would go to Orono tomorrow and check out the convenience store. And check out Christopher's mother. But just now the sky was blue and she would have a lovely, uninterrupted day with her Christmas baby.

It didn't take long for Faith to realize that iceboaters were a breed unto themselves. The men—and a few women—were completely obsessed, amazingly inventive, ridiculously courageous . . . and quite likely slightly nuts. Their enthusiasm was contagious and both her husband and son caught the bug immediately. Freeman was describing how he'd built his new boat and giving them a quick overview of the sport.

"You see, we have what we call the 'cockpit'—some call it the 'fuselage'—mounted on three runners. Now, my cockpit is built to the dimensions of my La-Z-Boy, which over the years has taken on a certain bodily configuration that I treasure."

"It looks like a triangle," Amy piped up.

"Yes, it does, and the triangle goes on top of these steel plate runners. Now, I have made them myself, but these factory ones hold an edge better. Made the sail from a Hobie Cat mainsail that some summer person left at the dump, found the mast and most of the hardware there too."

Tom Fairchild's face took on a wistful look. He loved picking the dumps in Aleford and Sanpere. Faith could always lure him to Manhattan with reminders of the great stuff he'd previously found curbside on trash days in her parents' Upper East Side neighborhood.

"How fast can you go in this thing?" Tom asked.

"Heard that one fella did seventy on Sebago last winter, but my top speed is forty-eight point nine. Willie gave me one of those handheld GPSs a while back, so that's how I know so exactly. Only problem with the thing is the batteries don't last long in the cold. I'd like to get up to fifty, but I'm doing pretty respectable for boats built from scratch."

"'Respectable'! That's fantastic. It must be great!" Tom said. Faith looked out at the boats whizzing along the surface of the pond. She couldn't see the end and wondered how it got its name. The pond was actually a good-sized lake, almost 7,600 acres in size. Whoever Walker had been, he or she must have been myopic. The scene in front of her was a treat for any eyes, though. Some of the sails were bright colors—one rainbow striped—and the icy surface of the pond provided a glistening backdrop. Freeman had told them conditions were near perfect today—"Iceboater heaven" he'd said, the ice still pure and clear of much snow and no slush at all. They'd been out checking its thickness since early that morning and from one end of the pond to the other it was well over the five inches they needed to be safe. The cloudless blue sky suggested summer months and, as she'd told Ben earlier, the bright sun gave an illusion of warmth. She was enjoying herself.

"They do seem to be going fast, Freeman," she said. "How do you stop?"

Willie, Mark, Freeman, Tom, and every other male in her vicinity froze.

"Stop?" Freeman said. "Well, now, that's not the point."

"You mean there's no way to stop? No brakes?"

"You can head into the wind. That slows her down," Willie explained. "But pretty much the boats are kind of like turbocharged go-carts with the handling and g-force of a jet."

They'd drawn straws and Mark had won the privilege of taking *Yellow Fever* out on the ice for her maiden voyage.

Freeman saw Faith eyeing the name on his boat. "Nan wanted her flower boxes painted yellow, then changed her mind, so I had the paint. And the 'Fever' part is 'cause we get the fever in December, start looking for good ice and don't recover until spring. Last year we took the boats out one final time Easter Sunday and ate our dinners when it got dark. Nan and some of the others were a little miffed, but they're used to us."

Faith laughed. Mary Bethany's "little boys at heart" description was right on the money.

"Finest kind, Dad," Willie said as they watched Mark disappear down the lake.

"I'll get my camera and take a picture of him on the way back," Faith said. She also wanted to get some of the kids who were skating on a patch from which they'd cleared the light snow with a broom Freeman had in the pickup. Amy was teaching Missy how to do a figure eight.

As she walked back to the car, she heard Tom say, "Well, you know, I'm a fair enough sailor when the water's not frozen. Think I could have a try?"

All the Fairchilds had emerged from the womb knowing how to ski and sail. She'd known when they set out for the pond that Tom would never be able to pass up something like this. Some photos of him iceboating would be a shot in the arm for his parents, who had been as worried as she was during their son's illness.

And then there were the eagles. Circling and swooping about the mast tips, they seemed to be racing with the sailors below. It would be fun to use the video feature on the camera to capture the moment. She'd better check how much room there was on the memory stick and possibly delete some shots. Although there might be a blank one in the pocket of the case.

There wasn't. When it came to things like this—spares—there never was. She got into the car and reviewed what was on the camera.

It was going to be hard to pick one of the kids for her post-Christmas card. One of the ones in front of the "tree" made from traps and hung with pot buoys would make them happy—it had remained their favorite and they'd taken Tom to see it too. It was also certain to amuse the recipients. She doubted that any of them had ever seen a similar holiday yard decoration. On the way to Orono tomorrow when she was shopping for little Christopher in Bangor, she should have time to get the prints made. It wasn't taking long to go through the shots. Point and shoot was not infallible—she culled some slightly blurred ones and several that were overexposed.

And then there it was. Or rather, she was.

Faith knew the pictures were there. Had considered stopping her editing before she reached the ones taken by the sleigh. Those photos she'd made impelled by the need to do *something*. She looked up and stared out the front windshield. The pond was surrounded by tall pines that had been limbed up, leaving thick, pencil-straight trunks devoid of branches. She had a clear view and could see flashes of color. The boats. The skaters. A lively scene. Alive.

She looked back down at the camera, at the still figure in the sleigh, and thought angrily of the desecration of human life the act represented. Aside from the murder—humankind's most heinous act—there was the deliberate placement of the body next to the mannequins. She was sure it was not simply a matter of convenience that the body had been placed where it was. It was meant to indicate that Norah was of no more importance than a plastic doll.

Faith was glad Earl had told her about the Rohypnol. She hoped Jake knew by now—and everyone else who loved the girl. Norah hadn't known what was going to happen to her. They could take some slight comfort from that. But someone else had known. Someone, or more than one. Faith advanced to the next picture and looked at the snow. There was definitely more than one set of footprints, aside from Faith's. Earl had said they would have been left over from the weekend. Faith tried to remember whether there had been snow the night before she'd found the body. She thought there was a dusting on the deck when she'd looked out that morning. The morning when everything seemed brimming with possibility—Tom's health restored, the kids in fine shape at school and at home, her own mind and body starting to relax from some of the stress that had been so relentless during the fall. But yes, there had been a dusting of snow. She was sure.

Norah wouldn't have left prints, even if she had been wearing both her shoes. Faith found herself wondering what the shoes looked like. "Shoe." Not "boot." Tom said they'd found a shoe in Jake's car. This wasn't shoe weather; it was boot weather. This meant Norah hadn't planned to walk far.

The throw had been pulled up close to the girl's chin, but Faith had been able to see that she was wearing a thin silk blouse. Again, not appropriate garb for the time of year, although she had been at a party and must have worn a coat or jacket on top.

There wasn't much in Faith's photos that the police wouldn't have subsequently photographed. Maybe they'd be able to tell how many people had carried her to the sleigh from the shots she, and they, had taken. More than one; no more than three was her guess.

She advanced the camera until she got to the last picture, stared at it, and knew that she'd have to sit a moment before joining the iceboaters. The last shot had been a close-up of the sleigh's contents: a pile of presents gaily wrapped in waterproof oilcloth and tied with plastic ribbons along with the incongruous brown paper bag with what Faith imagined were disposable syringes and other necessities for an addict. The name of a store was stamped on it in red and the bag looked soggy. Proof that it *had* snowed that night, but not much. The sun must have quickly melted what had fallen. Faith recalled that she had noticed the printing on the bag, but what she hadn't taken in earlier was the name, clearly visible on the left side: "Sammy's Twenty-four Hour Store." Sammy's Twenty-four Hour Store! A duplicate of this bag was wrapped around thousands of dollars and hidden somewhere on Mary Bethany's farm. Faith closed her eyes. The streaks from the dampened ink looked exactly like blood.

Daniel Carpenter was not the type of person who gave up easily when it came to getting what he wanted. It was this attitude that had made him the top Realtor in Portland and its surrounding Gold Coast towns. He had a particularly uncanny ability when it came to obtaining new listings. Competitors complained that "Daniel Carpenter knows you're going to sell your house before you do."

After Miriam called with the news about the baby, he'd immediately sprung into action, first checking the caller ID. When he saw that it read "Private Caller," he went to his computer and entered her name. Daniel had embraced the new technology years ago. He was the first in the area to have a Web site featuring virtual house tours and he regularly surfed the Web for information about both buyers and sellers, discovering early on that there was little you couldn't find out about someone if you knew where to look. No phone was listed for Miriam Carpenter anywhere in the state. He checked every Carpenter. No one that could be Miriam. He googled her, looked at public records and credit reports. He expanded the search. As far as the Net was concerned, "Miriam Carpenter" didn't exist.

"Damn," he'd said to Brenda. "She may be using another name—and she definitely only uses a cell."

Brenda had nodded. "All the kids do that. None of them has a landline anymore. I doubt she's going by anything but her own name, though. Why would she? We'll have to find her another way, but there's no rush. I'm sure she's staying put wherever she is with the baby. Let's enjoy our Christmas and start looking Wednesday."

Anxious as she was to get her hands on her new acquisition, Brenda was savoring the moment. Anticipation—just like that ad for ketchup said. She was in a mellow mood, having already ordered an expectant-mother gift basket for herself like the one Charlotte gave Miranda on *Sex and the City*. A minishower. With express shipping it might even arrive before the baby. When Daniel went off to pick up little Daniel, she'd shop some more. It was a shame she didn't have a longer lead time. What she could get online was much better than in the local stores, but it would take a while to get here. Maybe she'd just buy a few things to tide them over while she waited for her orders from Bonpoint, Tiffany, and Saks to arrive. They could start with a cradle or bassinette, which would give them a chance to find the perfect crib. Possibly have one made. The room she now used for wrapping presents would make a perfect nursery. Oh, and she'd have to start looking for a nanny right away. No Swedish girls, though. Daniel was only human.

Wednesday a young couple who had been hesitating between two houses called and told Daniel both sets of parents were in town for the holidays and asked, would he be available to show them the houses again and perhaps a few more to give their folks an idea of what was out there? Daniel would, and could.

"She said she was going to college, remember?" he told Brenda as he was leaving. "See if you can find an actual person to talk to at UMaine, Bowdoin, Bates, Colby, all of them. You'll think of some story. She was supposed to come home for the holidays and didn't—is she on campus? That sort of thing."

"But she wouldn't be living on campus if she was having a baby. I know dorms are coed now, but I don't think they let students live there with their children."

"If we can find out where she's in school—if she still is—we can narrow our search and try the local hospitals. They don't keep you long these days, but she could still be there—or was. I can't get into patient information online, but they'll tell you by phone. Say you want to send flowers, a gift, whatever. You know what to do. With luck she'll have been discharged and we can get an address."

Brenda did as she was told, but when Daniel came home exhausted at five o'clock and poured himself some Maker's Mark to celebrate the sale, she'd had less luck than he had.

"Poodle, maybe this wasn't meant to be," he said, settling back in one of the oversize leather chairs in front of the fireplace, which Brenda had turned on. He could never understand why people wanted to bother with the mess real wood made.

The house he'd just sold was on the water and had been listed for four million—a price he knew he'd never get, especially these days. They'd offered a half million less, which was considerably more than the price he'd agreed upon originally with the owners. He'd also told the couple and their parents that they'd have to waive an inspection if they got it at that price. Well, they'd gotten it; so now all they had to do was close. Life was sweet.

Brenda poured herself some crème de menthe. She didn't like "those nasty whiskey drinks," as she called them.

"You told me you'd do this. You said you'd get the baby for me," she said evenly.

Daniel recognized the tone. They seldom fought, but when they did, this was always the lead-in. Brenda being reasonable. Brenda speaking in a calm, rational way. Soon Brenda would become Hurricane Brenda and there was no eye in that storm.

He spoke in a placating manner. "But, honey, how can I get the baby if I can't find Miriam?"

"You just don't want a baby. You could do it if you really wanted to. You lied to me."

The winds were picking up.

"Okay, I'll find her and get the baby. They have to be somewhere and I'm betting she stayed in Maine. Miriam was always a wimpy kind of kid, not the type who would go off to someplace new. I'll spend all day tomorrow on nothing else."

Brenda drained her Waterford crystal liqueur glass, set it down, and climbed into Daniel's lap.

"I'll still be *your* baby, Daddy. Don't you worry."

Filled with a sense of purpose and still glowing from his major sale, Daniel started hunting early the next morning. Miriam hadn't had many friends. None, in fact, that he could recall, but it was a shame they'd thrown out her yearbook when they got rid of everything she'd left behind. There was one girl, Sheila something, Miriam used to play with, and maybe they'd stayed in touch. Looking at the yearbook, he could have found her and called her family. How many "Sheilas" could there have been in the class? Now if it had been "Tiffany" or "Jessica" that would have been different.

He sat down to eat the tuna fish sandwich Brenda had made him for lunch. It was his favorite, but today it tasted like sawdust. He was getting annoyed. There was no record of births to anyone named Carpenter in the entire state. Even with the holidays, computers kept the records up-to-date. This meant she hadn't gone to a hospital or had, despite his conviction, moved away. All he had to go on was the conversation he'd had with her when she'd called to tell him she was continuing her education. He began to think out loud.

"She wouldn't have had the money for any of the private colleges in the state unless she got a scholarship."

"Well, she's smart, isn't she?"

"I guess. But still, I don't think they hand them out nowadays the way they used to. My gut tells me she's at a UMaine campus. You called all the offices and there were no answers, right?"

"Just a recorded message about being on vacation. I even tried department offices."

"What we need are the student directories for each of them. The library won't have them, and even if we could get through to the schools, they probably wouldn't give us the information. This society is getting too damn concerned with privacy!"

"Daniel! I know how to get the one for the campus in Orono!" Brenda clapped her hands together. Her rings sparkled.

"How?"

"That's where my friend Leila's daughter goes."

"But why would Leila have the directory?"

"She's what they call a 'helicopter parent.' I swear she'd be living in Teri's room if she could. I'm sure she grabbed a copy of the directory, so she could have the numbers of anyone Teri mentioned she was friends with, especially male."

Daniel was skeptical, but a call to the devoted parent produced the information that, yes, she had a copy of the directory kept with all her other phone books and would be happy to look up Miriam. What a shame they had lost her new address and how nice that they were going up to see her to bring the holiday gifts they couldn't mail. And even more of a shame that the job Miriam had taken to help pay for her own college expenses wouldn't give her enough time off to come home!

Brenda scribbled furiously, talked a bit more about how worrisome young people today were, and hung up. She held out a piece of paper. "We've got her now," she said triumphantly.

"I'll go first thing in the morning." Daniel Carpenter poured himself a shot of bourbon.

Piece of cake.

"I know you want to help Mary, sweetheart," Tom said, "but isn't there someone else who could go, or why doesn't she leave the baby here and take our car? That old truck of hers barely makes it to Granville. I thought we could go over to the country club and ski on the golf course."

The Reverend Fairchild was feeling great. Yesterday's iceboating had stripped the final threads from the cocoon of his illness and he wanted to spread his wings—with his wife for company.

"There isn't anyone else. And unless she's taught one of the herd to drive, Mary won't go any farther than Blue Hill. I just want to get her the bare necessities—more clothes, a proper sling to use when she's milking, diapers, bottles—you remember. The crib we borrowed from Pix for Amy and never gave back is still in the garage here and I want to take that over. I'll have to get some sheets, though. I want to do this for Mary. A belated Christmas present from us."

"Come here, gift o' mine," Tom said, reaching for his wife. Outside Ben and Amy were tossing tiny snowballs at each other, scooped up from the fluffy two inches that had fallen early in the morning.

"And do you have to leave right away?" Tom motioned toward the ceiling. "I thought this might be the perfect occasion for some quality adult time upstairs."

Faith hugged him hard. "What's that line about having 'world enough and time'? I know Marvell was addressing his Coy Mistress and I'm not being coy. There will be time—many times."

Tom kissed her, and in a voice suggesting slight regret, but hope for a Plan B, said, "Hey, why don't we all go? Maybe see a movie in Ellsworth?"

Faith had been deliberately vague about where she was going. Orono was in a different direction from Ellsworth. She was feeling slightly guilty at keeping so much from Tom. It wasn't what they did—wasn't what their marriage was about. But she didn't want to upset him when he was coming along so well—or so she rationalized. Still, it was true. He would be upset—the last thing she wanted, especially now. She felt an almost painful surge of love for him, the kind of feeling you don't have until you're faced with an illness, or worse.

"You know you would hate it, and so would the kids. The after-Christmas sales bring out the beast in everyone and the stores will be packed." L.L.Bean online was as close as Tom normally liked to get to retail. Faith had often thought his choice of profession might have been dictated in part by the simple nature of wardrobe choices—and the robe also covered a multiple of fashion sins.

"I'll be back as soon as I can." She kissed him hard. It was full of promise. Promise of Plan A. "Why don't you take the kids skiing? Missy might be able to join you and could use mine. She's pretty tall."

The Sanpere Country Club had been started in the early twentieth century by a group of locals who had been bitten by the golf bug. The club had an excellent nine-hole course plus two tennis courts. It was open to anyone—no blackballing here—and the cozy little clubhouse served up excellent lunches during the summer season. She'd have to pack something for her gang now.

Tom held her closer. "I swear if I didn't know that Mary and her Nubian goats existed, I'd think you made the whole thing up so you could sneak out and meet your secret lover. Mary Bethany. Bethany—the village where that other Mary was born. A baby, Christopher, turning up on Christmas Eve." He settled back, still with his arm around his wife. He was loath to let her go. "I've always felt sorry for Mary—or rather Miriam, which is the Hebrew. She was as sorely tested as Job. It can't have been easy for her. Some sources put her age as young as thirteen when she became pregnant out of wedlock. The gospels don't tell us much about her, barely mentioning her by name, but it's not hard to imagine how the good people of Nazareth would have treated her."

Faith agreed. "I always thought it was a little mean of God to leave her on her own for so long while Joseph was off building houses. Here she is betrothed and all, picking out pottery patterns, then suddenly she's getting more full with child by the day. She knew she was a virgin—but it took a while before it was all sorted out. I've always imagined her as a feisty lady. She had to be."

"Joseph stuck by her, though."

"Yes, I'll give him that—thanks to one of those convenient dreams people in the Bible always seem to have. But when it came time for the blessed event, why did it take so long for him to find someone to deliver the baby? Mary was on her own again in that stinky barn—or cave if you want to believe James—having the baby all by herself."

Mary—or Miriam, Maryam, Maria—had always seemed very real to Faith, especially when she became a mother herself. She pictured her not so much as the meek and mild blue-clothed woman in Renaissance portraits—although they were beautiful— as clothed in a linen shift she'd woven under her own mother's instruction, working hard in the hot sun, an active, vibrant presence. A woman who said yes to God's emissary—"Let it be according to your word"—perhaps sensing even then that the fruit of her womb was destined for a short life on earth. A much beloved son. One of Faith's favorite parts of the Bible was that wonderful scene at the wedding in Cana where Mary notices that the caterer must have messed up the wine order and tells her son to get busy changing the water into Merlot. When the servants balk, she's firm—"Whatever he say to you, do it."

Faith's mind moved back to the present and she stood up.

"But, speaking of Marys, I have to go. The sooner I leave, the sooner I'll—"

"I know, I know, and say hi to your secret lover."

"Hi, lover."

Why hadn't they arrested him?

Jake Whittaker wished it weren't school vacation for the first time in his life. Without the routine of classes and the burden of homework—the teachers had gone easy on their students—there was nothing to keep him from thinking about what had happened and what might happen.

He didn't want to see anyone, but he'd gone to Davey's in the early morning hours after coming home from Ellsworth, after all hell had broken loose. He had to warn his friend and be sure they had their stories straight.

Davey had a room the size of a closet on the first floor behind the kitchen. Last year he'd convinced his mother to move her preserves to the basement and let him have the space. Jake had helped him paint it and hang up some posters, so now it was all his. It had a small window, which he never locked. Nothing in the house was. He'd been startled out of a very sound sleep by Jake's sudden appearance at his bedside, but had quickly thrown on some clothes and gone out the way Jake had come in. Neither said a word. Davey never chanced the kitchen door when slipping out at night. His mother could sleep through a nor'easter, but would be down the stairs the moment the knob turned.

Larry's truck was parked out behind the house on the gravel

drive and they got in. Jake hadn't worried about anyone noticing footprints in the snow by Davey's window; you'd have to be looking for them. But Larry was as particular about his truck as Jake was about his car. Nobody, but nobody, touched it without permission. They'd been careful to walk in the tire tracks and kicked their boots off before climbing in the cab.

"How are you, man? I guess they haven't arrested you or anything." Davey had heard that Jake had been taken to Ellsworth for questioning about Norah's death—seemed like every old woman on the island wanted to make sure he was informed about the turn of events—but he'd had trouble taking it in. This was Jake they were talking about. *Jake.* He couldn't remember a time when Jake hadn't been his best friend. The guy could never do something like this. Somebody had gotten things totally screwed up. He hoped Jake would sue them for a million dollars. What was it Mr. Trask had been on about the other day? Slander. That was it. Libel was the other kind. Sue them for both. Sue the whole damn island. Hell, the state too and the cops.

His brother always had a pack of cigarettes in his glove compartment and Davey lit one for himself and one for Jake. This wasn't a time to think about breaking training.

"You can't repeat any of this," Jake had said.

Davey had agreed.

"I want us to be sure we're telling the same story, because I know the cops are going to start questioning everybody I ever said hi to in my life. They don't know that you were at the party, or your brother. So, remember that. You were never at a party that night. Reverend Fairchild knows someone was with me, but I told him I wasn't naming names and I'm not. I don't care what they do to me, but if you get kicked off the team too, we're goners for the district, and totally forget about the state."

Davey shook his head. He was blinking back angry tears. Everything was turned upside down. "I don't get it. You're the last person to ever hurt Norah. Don't the stupid bastards know that!"

"My lawyer—I have a lawyer, weird, huh—says that they're trying to make me look like that drugged-up preppy killer guy in New York or the rich one in Connecticut. Like Norah and I were, you know, fooling around, and maybe I got rough or maybe she said to stop, but I didn't."

"No way! I hope they do pull me in. I can set them straight on a few things."

"Look, when they do," Jake had said, "say as little as possible. Tell them the truth—just not everything. Yeah, you can say I don't do drugs—and wouldn't do that other stuff—but keep yourself out of it, okay? Like my lawyer says, 'Don't answer questions they're not asking.'"

"This is like a movie. I mean I can't believe it's happening to us in real life. Here on the island. Norah murdered and they think you did it? Everything's totally messed up. Why? Just give me one good reason why they would think you did it."

"They found her shoe in my car. That's why, my friend."

The shoe. Those foolish, bright red shoes with the high heels.

They'd parted and now it was Friday. Jake was up in his room. Everybody was moving around the house on tiptoe. The radio, which his mother turned on when she got up and left on until she went to bed, was silent. He didn't know why, but it was pissing him off. Didn't they have places to go? His father was skipping work. He couldn't remember when his father had stayed home like this, not even when he had the flu or the time he was on crutches with a broken ankle. He thought about going downstairs and telling them to get out—or maybe walk out the door himself. Too much effort.

They were acting like someone had died. Like when his grandmother, who'd lived with them, was passing. Well, someone had died.

He couldn't concentrate. Couldn't read. Nothing. He thought about calling Reverend Fairchild. Jake planned to take what Norah told him about her father to the grave, but he had to talk to someone about the way he was feeling. That if he hadn't gone looking for her, she'd still be alive. He'd gone over and over the whole night. What he could remember of it, that is. But he was sure of two things. That while he'd been outside peeing, someone had put something in his soda can that knocked him out, and more important, he was sure that they'd been followed. And that someone hiding in the trees by the shore had overheard everything they'd said.

Jake would never forget those words, and everything else, how Norah had felt in his arms, the moon on the snow, the raucous cry of a lone heron—so at odds with the beauty and grace of the bird. No, Jake would never forget any of it. He knew now that Norah had protected him. Made certain not to use any names, so he'd be in the dark. In the clear. She'd saved his life. The life he didn't have much use for now, since he'd been responsible for ending hers.

The years ahead seemed like just something to get through until he could be with Norah for good. He thought he'd known what the world was like, but he hadn't known anything. They had snuffed her out as if she were no more than a fly on the wall. He'd felt nervous in that house, but only now thinking back did he realize he'd also been scared. Evil. He'd been in the presence of pure evil. Maybe the reverend could explain it to him. Explain how God could let something like this happen. Jake thought he was all dried up, but the tears started oozing out again. He and Norah were going to be so happy. Everything was going to be perfect.

Why hadn't they arrested him?

After she'd stumbled in the woods, he thought he'd touched both shoes when he'd helped her put the one that had come off back on. In any case, his prints were certainly all over that one. He tried to picture it—was it the right or left? Left, he was pretty sure. Maybe it was the right one that was in his car. They'd have lifted whatever prints were on it by now, and if they'd been his, he'd be in a cell. He'd told his lawyer about this part of the night—how the shoe had come off—and she'd said to wait. "Answer what I tell you to answer." The old "don't answer questions they don't ask."

She did have him give them some blood and urine after they'd talked, and he said they wouldn't find anything there that wasn't supposed to be. He hadn't even had a beer after Christmas dinner when he was in his grandfather's barn with his dad and uncles looking at the new iceboat. He'd worked on it some, especially the mast and sail, trying something new to increase her speed. He'd junked his own boat for parts.

They'd taken some of his hair too. What was that for? He guessed he should have asked his lawyer—or the cops—but he found he mostly shut up around all of them. He remembered a picture in a book he had when he was a kid. It was all about the Greeks, their gods and goddesses, and had a lot of cool stories. The picture he was thinking of was of this dumb girl Pandora who was so nosy she opened a box she had been told never to touch and let out all sorts of terrible things into the world. That's how he felt. That if he opened his mouth and started to say more than a few words, all sorts of awful things would tumble out into the open. What had he done with that book? He wanted to read the story again.

Why hadn't they arrested him? He kind of wished they would.

Jake had been sitting at his desk, staring at the bleak winter landscape. The sky was graying over. Could be some weather. His yard was one of the few that wasn't jammed with traps hauled out until spring, just the couple of dozen he set with Davey.

It was only nine in the morning. What was he going to do with himself all day—and the next day and the next?

He lay down on his bed. Probably at this very moment, the cops were taking his car apart. He didn't want to think about it. They were looking for drugs—and more evidence than the shoe that Norah had been in there. But he'd never given her a ride. He'd told them that much.

She'd ridden in his car, though.

Was she already dead? He slammed his fist into his pillow.

CHAPTER 9

"I'm sorry, but I don't operate my bed and breakfast during the off-season. They should have told you that at the market."

Mary had been startled by the sudden appearance of a big fancy car coming up the long drive that led to her farm from the main road, but not so startled that she hadn't quickly erased all evidence that a baby was living in the house. It wasn't hard. She had prepared herself for the possibility—the eventuality. She took Christopher himself out through the shed and across into the barn, placing him in one of the mangers well away from the goats. He was such a good baby, but even if he did start crying, the nannies would more than drown him out.

"I must have misunderstood. My name is Dan Carpenter, by the way. I own a real estate agency down in Portland and I'm up here to check out a property."

Mary's eyes narrowed. Skunks, that's what they were. The local agents had given up on her long ago, but there were new ones all the time. Telling her what she could get for waterfront on Eggemoggin Reach, what a genuine Down East saltwater farm would fetch. She knew what it would fetch. More skunks. Skunks who would have the farmhouse down in two minutes and put up some sort of hotel-looking place with a tennis court.

"I am not interested in selling my property, Mr. Carpenter. Good day." Mary started to close the door. He'd come to the front, which had further alerted her that he was a PFA—person from away.

"No, wait. Please. I'm sorry. You've misunderstood me. I'm not interested in your property. I mean, of course I'm always interested in property, but that's not why I'm here. I simply need a place to stay for the night."

"They should have sent you to Granville. There's a motel that stays open year-round there and I can't imagine they'd be full, even with the holidays." Mary started to close the door again.

But Dan Carpenter was very good at what he did. He was used to people trying to close doors in his face—and equally used to getting his foot in them. He'd arrived on the island around noon and headed straight for the market. Next to the post office, the market in any small Maine community was the best grapevine, and the post office only worked if you were local. So, he'd picked up a few snacks and mentioned at the register that his daughter had stayed at a bed and breakfast run by a woman who kept goats. His daughter had recommended it as a place to stay.

"That would be Mary Bethany," offered the teenager with a singularly repulsive Goth look who was minding the till. Dan had been in luck. Anyone older would have either asked him what his business was that meant he had to stay the night on Sanpere, or more likely, simply grunted, rung up his purchases, and taken his money.

"She won't let you stay, though. Isn't open now. Better go to the motel in Granville." The boy was a veritable hydrant of information.

But Dan had gone to Mary's after looking up her address in the phone book thoughtfully offered for free by the local island newspaper. A stack of them rested next to the display of motor oil at the entrance to the market. It was one of those typical Maine places that sold everything you needed and nothing you didn't.

He'd cracked tougher nuts than Mary.

"Please, I'm sorry to have troubled you, but could I call the motel? I don't want to drive all the way down there and find they haven't any room at the inn." He gave a little chuckle to show how very, very harmless and how very, very charming he was.

Mary grudgingly opened the door wider and led the way into the kitchen. "I'll call Patty and see. You sit here." She pointed to one of the chairs at the table and turned to the phone on the wall.

"Did I hear a baby crying? Are your grandchildren visiting for the holidays?"

Instantly Mary swung around.

"Those are my goats, mister. I don't have any grandchildren and there are no babies in this house. Now, why don't you take yourself down to Granville? I don't think I care to call Patty after all."

Dan Carpenter stood up and started walking toward Mary. She grabbed the phone again and he stopped.

"Look, I know Miriam is here with the baby. You are going to be in major trouble for hiding them if you don't get them right now!" He glared at Mary and loudly shouted, "Miriam, come here this instant!" There was no answer. He broke the silence. "My daughter, Miriam, is mentally unstable. I don't know what kind of story she's told you, but she's not fit to raise a child. She's a thief, a drug addict, and an alcoholic, just like her mother. A pathological liar too. I'm only thinking of the baby. My grandson."

Mary had listened and watched impassively, her hand still on the phone.

"I don't know anything about your daughter," she said calmly. "She is not here. And, as I told you before, there are no babies in this house. I'd say you were welcome to search the premises, but then I'd be the liar. You're not welcome at all. You came into my home under false pretenses and now I want you out." She was dialing a number as she spoke the last words. When someone answered on the other end, she turned back to face Mr. Carpenter.

"Earl," she said pleasantly. "I have a man here bothering me. Could you come over right away? And, Earl, bring your gun."

An early riser, especially when compared to his wife, Daniel had been on the road by 6 A.M. The drive-thru at McDonald's provided breakfast with enough coffee to last him the trip up the turnpike to Orono, where he'd planned on waking Miriam up— or maybe not. If she was sound asleep and the door open, he might be able to simply spirit the baby away. He'd Google-Mapped her address and the neighborhood was not a savory one, confirming what had in his mind become a fixed belief that he was saving his grandson—soon to be his son—from a life of squalor or worse. As the sun had pierced the early morning fog, he saw himself in a truly righteous light.

He'd parked and gone into the building; the lock on the front door to the vestibule was broken. Scanning the mailboxes for Miriam's name, he'd stopped at the one for a top-floor apartment and headed up the grime-encrusted stairs to her door. But there was no reply to his repeated knocking or his eventual shouts— "Miriam! I know you're in there! Miriam, answer me!"

It looked as if he'd be spending a long day in his car, waiting for her return. Where else could she go with such a new baby? She *had* to be here. He'd turned his steps back downstairs when, he thought, his mission continued to be blessed. He ran into her neighbor Ellen. And Ellen told him where Miriam might have gone.

Afterward, on the drive to Sanpere Island, Daniel Carpenter continued to feel optimistic. And even when Mary Bethany turned him out of her house, he did not give up. He should have known better than to listen to Ellen. Ellen, whose last name he hadn't gotten and didn't need. She was a loser and exactly what he'd expected a friend of Miriam's to be. Her heavy musk perfume did not begin to cover the other aroma in her apartment, where she'd invited him in, telling him that she hadn't seen Miriam recently.

"Do you think she's in Orono or maybe she went someplace else for a while?" he prodded.

"Wow, are you really her father—cool."

"Stay on track, missy," he muttered to himself, and said, "Someplace else. A trip."

"You mean like a vacation?"

He'd almost given up and then Ellen came through—or so he'd thought.

She'd caused him to waste time driving all the way to Sanpere, but it was still early. When he returned to Orono, he intended to sit in the building right outside her apartment door; the door that Ellen had confirmed was Miriam's. "And Bruce's, only he's away. Canada?" Daniel didn't care who Bruce was. He could be the father of the child, but if he were, he wouldn't be for long. Ellen had added, "With Tammy," and Daniel put him out of his mind completely.

After a few minutes, he'd believed the woman with her goats. Miriam had never been much of a nature girl; despite all the summers they'd sent her to camp. It was unlikely she'd have formed any kind of friendship with someone like Mary Bethany in such a godforsaken place. And the goats? The kitchen had reeked of them. He increased his speed. He was through the notorious speed trap in Searsport. At this rate he might even have time to grab some lunch.

❄   ❄   ❄

On the way back from the market Miriam ran into Ellen the Airhead on the stairs. They called her "the Airhead" not because she was spaced out on drugs but because she was very, very stupid. She was also usually spaced out on drugs.

"Hi, how are things?"

Miriam was always pleasant to Ellen, especially after the girl had confided that her parents sent her a check every month on the condition she stay away from home—a wealthy suburb outside Boston. How sad was that, Miriam had thought—and how convenient for them. Out of sight, out of mind. And in Ellen's case the latter was quite possibly true.

"Oh, hi. Wow, you're so lucky. Your dad totally rocks."

"My what?"

"Your dad, like not your mom. Your father."

Miriam froze and slowly said, "How do you know my father?"

"Well, silly, he was here to see you, wasn't he?"

Ellen looked a little tentative. Was Miriam mad at her? Her voice sounded kind of mad.

"When was he here?" Miriam worked to keep her tone light, and casual, as if asking the time—although telling it wasn't one of Ellen's fortes.

"Today?" Was this the answer Miriam wanted?

She didn't have a moment to spare, but if she rushed the girl, she'd go to pieces and Miriam wouldn't find anything out. She'd seen Ellen fall apart over less.

"Hey, have you got any of that great coffee you gave me before? I could use a cup."

Sitting in Ellen's cluttered kitchen with a mug of instant that she didn't want, Miriam walked her through the morning. They'd moved past getting up and getting dressed and reached the encounter on the stairs.

"Think hard. Think about how he looked. An older man. Tall with dark hair."

"Dark hair," Ellen repeated obediently.

"Great." Miriam patted Ellen's hand and was soon rewarded for her patience with a flash of almost total recall on the girl's part.

"He said he was your father." She hesitated.

"He was . . . is . . . my father. It's okay. Then what did he say?"

"He was like looking for you, and I go, I don't know where she is. Not Canada, but maybe, maybe on Sanpere Island with that goat lady."

"What!" Miriam screeched. "How do you know about Sanpere!"

"You told me." Ellen stuck out her lower lip. "You didn't say it was a secret. Last summer. You told me all about the nice lady with the goats on Sanpere that you and Bruce stayed with. Hey, you didn't finish your coffee."

Miriam was out the apartment door in a flash, taking the stairs by twos. Even if her father had somehow managed to snatch Christopher away from Mary, Miriam would pass him on his way back home, follow him to his doorstep if need be—and call the police. The idea of having her father arrested for kidnapping was extremely pleasant, and it was only when she thought about what he'd say in his defense—that his grandson had been abandoned by his mother, left in the barn of someone she barely knew—that Miriam realized how precarious her situation was. She had to stop him without involving the authorities.

She should have dropped her groceries on Ellen's counter and headed straight out, but she wanted to pack her knapsack. She should have done it earlier, she thought as she also frantically tried to think of someone with a car she could borrow. It had been easy the afternoon of Christmas Eve. She went to a party on the other side of town that she'd heard about and took the keys from the drunkest person there. Today, a workday, was different.

She debated whether or not to call Mary Bethany, but she didn't want to alarm her. For all she knew, Mary might call the police, the state police. There weren't any police on Sanpere, which was one of the reasons Miriam had picked it. That and Mary. Mary would take care of the baby. She'd raise him to be a good man. Miriam didn't care whether her son went to college, made money, or did anything other than raise goats. All she cared about was that he be as honest and kind as Mary Bethany was. She started calling around to find a car and finally located one, arranging to go get it from a classmate, Cindy.

Hastily, she did up the straps on the knapsack. She was pretty sure Mary wouldn't be fooled by whatever story Daniel Carpenter cooked up, but Miriam needed to give her some sort of letter that would say Christopher was hers. That she was surrendering her parental rights to Mary. That would keep her father away. Mary could use some of the money for a lawyer if she had to.

Stupid, stupid, stupid. She angrily blew a stray strand of hair out of her eyes. How could she ever have called her father!

She was ready to go. Suddenly she looked at where she had been living for over a year—the stained and sagging couch, a few beanbag chairs, a coffee table scrounged from the trash. It was covered with white rings and cigarette burns. The place stank—stale air and more. The doorknob was greasy. She turned it and pulled the door open. Pulled it open and stepped back into the room.

"Hello, Miss Miriam. Glad to see you're finally home. We've been looking for you."

"For you—and the money."

Duane and Ralph. Two of Bruce's out-of-state suppliers. Very, very scary guys. Miriam let the knapsack slip from her shoulder. She let her whole body sag. Then she sprinted past them, slamming the door behind her, and ran out of the house into the street as fast as she could.

Ralph and Duane. How could *they* have connected her to the cash she'd taken for the baby from the storage container down in Brewer? It was one that Bruce didn't think she knew about. He was still in Canada—there hadn't been any empty beer bottles on the counter or pizza boxes, the staples of his diet—and he couldn't know the money was missing. She'd counted on that, and even if he did find out when he returned, he wouldn't associate her with the theft.

She hid behind the Dumpster in the parking lot of the convenience store across from the apartment and watched the two heavyset thugs come roaring out screaming her name. They had been to the apartment only once before. Mostly Bruce met them down in Belfast or in Bangor. He didn't want them at the apartment. Too risky. She watched them go to the end of the block in either direction and circle the house. Ralph yelled, "Bitch, we know you're out here, so listen up. We will find you!" Duane had his cell phone out, but put it back in his pocket right away. Miriam assumed he was trying to call Bruce wherever he was, and she blessed Maine's erratic cell service. Her mind was racing. Bruce must have come back early and gone to Brewer to stash the prescription drugs he'd brought across the border—that very long border impossible to patrol, just as Maine's very long coast was in better weather. By land or by sea, Maine had always been a smuggler's dream and a law-enforcement nightmare. He'd discovered the money was missing, figured out it had to have been Miriam—who else?—and sent Duane and Ralph to grab it, and her. It was probably money he owed them. And they wanted it now.

The trash in the Dumpster had been ripening since the holiday and she felt slightly nauseated by the smell. The sky was getting dark and she remembered hearing someone in the market say she was stocking up on milk, because a storm was coming. She breathed through her mouth and curled into a tighter ball.

After loudly describing in graphic detail what they'd do to her when they found her, the two got in their pickup and tore off, burning rubber. The Chevy was tricked out with flames airbrushed on the sides. Perennial adolescents: totally amoral, psychopathic ones. But she couldn't think about them—or Bruce—now. She had to head down to Sanpere and try to intercept her father on his way back. She wasn't altogether sure how she was going to do this. She certainly didn't want to endanger the baby by trying to cut the car off on the road; she'd think of something.

Her father's car was new to her, but she'd never known him to drive anything but a Mercedes. Daniel Carpenter was loyal—to brands, anyway.

Once she was sure Duane and Ralph were really gone, it didn't take her long to walk to Cindy's apartment and pick up her car keys. Cindy was living with her boyfriend and using Miriam's address for her parents. She stopped by to pick up the mail every week and score some dope. Her parents never called, because dutiful daughter that she was, Cindy had arranged a weekly time when she would call them, saving them the long-distance fees, since "I'd probably be in the library anyway and you'd just get my roommate, Miriam." Cindy also had had Bruce take a picture of Miriam and her on the couch with a stack of books on the coffee table, so she could send it to her parents. They lived in Duluth and it was highly unlikely that they'd be dropping by unannounced. Miriam had been impressed by Cindy's thoroughness, but college students in general were a pretty crafty bunch, she'd noticed—or maybe it was that parents just wanted to believe.

As she drove off, she looked at her watch. Less than twenty minutes ago, she'd been sitting in Ellen's apartment.

She was passing through Bucksport when she saw her father's car. It wasn't hard to miss. There weren't too many silver Mercedes S500s (have to have a killer car to impress the buyers and sellers) around at this time of year. The summer people—those who weren't green and driving hybrids—were going for the SUV version in the absurd belief that they were blending in ruralwise. To really blend in, they'd have to drive a pickup over ten years old with vanity plates that combined your initials with your girl-friend's, your wife's, or your kid's.

Miriam thought fast. Her father had obviously been down to Sanpere if he was coming this way. He might or might not have Christopher. Suddenly she was furious. She pulled into Hannaford's parking lot, did an adrenaline-fueled U-turn, and followed him. He wouldn't know Cindy's car, or any other car Miriam might be driving.

It was easy to keep the big silver car in sight. She'd tail him until he stopped for gas or a bathroom break, then act. If he didn't have Christopher in the car that would mean the baby was still safe with Mary. If he did, she'd grab the baby and run, making a scene at the rest stop or wherever when her father resisted, as she was sure he would. Not just any scene, but a pull-out-all-the-stops one. Her fa-ther hated scenes and she was sure she could draw a crowd. The so very public mention of his name and his agency might be enough to get him to give up and leave. She was sure the whole kid idea was Brenda's. Her father wasn't the paternal type, as she knew only too well. Thinking about her years with him, she grew more and more angry, her mood matching the darkening sky. Daniel Car-penter wasn't fit to raise any living thing, and—most important—Christopher was her baby, not his!

She was surprised when he didn't turn south toward Portland. What was he doing? Where was he going? He was speeding up too. Well, so would she. Except she'd have to stop for gas. Damn. She followed for a couple more miles and saw him turn. Okay. She was sure she knew where he was going now. Back to her apart-ment. But why?

Besides hitting the Bangor malls for baby things and driving to the twenty-four-hour store in Orono, Faith didn't have a plan. If she found Miriam, she'd talk to the girl, make sure she knew what she was doing, and then what? Ask her where the fifty thousand dollars came from? Get her to sign some kind of papers, so Mary could adopt Christopher?

She decided to hit the mall first. She'd gotten a later start than she'd planned, but a practiced shopper, she was sure she could get the baby essentials quickly. The lines at the registers had been long, however, and it seemed that every one she chose turned out to be behind a customer who needed a price check. Finally, late in the afternoon with a threatening sky and lengthening shadows, she turned the loaded car north away from Bangor toward Orono. It wasn't far, and once there she only had to ask twice to find the convenience store.

As she had suspected, it was a mom-and-pop operation, a cross between a market and a five-and-dime—only those long-ago treasure troves had morphed into dollar stores now. Sammy's had a little bit of everything from beef jerky to Rolex rip-offs and dusty plastic poinsettias, still on sale from the last few Christmases. It was located in a mixed residential/commercial area. There was no Sammy in evidence, unless the tired-looking older woman at the counter was named Samantha. Faith picked up a slightly faded package of colored construction paper for Amy and an ancient balsawood model-airplane kit for Ben. At the register, she added a Milky Way for Tom. She'd check the expiration date in the car.

As the sale was rung up, she said, "I wonder if you might help me. I'm supposed to drop off a Christmas gift for a friend of mine. It's for her niece, who lives around here. I've misplaced the address, but the niece's name is Miriam. She's tall with long dark hair that she usually wears in a braid down her back. Do you by any chance know her?"

"Sure, I know Miriam. Comes in here a lot. Always polite. Not like some. She lives over there. I'm not sure which apartment, but I saw her this morning, so she's probably home."

Faith looked through the window—obscured by HOLIDAY

GREETINGS sprayed on in white by a liberal but unsteady hand—
and saw a rundown house that had obviously been carved up into
apartments for students fleeing dorm life, or just fleeing.

She thanked the woman and walked slowly across the street.
The front door swung open and she stepped onto a litter of junk
mail. There were six mailboxes; each card had several names. Some
had been crossed out and new ones scribbled above. She studied
each as if it had been the Rosetta stone. She knew she wouldn't find
"Miriam" or "Bruce Singer." But she wasn't finding anything remotely resembling them. No initials *M* or *B*. No *S*'s. When people
put down false names, they usually stick to their own initials, even
if no monogrammed luggage is involved. A question of human
nature. Or they choose a similar name, as in a similar occupation.
"Singer." No "Chanteuses," "Vocalists"—what other synonyms
were there? Preferably synonyms that made sense. She went back to
the cards and searched again. And there it was. Apartment 4B. One
word in minuscule writing written above some others: "Carpenter." The Carpenters. Karen Carpenter. "Singers." Miriam Singer;
Miriam Carpenter? Faith pushed the buzzer. There was no answer.
She wasn't even sure it was working, so she started climbing the
dark, narrow stairs. If there was a "4A," it had vanished into a black
hole. 4B was the only door at the landing on the top floor. After
knocking loudly on the flimsy, hollow door—she debated giving it
good shove—for what seemed like ages, Faith was forced to conclude that Christopher's mother wasn't home.

She retraced her steps and almost bumped into a young woman
coming out of an apartment.

"Excuse me," Faith said. "I'm looking for Miriam. She doesn't
seem to be home. Do you know where she is or when she might
be back?"

The woman—young, very thin with long, possibly blond hair,
hard to tell it so needed a wash—cried out, "Miriam! It's always
all about Miriam." And pushed past Faith.

"Okaay," Faith said aloud, and crossed the street. She'd ask if she could leave a note for the celebrated Miriam at the convenience store. The woman at the counter had been replaced by a short, balding man. Sammy?

"I just came on, so I haven't seen her today. She's around, though. Came by last night for some orange juice," he said, and gave Faith a sheet of paper. She wrote a brief note, knowing that it would most certainly be read.

Dear Miriam,

Your gift arrived safely. Could you get in touch with Mary when you get this? She's fine and would love to see you. Her number is 555-1550.

All the best,
Faith (a friend of Mary's)

Faith debated whether to include her number as well, but someone else, most likely Ben, might answer the phone, and Faith's cell didn't work on the island. She folded the paper over and wrote Miriam's name on the front, handing it to the man behind the counter. He tucked it by the register and said, "Nice girl, Miriam. Not like some."

Apparently this was the prevailing opinion at Sammy's, Faith thought, and left.

Back in the car, glancing in the rearview mirror, she could see the bags filled with baby paraphernalia. She understood the whole grandmother thing better now. The grandmother thing that awaited in the far distant future. Shopping when you had an infant was a chore, even if someone else was watching your precious bundle of joy at home. You were fatigued and in a rush. Today she'd lingered over the tiny garments, amazed that her children had ever been so small.

And now she was remembering the wonderful smell her babies had had—a milky sweet smell. A smell she realized with a start that only a mother or grandmother could love. The notion speeded her along. She wasn't speeding now, though. There was actually traffic. In Maine.

As she drove, she was thinking of how pleased Mary would be that Faith had discovered Christopher's mother's name and address. She hoped Miriam would call. Otherwise they'd have to figure out another way to make contact. There might not be time to come back up before the Fairchilds had to return to Massachusetts —and what excuse could she give Tom? She'd think of something, though. Knowing where Miriam lived—and she was most certainly in residence according to the people at Sammy's and the strange girl in the same building—meant they could eventually get in direct contact with her. The old "I know where you live."

The afternoon light was fading fast. Faith speeded up; cars were thinning out now. She hated driving at night in Maine. Even in the summer the dark was very dark. She wanted to get home before night fell, when even your high beams couldn't pick out the twists and turns in front of you. A few flakes of snow were starting to fall. She hadn't heard a weather report, and as she switched on the radio, she heard a muffled pop, which she assumed was coming from the speaker until it was followed by the dreaded flap, flap, flap sound that meant a flat tire. All those potholes down on Sanpere.

She was still on the main road, and pulled over to the side as far as she could. Faith knew how to change a tire, but she didn't want to in the dark, and searched for the AAA card in her wallet. She tried her cell—no bars, but there was a gas station within sight. Glad that she had on her long down hooded parka, even though she thought it made her look like the Michelin man, she set her flashers, got out of the car, and headed up the road straight into the wind.

❄ ❄ ❄

Mary Bethany had been sure her words would get Daniel Carpenter out of the house. Bullies were usually cowards. She was eager to tell Faith what had happened and was especially looking forward to telling her all about the call she had put through to the small Granville library, knowing it was closed, and not Sergeant Earl Dickinson of the Maine State Police. Earl did patrol the island, and he lived here, but Mary hadn't wanted him around any more than she had wanted Daniel Carpenter.

She went to the barn and decided to stay there with Christopher until dark, when it would be easy to see headlights, although she wasn't expecting anyone. But she hadn't been expecting Miriam's father either. "Better to err on the side of caution" had been one of her mother's favorite sayings, and in this case, Mary agreed. She'd told Faith to wait until tomorrow to bring the baby things over. The poor woman hadn't had hardly any time with her family these last few days. This meant that any lights Mary saw would not be welcome ones.

Christopher was sleeping so soundly, a warm little bundle hidden away against the straw in the manger, that she didn't want to disturb him by moving him to his basket, which she'd retrieved from the pantry, where she'd hastily shoved it earlier. The nannies were content for once and continued to greet her cheerfully. Christopher didn't move a muscle, so Mary turned her full attention to the herd, starting with Dora, her oldest goat—the queen. Her coat was longer now that it was winter and Mary kept it, and that of the others, free of tangles, running her fingers through it now in a gesture of affection. Then she spent time with each of the others in order of age. You had to do it this way or they got upset and confused. It was the same order for milking, grooming, everything. Each goat knew her place. No one tried to squeeze ahead. They all got along together and with her. Faith was going to bring her some baby books, which would be a help, but Mary thought raising goats and raising children were much the same. Of course she wouldn't have to make ear splints for Christopher. Sometimes Nubians are born with folded ears and they have to be splinted for a few days, otherwise they'll stay that way. She looked at the herd with pride, shining coats and straight ears. Christopher weighed about as much as a newborn kid too from the heft of him. Could be he was even a little more. She could tell from the way he felt in the sling. She'd also had to use one once for a tiny kid who was doing poorly after opening up her muzzle on a nail she'd worried loose. Goats are very curious, and childproofing a house would be child's play—Mary smiled to herself—compared to goatproofing the barn and pasture. And the nannies were social creatures, like people. Except me, she thought ruefully, and the enormity of what she was contemplating struck her. Raising a child!

She continued to sit and reflect on the last few days, stroking the youngest goat, Sheba, who had a particularly appealing face. Trusting, innocent. Yes, it was in the Bible, but Mary never could understand the Almighty's choice of a goat to bear the sins of the world, abandoning it with all that wickedness in the wilderness—the scapegoat. Why not a scapeox or a scapesheep? Those were around back then too.

Christopher gave another of those sweet little baby sneezes and Mary decided it was time to get moving, although the barn was warm as toast and she hated to leave it. Besides the coziness, it was the way the place smelled. Nannies didn't stink the way bucks did, just gave off a kind of living-things aroma.

The second milking done and goats fed, Mary went back into the house with the baby. She would have to make cheese tomorrow. The nannies were giving more milk than usual, and even with Christopher's consumption, she had too much.

Mary loved making cheese. Anne Bossi at Sunset Acres Farm

over in South Brooksville had given her the recipe years ago and Mary had taught herself, soon turning out a soft, spreadable chèvre. Every time she added the rennet and returned the next day to her curds and whey, she was as pleased at the way nature worked as she had been the first time. Faith had been the one to suggest adding herbs, besides salt, and eventually sun-dried tomatoes, mixed peppercorns, and other things for more varieties. Mary was proud of her cheese-making room—it was so clean it truly sparkled—and the inspectors had never once found anything to criticize.

In the kitchen she stoked the woodstove and settled back in the rocker to feed the baby. Full circle from milking the goats. The house seemed very quiet. The creaking of the rocker on the old linoleum began to get on her nerves, as it never had before. She got up and went into the parlor to finish the feeding, turning on the television Martha had brought all those years ago. Mary had kept it mostly for the B and B guests, but she sometimes tuned in to the news or a PBS show. The early news was on now, and she settled into the sofa to watch while the baby drank. His mother must have bottle-fed him, Mary realized. He wasn't missing her teat.

First they tantalized you with the weather, not actually telling you what it was going to be lest you turn to another station or, heaven forbid, switch the set off. It was going to be—something. Then there was more about Iraq and Afghanistan. Mary thought about a twenty-year-old Christopher going off to fight some war and prayed that by that time the world could come to some sort of truce. Not liking one another. Just a truce.

"This just in. Police are investigating a homicide in Orono and we are live at the scene. Steve, are you there?"

Mary sat up straight, unmindful of the baby on her lap for the moment. A reporter was standing in front of a shabby-looking dwelling, the sidewalk cordoned off with those yellow scene-of-the-crime plastic ribbons. Yellow ribbons for hope; yellow ribbons for despair. She'd never thought about it before.

"Yes, I'm here, Cheryl. Police are not releasing the name of the victim, pending notification of next of kin, but according to our sources here, he was a Caucasian male in his late twenties who lived in the building behind me in an apartment on the top floor with several other people. Again, the police have not released any information other than they are treating the death as an apparent homicide."

"Do we know anything about how and why this might have happened?"

"Our preliminary sources have indicated that the cause of death was a stab wound in the chest, but police are neither confirming nor denying that. We have also been told that drug paraphernalia and a large quantity of heroin were found in the apartment."

"Thank you, Steve." The picture shifted back to the studio, and the anchor, face carefully composed in a serious expression of regret—and condemnation—said, "A homicide in Orono. We're at the scene and will keep you informed. Now, how about those Celtics, Larry?"

Mary reached for the remote and muted the sound. It wasn't just that it was in Orono, it was what she had seen as the camera panned past the flashing blue lights and knots of curious—or prurient—onlookers to a small block of stores. Sammy's Twenty-four Hour Store was right on the corner.

She had to call Faith.

Had she waited for the weather report, Mary would not have been surprised at the way the wind picked up an hour later, or at the snow that began falling in horizontal sheets shortly after. She gathered flashlights, candles, and blankets, setting up camp in the kitchen. There was plenty of stove wood. The house's wiring hadn't been replaced—in her lifetime anyway—and she often lost power just in a stiff breeze, so the possibility was not alarming. Possibility became probability as the howls from the heavens increased their ferocity. The phone rang and it was Tom. When she'd called the house earlier, he'd told her his wife wasn't back yet. That she'd had a flat tire.

"Faith still isn't here," he said. "How could it take her so long to come from Ellsworth? Unless they can't fix the tire? Anyway, the reason I'm calling is that I'm going to come and get you and your nephew. This looks like it's going to be a big storm, Mary. We're bound to lose power and you could be snowed in for days."

Confused for the moment by the reference to her nephew and quickly realizing he meant Christopher, Mary told Tom, "It's happened before. We'll be fine. I have plenty of wood if the furnace goes off. Besides, I don't think you have room for the two of us plus six goats."

"I was afraid you'd say this, but promise you'll call if you change your mind. Faith has the Subaru we keep at the Marshalls' when we're not here, and our other car, the one we drove up in, has four-wheel drive. If you change your mind once it starts piling up, I'll be able to get you."

"Thank you. You're very kind. Best stay put in weather like this. I feel terrible having Faith on the road doing a favor for me," Mary said. "Doesn't she have one of those cell phones? I'd like to call her."

"I can give you her cell, but it probably won't have service. She's been calling me all day from public phones," Tom said.

Mary *did* feel guilty at putting Faith to so much trouble, but she didn't want to call only to apologize. She needed to tell her about the murder. Maybe it was a coincidence that it happened in Miriam's neighborhood, the neighborhood they thought was hers from the location of the convenience store. But Mary wasn't a big believer in coincidences. Life was strange enough without adding serendipity.

There was only one person at the gas station, and after saying he'd "take a look," he proceeded to take a very long time talking to someone named "Elwell" on the two-way radio. Apparently Elwell was out on a call with the lone tow truck and having trouble finding the party in question.

Faith sat in the office whose sole decoration was a Pennzoil calendar still turned to November and tried not to panic. The snow was coming down heavily and she wondered whether she should go back and turn off her flashers to save the battery. But if it did go dead, she could get a jump here. Thirty minutes came and went. She tried pacing in front of the desk, hoping to catch the man's eye, but he was resolute in his inattention. After Elwell, another call had come through, apparently from his wife—or a woman with whom he was familiar enough to call "honey." Finally he stood up.

"Well, now, you say you have a flat?"

She led the way back to her car and left him to it. He was back almost immediately, interrupting her vigil in the office with, "Need some tools."

"Is there any place nearby where I could get a cup of coffee?" She would need the caffeine for the drive and at the moment wanted something, anything, to wash the taste of gas and other garage smells from her mouth. Plus she was cold. Even with her L.L.Bean arctic special.

"Dottie's down the road might still be open."

Faith started off, but soon turned back. There wasn't even a glimmer of light ahead. Dottie, a sensible Maine woman surely, would have closed up.

She was startled by the ring of her phone, had thought she'd shut it off. Before it could stop or lose service she answered.

"Hello."

"Oh, Faith, thank goodness. It's Mary. Is your car fixed? Where are you?"

"Not yet, but soon. I think I'm near Bucksport."

"It's turning into a nasty storm. You should find a place for the night. There's one of those chain motels in Bucksport that should be all right. Go there." Mary's voice was insistent.

Faith peered out at the dense white curtain in front of her. Where was a Saint Bernard when you needed one?

"I think you're right. In case I can't get him, will you call Tom and tell him?"

"Yes, and Faith—"

"Oh, Mary, I hope I don't lose service," Faith said excitedly. "I have so much to tell you. I found out Christopher's mother's name! It's—"

"Miriam Carpenter," Mary said matter-of-factly.

"How on earth did you find this out? Is she there?"

That was the only logical explanation and Faith was momentarily miffed. Although she and Mary were a team these days, Faith had been thinking of herself as the field captain. She had been so clever at putting two and two together, or in this case, many more numbers. And why was it "two and two," anyway? In her experience, things came in triple or even quadruple digits.

Mary quickly told her about Dan Carpenter's visit.

"He wants Christopher. That's obvious. But he doesn't want his daughter. I'm sure she would have been upset if I'd given him the baby. I didn't lie, but took a page from your book and left a lot out. Faith, he scared me. I'll never let Christopher go to him. When Miriam was saying a 'good man,' I know she wasn't thinking of her father. But I haven't told you what was on the news just now. There's been a murder in Orono and I could see

that convenience store—Sammy's—when the camera was film-
ing the neighborhood around the house where the police found
the body."

"Who was killed?" Faith asked anxiously. Could it have been
Miriam? She calmed down. If it had been, Mary would have mentioned it right away.

"They're not releasing the name yet, but he was white and in
his twenties—and there were drugs in the apartment."

"Can you describe the building?"

Mary did. Faith could have described it herself. It was Miriam's
building and Faith was pretty sure it was Miriam's apartment. The
top floor.

Miriam hadn't been killed, but was she the killer?

Almost an hour later, Faith had wheels again, but the snow was
falling so fast and furious that she took Mary's advice and pulled
into the motel's parking lot. It was pretty full and she hoped they
would have a room.

Power went out all over the island at 9:45 P.M. Since a good many
people were already in bed, this posed no hardship for most. Keeping the fire going and trips to the bathroom would be nippy, but
this was what winter Down East was all about.

With the storm raging outside, Mary felt a deep sense of peace.
Once again, she wondered if Christopher was an unusually good
baby. He got hungry about every four hours and let her know by
slightly increasing the frequency of the little noises he made—
noises somewhere between a cry and a bleat to her ears. Sometimes he hiccupped and it was real comical. He was sleeping now
and she thought she would nap in the big armchair. She checked
the fire, kissed the baby, and curled up in the chair.

At first she thought the knocking at the door was a dream. She
struggled to pull herself awake. Conscious, she realized the storm

must have torn a branch loose and it was knocking against a window. She hoped the glass wouldn't break.

But it wasn't a dream or a branch. It was real knocking at her kitchen door. She jumped up to look out the window, then quickly pulled the door open. A woman was standing in the snow that had piled up on the top step and all but fell into Mary's arms.

"It's all right, Miriam. I've been expecting you," Mary said.

CHAPTER 10

The driving hadn't been too bad until she turned off the main road at Orland, and even then Miriam had gotten lucky. The town plow was lumbering along ahead of her. She could barely see through the windshield, but kept following the truck's taillights. The car's heater was working all right, but the radio had conked out. She was thankful she'd taken the time to get gas earlier. Once she'd figured out where her father was heading, there was no rush, so she'd paused to fill up. She wasn't in a hurry after all. Just the opposite. She'd needed to think. He wouldn't have been heading north unless he had been going to her apartment, and that meant he didn't have Christopher. She'd wished Ralph and Duane had stuck around as a welcoming committee. Torn between her disinclination to return to the apartment ever again and her desire to have it out with her father once and for all, Miriam had found herself driving north too. She had to make him understand that there was no way he could take her child. He'd taken her childhood. That was enough.

How many hours had passed since she'd seen his car parked on her street, quickly pulled into a space outside Sammy's, and run upstairs to the apartment? It seemed like days, even weeks, but it was hours. Only a few hours.

Afterward she'd come back down and gone into the store. Sammy had taken one look at her and led her to a chair in the back.

"Are you okay? You're white as a sheet!"

"I'm fine. No problem," Miriam said. She was shivering.

"Let me get you some coffee. And some lady left a note for you."

"A lady left a note for me?" Miriam was having trouble taking anything in, seeing only the room across the street. The room with so much blood.

"Yeah—blond, kind of classy, thirty, maybe a little older. Name's Faith something."

Miriam shook her head. "Don't know her."

He returned with the coffee and the piece of paper Faith had left. Miriam scanned the message and got up quickly.

"Could you give me another cup too—a large? I've got to go."

This had all been hours ago. She deliberately kept her mind from the recent past and focused only on the road ahead. The wiper blades kept freezing. She'd had to stop twice to clear the ice from them and her fingers were still numb. Her gloves were soaked through and her hands were warmer without them. She hated driving in bad weather.

She was tired. More tired than after the baby had been born. More tired than she'd ever been in her whole life. By the time the plow truck turned toward Castine and left her without a guide, Miriam wasn't sure she could make it to Sanpere. But she had no choice. No choice at all.

Don't think about it, she told herself. Don't go there. It never happened. You were never in that apartment.

She made it as far as Sedgwick, getting out every few miles to clear the blades. Then, seeing headlights behind her, she pulled over and flagged the 4x4 with its plow up that was barreling along behind her.

"Pretty rugged night to be out," the teenager commented when she slid into the cab.

"Yeah, well, my mom's sick and I have to get down to Sanpere."

"I don't want to get stuck on the bridge. I'll take you as close as I can."

Miriam closed her eyes. The warmth of the truck enveloped her like a quilt. The radio was working and tuned to an oldies station.

> *If I were a carpenter and you were a lady*
> *Would you marry me anyway*
> *Would you have my baby*

But she was the Carpenter, she was the lady, and she had had the baby. Miriam had heard the song before; she knew the refrain.

> *Save my love for loneliness*
> *Save my love for sorrow*
> *I've given you my onliness*
> *Give me your tomorrow*

Still she cried; hot tears ran down her cheeks. Cried silently, looking out the side window into the darkness, her eyes wide open. Exhausted as she was, if she shut them, it would all come back. The room. The blood. No tomorrow.

"Stay with me. I can't let you out here. It's freezing. You'll never make it!" The boy grabbed her arm. He'd slowed near the bridge and now he'd changed his mind. She pulled her arm away.

"I'm not going to mess with you," he said. "Nothing like that.

I'll drop you off at my sister's. She'll be glad to give you a place to stay. You can't get to Sanpere tonight in this storm."

Miriam was tugging at the door.

"I'll be fine. I have really good boots and this parka is supposed to be what those guys who live down in Antarctica wear. I got it at the Bean outlet. Don't worry—and thanks a lot."

He wasn't ready to give up. He was only a few years younger than she was. The hood of the gray sweatshirt he was wearing under his jacket was pulled up. He smelled like cigarettes and WD-40, like a million other guys his age in Maine.

"You won't help your mother much if you turn up dead yourself."

She had the door open. He was forced to slow down almost to a stop.

"It's okay. Really. And thanks for the lift."

She was out and away from his headlights before he could say another word. It would have been impossible to explain to him that she didn't care whether she made it through the night or not. She cared only about reaching Mary's. If that wasn't what was going to happen, then that would be it.

Getting across the bridge was surprisingly easy. The high winds had kept the snow from piling up and there was no danger that Miriam would be blown into the frigid waters below. Unlike other suspension bridges that allowed for a scenic view, the island bridge had solid five-foot-high walls and was all business. At the top, it was hard to keep from sliding down the other side; the roadbed under the snowfall was treacherously slick. The wind blew the falling snow into her face. It felt like grains of sand, sharp and painful. Tiny knifepoints. She ducked her head down against her chest and pulled her hood more tightly closed. Knives. She couldn't think about knives.

Back on land, Miriam was sorely tempted to stop at the first house. It was dark, no lights at the window. She'd expected the island, like most of the mainland, would have lost power. Yet, she knew a house was near. She could smell wood burning. A woodstove or a fireplace, maybe both. The pungent aroma meant there would be warmth—a warm room, warm clothes, something warm to drink. But how to explain herself? What was she doing out on a night that wasn't fit for man or beast? And tomorrow, when power was restored and the news came on, what then? She trudged past the smell and all the others that beckoned until she came to Mary's road, perpendicular to the Reach, parallel to the bridge. It wasn't snowing as hard now and thankfully she'd recognized the turnoff. Once Miriam started down it, there wouldn't be any more houses. She'd make it—or not.

"First we have to get those wet things off. It's all right. Your baby is safe. Hush, don't try to talk."

Mary ran upstairs and pulled a flannel nightgown, sweaters, and socks from her bureau. She'd eased Miriam into the big chair, after dragging it closer to the stove. The girl was barely conscious. As she stripped her wet clothes off, Mary was relieved to see Miriam's skin was pale but not dead white. No frostbite. She rubbed the girl's feet and put on several pairs of socks, then wrapped her in a blanket before undoing the frozen braid that hung like a poker down her back and dried her hair with a towel. The girl had not tried to say a word, but Mary could feel Miriam's eyes following Mary's every move. She heated some whey and honey on the stove, then fed it to the young mother with a soupspoon. After she'd consumed half the cup, Miriam took it herself and drank.

"More," she whispered.

After she finished the second helping, she slept.

Mary had moved Christopher's basket next to Miriam where she could see him. Now she stationed herself in the old rocker and kept watch on them both through the long, dark night.

❄   ❄   ❄

"Do you have any rooms left?" Faith asked the desk clerk anxiously as she eyed the couch in the crowded lobby—orphans of
the storm. This was about the only place in the area that stayed
open during the off-season. A very large man was sitting on the
couch and she hoped that didn't mean he was staking a claim for
the night.

"Not really." The young man paused and Faith jumped in.

" 'Not really.' That sounds like you do have something. I'll take
anything."

"What we have is a room that's still being redone. No TV or
phone in service, but I could have the bed made up and give you
some towels. The bath's all set."

Bath. The magic word. A long, steaming hot bath.

Bed. Even more magical. She might even skip the bath.

"I'll take it."

"Okay. Sue's just about to leave, but I'll get her to make the
room up for you."

"I don't want to keep her. It's getting pretty bad out there.
Why don't you just give me the linens? I can do it myself."

Pete—as his badge noted—looked at her askance. It was as if
she had suggested something unspeakably kinky.

"Susan will make up the room. That is her job," he said firmly.
"You are welcome to wait here."

Given that the choice was of the lady-or-tiger variety—the
lobby or the snowstorm—Faith obediently perched on a chair near
the counter. The man on the couch was easily 250 pounds and
taking up most of the room.

She closed her eyes for a moment. After her tire was changed, it
had taken forever to get this far. She had greeted the train cars and
huge stacks of pulpwood outside the paper mill, recognizable even
in the blizzard, with relief. She was in Bucksport and near the
motel. It was eerie to see the mill, open round the clock 365 days

a year, shrouded in white, completely silent at this distance, the smokestacks with their clouds of steam. Steam. Her eyes opened and she thought about a bath again. Yes, she could do this. She was exhausted, but a bath first, then bed.

She was so tired, she realized, that she wasn't hungry. Of course as soon as the thought crossed her mind, she got hungry. The Milky Way bar she'd purchased for Tom at the convenience store served as an appetizer—a slightly stale amuse-bouche. She needed more. The lobby offered several vending machines and soon she was contentedly feasting on peanut butter crackers and Mountain Dew. The sweetness of the soda offered a witty counterpoint to the saltiness of the cracker; she laughed to herself, and decided she needed another package of the orange crackers to finish off the soda. Passing the phone on the way to the machines, she realized she hadn't told Mary that she'd left the note for Miriam at the convenience store. The note with Mary's phone number. Possibly Miriam had already called, but Faith thought she'd try to get through and alert Mary as to the possibility. Mary had a landline, so even if the power was out on Sanpere, it should go through. Power was still on here in Bucksport and presumably was up in Orono too.

She pulled out the calling card she always kept in her purse for just such an emergency. Gone were the days when the Coach saddlebag she favored for every day was filled with juice boxes, crayons, Teddy Grahams, and the like. They'd been replaced by new essentials. She could never understand how those women who carried a tiny clutch, or no purse at all, survived.

"I'm in the motel," she said when Mary answered.

The man on the couch got up and was fishing in his pocket for change. He obviously wanted to use the phone. She spoke more rapidly. "Everything's fine, but I forgot to tell you that I left a note for Miriam with your phone number at that Sammy's convenience store, so she may call or even show up, although that depends when she got it. The driving would be impossible now. Anyway, someone wants to use the phone, so I have to get off. Could you call Tom again and tell him I did stop here? There's no phone in my room. I'll call you tomorrow when I get to Sanpere and hopefully can bring the stuff over."

As she hung up, Pete called out, "Mrs. Fairchild, your room is ready."

She gave the man waiting to use the phone a radiant smile.

Bath. Bed.

Greatly relieved that Faith was riding out the storm with a mint on her pillow or whatever the equivalent was at the place she was staying, Tom turned his full attention to his kids. He'd always loved the combination of fun and fear that a power outage meant when he was young. Ben and Amy were the same. Two full pro-pane tanks at the back of the house had meant hot water for baths, and afterward he'd been able to heat up some of the pumpkin pie soup (see recipe, p. 246), that Faith had left. She always made it around the holidays and it was a family favorite. The smell of nutmeg and the other spices still lingered in the air. The kids were snuggled in sleeping bags in front of the woodstove; Tom claimed a couch. The house was almost too well insulated and he soon had to toss off his down comforter. He was reading E. B. White's *Stuart Little* out loud. It was the kind of book that knew no season. The Little family had just presented Margalo, the walleyed vireo, with a tiny cake in thanks for saving Stuart's life.

"Keep going, Daddy," Amy begged.

This wasn't a night for strict adherence to bedtime and Tom kept reading until Amy's regular breathing and Ben's drowsy "I'm not asleep" told him it was time to stop.

The storm was at full throttle. He couldn't see the cove and the wind was flinging what was coming down against the plate-glass windows with the force of a pile driver. He wasn't worried that they'd break—they'd opted for the top of the line, double paned. He wished Faith were here beside him not because he was worried about her—by now he'd bet she was sound asleep—but because she'd appreciate the wild beauty of the scene outside.

It had been an odd time, this time in Sanpere. First of all because Tom wasn't where he should be, had been for all of his adult life. In a pulpit at Christmas. Not lying on a couch—or sitting in an iceboat. Although that had been great. During the worst of his illness, he'd despaired of ever feeling like his old self and hated the thought that he might be a burden on Faith. It was actually pretty selfish, he reflected now. Pretty pathetic. Still, it had been his very own black cloud and wasn't entirely gone until the other day flying down Walker Pond under an impossibly blue sky, literally racing with eagles.

He'd felt a bit dislocated to be here at Christmas, but dinner with the Marshalls and the joy of being just the four of them with no services to rush off to had set in. Even Norah Taft's death, and Faith's discovery of the body, had been sad, tragic, but not something that touched them directly. Then he'd gotten involved with Jake. Ever since the ride to Ellsworth, Tom kept thinking of the boy and what he and his family must be going through.

Ben's blond head—the same color hair as his mother's—was poking out of his sleeping bag. Tom felt an overwhelming desire to wrap both kids in cotton wool until they were, what? Twenty-one? Thirty? Keep them safe in an unpredictable and dangerous world.

Tom got up to get himself a snack. Again, he wished Faith were here—and not to look outside, but inside. He needed to talk to her. She'd understand.

It was close to dawn. When Mary returned from the 6 A.M. milking, Miriam was sitting at the table. She was reading the Sanpere local paper with such intensity that she didn't look up until Mary said good morning. Startled—and pointing at the paper—she said, "I know this girl. Except her hair was different and she said her name was something else. It began with a *Z*."

"Zara, but everyone on the island knew her by her given name, Norah." Mary sat down next to Miriam. Christopher was still sound asleep. He'd awoken an hour ago and Mary had fed him. Miriam hadn't stirred.

"It says she died, but not how." Miriam turned a stricken face toward Mary. "How did she die? She was so young."

"At first they thought it was a drug overdose, but now the police think she was murdered."

The color drained from Miriam's face as she whispered, "Murdered." She sat very still, and then said, slowly, "She was just a kid."

Mary waited. There really wasn't anything to say. Either Miriam would tell her more or not.

"I thought she was a runaway. She'd come to the apartment for, well, for drugs. Bruce had her dealing to pay for what she wanted. Then she was gone for a while. I was happy, because I thought she'd returned to her family. She seemed like the kind of girl with a family if you looked past the tattoos and the way she dressed."

"She left her mother," Mary said, "and a whole lot of people who thought of themselves as family. The police are talking to her boyfriend. He's from the island. In high school, like she would have been. Quite an athlete. We all think a lot of him."

"He didn't kill her."

"Nobody here thinks he did."

"I need some paper and a pen, Mary. I need to write down that I'm surrendering my rights to the baby, giving him to you. And something else. Paper and two envelopes."

"I've got plenty upstairs, but are you sure you want to do this? Look at him."

Miriam glanced over at the baby, then back at Norah's photo in the paper. It seemed to hold her gaze more than the infant had.

"I'm sure. Absolutely sure. Always have been. How about you? I never thought that you might not want him. I guess I was kind of thinking of him as another one of your herd." Miriam smiled. She had a joyful smile at times, Mary thought.

"I'm honored that you regard me as someone who would raise your son the way you think he should be raised. And yes, I want him," she said gravely.

It was a moment for a hug, or failing that, a handshake. Miriam did neither, but stood up and placed the baby, his eyes slowly opening to the new day, in Mary's arms.

"I believe this belongs to you."

When Mary returned with the writing materials, also taking time to put on fresh clothes, she noticed two things: Miriam was flushed and the boots she'd been wearing when she arrived had a thin layer of white. The boots were by the door in exactly the same place Mary had put them hours earlier, but now there was a coating of fresh snow on the toes. What had Miriam been doing outside? What possible reason could she have had to go to the barn—the only destination?

Mary hadn't mentioned what she'd seen on the news—the murder of a young man she was almost certain was Bruce, the same Bruce who had come down to the island with Miriam last summer and who was probably the baby's father. The same Bruce who had supplied Norah with the drugs that took such a deadly hold of her. What was Miriam thinking after she saw Norah's picture in the paper? Something that linked Bruce to the poor girl's death?

Faith Fairchild would help straighten everything out, and although she assumed Faith would first go home to her family, Mary hoped she would come by today. John Robbins kept Mary plowed out and she always told him to do her last—she didn't have to get to the main road. She was tempted to call him, so Faith could get in, but with a storm like this, she didn't want to bother him. Miriam must have driven a car from Orono and left it someplace on Route 17. So, she wasn't going anywhere and the thought filled Mary with a sense of satisfaction, peace even. The girl could stay for as long as she wanted. Sanctuary.

"I have to start some cheese," she told Miriam. "I won't be long."

It was already a bright sunny day—warm enough so the snow that clung to the trees was starting to fall in clumps to the ground. The weighted branches relieved of their burden sprang up like jack-in-the-boxes. She reached down and shook the snow from a bayberry bush. As she freed it from the ground, she caught a slight whiff of its scent.

It didn't take long to finish her chore and when Mary returned she felt as if she were walking into a storybook picture—one by Jessie Wilcox Smith or Tasha Tudor. Miriam was sitting in the big chintz easy chair again, Christopher cradled in her arms while she fed him. Her long shining dark hair tumbled over her shoulders, tumbled over the soft blue sweater she was wearing. She looked up at Mary, but finished singing to the baby, " 'I've given you my onliness / Give me your tomorrow' " before asking, "All's well?" The query was as soft and melodic as her singing had been.

The room was glowing—with the heat from the stove, the smiles of the two women, and the radiant baby. Mary felt the sense of peace return. Out in the barn, her thoughts had strayed to the murder in Orono. She'd calculated the probable time of death the news had announced and measured it against the time of Miriam's arrival at the house. She couldn't have been in Orono at the time in question and made it down to the island in the storm. Or could she? Suddenly the warmth in the room became a suffocating blanket of heat and Mary went over to the window to open it a crack.

"Dear God! Something's wrong! It's Faith, but . . ." Mary didn't finish her sentence but raced for the phone. Miriam hadn't moved. "Quick, you've got to take Christopher and get out of here! Run!"

The snow was so soft that small, sparkling eddies swirled about Faith's feet as she made her way to her car. The surface caught the morning light, turning the motel parking lot into a blanket of diamonds. She'd slept, well, like a baby, and when she'd opened the curtains even the sight of the hideous new Penobscot Narrows Bridge couldn't dampen her spirits. It looked as if it were made of string cheese, a dismal comparison to the graceful copper-colored suspension bridge still standing next to it. Yes, the old bridge was near to collapse, so better a safe span than the ever-increasing possibility of plunging into the swift currents below, but did it have to be so ugly?

Pete was still on duty and had managed to get coffee and doughnuts from somewhere. Faith gratefully drank two steaming cups, accompanied by two very sweet powdered-sugar doughnuts. She settled her bill—he insisted on charging only half price even when Faith, in gratitude, offered to pay the full amount. It had been a real port in the storm. She left a large tip for Sue and Pete himself, then, hearing the roads were clear, set out on her way. She paused to call Tom and told him she'd be home in about two hours. Bucksport was normally much less, but the side roads through Penobscot and Sedgwick might not be in great shape.

A man was just finishing scraping the snow and ice from her front windshield. The back was clear.

"Why, thank you!" she said.

"Compliments of the management," he replied.

Making a mental note to write to the president of the chain, Faith got behind the wheel and the car started right up. She backed out of the space and turned toward the exit, stopping to check for an oncoming car.

"Just keep driving, ma'am. Keep your eyes on the road. I'm not going to hurt you."

The words came from the backseat, where the speaker had been crouched, and were accompanied by the unmistakable feel of the barrel of a handgun, cold against the back of her neck. She felt the coffee and doughnuts she had just consumed rise into her throat and swallowed hard, keeping her mouth shut. If she spoke, she would scream, and if she screamed, he would do what? Pull the trigger? Could she chance it? He loomed large in the rearview mirror, a greasy watch cap pulled low on a tangle of dark brown hair that merged with a beard of the same color and texture. It was the man who had been in the lobby the night before. The man on the couch. His eyes were tiny pinholes in the mass of flesh surrounding them and it was the eyes that convinced her. He would pull the trigger.

She knew it wasn't a carjacking and his next words confirmed her fears.

"You just head for Sanpere and whoever you talked to last night. I'm not interested in whatever stuff you're delivering. Just Miriam. You'll be fine, unless you try anything funny. This is to do with her, not you."

Faith took a deep breath and started to make the turn. Out of the corner of her eye she saw the good Samaritan who'd cleaned her windshields start to get into his truck, which was parked next to the street. She could lean on the horn. Whoever the madman in her rear seat was, he couldn't be so crazy that he'd shoot her with a witness so close by.

"Don't even think about it." Her captor leaned so close to her ear that she could smell his breath. He'd had the doughnuts too. "Name's Ralph and Ol' Duane out there? He's with me."

❄ ❄ ❄

As she drove, Faith looked out at familiar landmarks: the Union Trust Bank and Radio Shack across the intersection, and there was Hannaford and Dunkin' Donuts. Things that were on Main Streets everywhere in the country. Normal, everyday things. "America Runs on Dunkin'." The slogan popped into her mind. What did these two men run on? What fueled them? She couldn't begin to understand. Or maybe she could. Maybe it was as simple as seizing whatever they wanted, whenever they wanted it, by any means. No spark of conscience lit up the eyes she couldn't avoid seeing in the mirror.

How could this be happening? People didn't get kidnapped at gunpoint in broad daylight. Not in Maine. Not her.

It was happening.

A car passed her. It was moving slowly and she darted a look at the woman in the passenger seat, mouthing the word "help." The woman smiled cheerfully and waved, mouthing something in return that could have been "hi." The car pulled ahead and was gone.

Faith was gripping the steering wheel so tightly her fingers were beginning to throb and she wasn't sure she could continue driving. Fear threatened to overwhelm the reflexes that were keeping the car moving.

"All's we want is the money. Our money," he said.

A justification?

Faith didn't pretend ignorance. As soon as he'd said Miriam's name, she knew what he wanted.

"I don't know where the money is, but the person who does will give it to you." She tried to keep her voice steady and calm— as if talking to a two-year-old on the verge of losing it.

He nodded. "That would be Miss Miriam." His tone made her name sound like an expletive.

"No, not Miriam," Faith said. "I've never met her and don't know where she is, but she left some money with someone on Sanpere and it's the money you want."

He didn't say anything for a while. Processing.

"Maybe you never met Miriam, but, ma'am, you said her name on the phone."

"If you heard that, you also heard that I said I'd left a note for her in Orono." Faith wasn't sure she liked being called "ma'am." She wasn't the Queen of England or the new schoolmarm. How old did this guy think she was, anyway?

She pictured Mary's farm in her mind. She had to have a plan ready for their arrival. There was no way she could let the two men simply walk in without warning Mary and calling for help. She didn't believe they would leave them unharmed after getting the money. No, these two men wouldn't leave Faith and Mary alive, able to identify them as kidnappers and more.

With Ralph and Duane, Faith was sure she now had all the pieces of the puzzle that had started with her discovery of the body in the sleigh even if she hadn't fit them together. The dead man in the Orono apartment must have been Bruce and the fact that Norah was found with a bag from the convenience store across the street meant she had been connected to him.

Trees. Mary's farm had lots of trees. And trees meant cover. Faith began to figure out what she could do. Figure out what she had to do to keep the three of them from being killed. Or perhaps it was four. Had Miriam gotten her note? Was she at Bethany Farm?

Ralph sat in total silence. It was terrifying. Faith began to abandon her thoughts of running once they were at the farm and weighed the pros and cons of deliberately skidding into a pole right now. His sudden voice jolted her.

"This person who has the money. They'll know where she is."

Ignoring the lack of pronoun agreement, Faith said, "No, she probably doesn't. That's why I was in Orono. To try to find Miriam. You'll get your money. You don't need Miriam for that."

He pressed the gun harder into the back of Faith's neck. She promptly abandoned any thought other than driving straight to Sanpere.

"We don't like it when people take things that belong to us. That's why we want Miriam."

At Bethany Farm, the scene inside the house and outside ricocheted off each other. Dashing to the window, Miriam saw a woman near a car at the end of the drive followed by Ralph. Duane had pulled up his truck behind them and was lumbering through the snow. They were moving slowly. Ralph weighed closer to three hundred pounds than two hundred and Duane was no Kate Moss. The woman, unencumbered by excess weight and in the lead, was nonetheless staying close to them.

Miriam felt unnaturally calm.

"Their names are Duane and Ralph and they want the money I left with you for Christopher. They also want to kill me."

Mary was dialing 911.

"Get your boots on and wrap the baby under your jacket. Go straight through the woods to the Harveys. Where we went to bring some squash last summer. Go by the shore, just in case you have to use the canoe. The Reach isn't frozen solid. The canoe's under a blue tarp."

"I can't let you do this!" Miriam said.

"Don't waste time, just get out of here! You've got to get Christopher away from them! I'll give them the money."

Out in the snow, Faith was eyeing the thick stand of tamaracks close to the house. The two men's labored breathing was audible. She could definitely outrun them in this deep snow and warn Mary. As she'd imagined earlier, the trees would provide cover and she could go in through the shed. If the money was in the house, they could toss it out a window and that might satisfy them. It was a vain hope, but it was the only plan she had.

She was at the trees before the men knew what was happening.

"Hey! Stop! Dammit!" Ralph yelled and she heard the shot, which missed her. The next one might not and she sprinted for the shed, a streak of color against the white snow—a moving target.

Safely through the kitchen door, Faith almost collided with Miriam, who was standing immobilized as Mary pushed her boots at her.

"Go with her, Faith! Take the baby! I've called 911 and told them the house was on fire and we needed police and an ambulance too. I'll stay and give them the money."

Sirens, lots of sirens. Faith only hoped the volunteers would get there in time.

Faith grabbed Miriam and that action roused her into action. She shoved her boots on and headed for the back door. They could hear the men's voices closing in on the house.

"Hurry!" Faith cried.

"You take the baby," Miriam said, pulling on her parka and handing Christopher in his sling to Faith. At the door, Miriam called to Mary, "Don't stall. Tell them where the money is right away and follow us! You don't know what they can do!"

Outside, the sun was almost blinding. The two women ran toward the woods across the old pasture behind the house.

"I think it's Miriam! She was here and she's getting away!" yelled Ralph. He called to Duane, "Come on!"

"There's someone in the house," Duane said. "I saw the curtains move. She may be trying to trick us into following somebody else. I'm going in! You follow those two." He was at the front door and started kicking at it. "Open up, bitch. We know you're there!"

Inside, Mary decided to ignore Miriam's advice. The longer she could keep them out, the farther ahead the others would get. Ralph had stopped running—to catch his breath—and was looking toward the house to see what Duane was doing.

The door was solid oak and Mary had hopes it would last until help arrived.

"Sonofabitch!" Duane hopped on one foot, rubbing the toe of his boot, then went back to the truck for something stronger. He saw Ralph and yelled, "What are you waiting for? Keep going, asshole!"

Ralph took off again; the two figures were in plain sight, but nearing the woods. Duane shook his head and smacked his fist on the side of the truck before he reached into the bed to get a crowbar. He didn't know what was going on. Mostly his life was pretty simple. He got what people wanted, gave it to people to sell, and they handed over a lot more money than he had paid in the first place. Maine. What kind of a place was this? Nothing but trees and maybe moose. That's what he'd told Bruce two years ago when he wanted to leave Massachusetts and start up the business here. Volume. That was the point. Bruce had convinced him there were plenty of people looking for what they had to offer and he'd been right. Not as straight with them as he should have been, but he and Ralph had taken care of that. Bruce wouldn't be skimming off the top anymore.

Duane retraced his steps. No, he didn't like not knowing what was going on. He felt better thinking about what he was going to do to Miriam when he got her—and he would get her.

"Who are they?" Faith managed to gasp as they neared the woods and safety.

"Drug dealers, big-time on the East Coast. They think I stole some money from them."

There was no mistaking the sound that split the air. Faith had heard it earlier; Miriam hadn't.

"Oh, shit," said Miriam. "Ralph's got a gun."

❄   ❄   ❄

As soon as Mary saw Duane approach her door with the crowbar, she opened it.

"There's no need to damage my property. What do you want?"

"Fer sure I'm not here for a friggin' cup of coffee. Now get Miriam and get the money."

"I don't know what you're talking about," Mary said. Help was on the way.

Duane took a step toward Mary and grabbed her wrist. Then, hearing the sound of the goats from the barn, he leered at her.

"Like animals, do you? Think I'll take a look at the critters."

"No!" Mary cried, pulling free. "Don't you dare go near my goats! I'll give you the money. Miriam isn't here. She ran off when you drove up. You could see that."

"Well, now, this is much better. Ralph will take care of Miriam. Okay, grandma, let's get the cash—and it had better all be there."

"You stay here; I'll bring it to you." Where was the fire truck? Why hadn't at least one volunteer arrived yet?

"No, I think we'll stick together."

"It's in the barn." Mary hated to bring him anywhere near her nannies. They'd be upset for days, but there was no choice.

When she opened the door, the goats' bleating increased. Just as she feared, they were panicking. It was as if they knew exactly what was happening. Mary paused to try to calm them, but Duane told her to hand over the money and hand it over fast.

She walked over to a pile of small square bales of hay—she bought it like this rather than in the rolls, because it was easier for her to handle. Easy to handle the other day when she'd hollowed out the middle of one and replaced the straw with the money.

"Here." She shoved the packet at him. "Now get out."

Duane opened it up. "Looks like it's all here, but I think I'll just count it to make sure. Could be you wanted to use some of it for a new billy goat." He laughed. It wasn't a pleasant sound. Mary didn't correct him as to the gender of her herd. The longer he took the better. She was straining to hear the sirens, but the only sound was her goats' piteous racket, louder than ten fire engines.

"Now, now, what's this?" Duane snarled. "There's two thousand dollars missing!"

"I don't know anything about that," Mary said firmly, backing away from him. "I haven't touched that money since I put it there."

"So I guess you musta taken it out before then." He reached into his pocket and took out a Buck knife, flicking it open. "That little goat over there. He needs a haircut."

Faith knew they were close to the shore. There had been a couple more shots, but since Ralph had to look down to follow their tracks, they'd been able to keep ahead of him. Mary's canoe was under a blue tarp. You could find just about anything under a blue tarp in Maine. Miriam tugged at it, freed the canoe, and dragged it to the shore. Mary had been right. The water in the Reach wasn't frozen the way it was in the smaller coves. There were chunks of ice, but they'd be able to get the canoe in—and then what? Faith certainly hoped Miriam knew how to paddle, because otherwise they were sunk.

"Get in! Grab a paddle and go! I'll push us off!"

Christopher had started to cry. Faith felt like crying herself, but saved it for later. The canoe teetered in the water. She didn't even want to think about what would happen if they capsized. A minute, two minutes in water this temperature?

Miriam was moving them along with strong, swift strokes. Faith tried to match the rhythm, but gave up and concentrated on calming the baby.

A bullet hit the water just behind them. Ralph was screaming at them from the shore. He emptied the gun as they pulled farther and farther out of range. Around the corner of one of the points of land that extended like gnarled fingers into the current, Faith could see the Harveys' dock. They were safe. And the emergency rescue vehicles must have arrived at the farm by now. Mary was safe too.

Mary *was* fine, but Duane was suffering from a nasty bite on the hand from Dora, the queen, who had been very curious about the bright shiny object in his hand. She'd slid through the gate from the stall that he hadn't closed properly when he'd reached for the kid, and lunged to explore the blade, encountering instead Duane's very fleshy palm. Before he could do more than just shove at the 180-pound pride of Mary's herd, the fire department, rescue corps, and a state police officer all poured through Mary's barn door. They arrested Duane immediately and sat down to wait for Ralph and the officer who'd gone after him. One of the volunteers took pity on Duane and poured more than enough iodine on his open wound before bandaging it.

"We can call the farm from the Harveys', and as soon as we reach Mary, they'll drive us back." Faith was nuzzling Christopher's tiny head, which seemed to be keeping him quiet.

Miriam maneuvered the canoe toward the dock, and Faith grabbed a line tied to the end of it, pulling them in alongside.

"Maybe we should put the canoe on the dock. No, it won't be here for long. We can moor it and someone will take it back to Mary." She stepped out and reached to help Miriam. The expression on the girl's face troubled her. They were safe. All of them. Why did Miriam look so sad?

Miriam fleetingly wondered what it would be like to be Faith

Fairchild. Mary had told her all about Faith this morning. Her life sounded perfect—happy marriage, kids, job, a direction in life. She sighed.

"Look, Faith, this is where I get off. Or rather, you get off."

"What!" Faith exclaimed.

"I'm not like you or Mary. I'm not a good girl. And I certainly wouldn't be a good mother."

"It's Bruce, isn't it?" Faith said. The cold dread she'd felt since hearing about the murder gave way to cold certainty.

"Kind of. I didn't kill him, though, if that's what you mean."

"Then who did? Those men? Duane and Ralph?"

"Pretty much. They got their licks in first. Bruce was holding out on them and they made sure he wouldn't do it again, but no, they didn't kill him. He was the proverbial golden goose for them and their gang. But, believe me, you don't need to know about this. Tell Mary that Christopher is hers. I left a letter in an envelope in the drawer where she keeps her dish towels. If that's not enough to convince the state, I'll sign whatever they want. Help her get a lawyer. She's got plenty of money. It was mine; don't let the cops have it."

By now Miriam was convinced the money was hers—wages for all the housekeeping and accounting she'd done—and certainly Christopher's. His inheritance from his father and all he was ever going to get from him, thank God.

"I thought this was going to be a whole lot easier." She sighed. "I decided last summer that I wanted Mary to be the baby's mother. When he was born, I wanted to give him to her even more. She's the best person I ever met. Tell her that. And also that the week I spent with her was the happiest in my life."

"Then why go?" Faith had been picturing a perfect happily-ever-after. Mary and Miriam—the two Marys—raising Christopher, goats, and vegetables together on into the sunset.

"I'm only twenty-one years old. Even if I were a good person, that's too young to have a child—at least for me. And I have to figure some things out, a lot of things."

"What about your family? Your father?"

"There isn't any family now, never was much of one. But don't worry, Daniel Carpenter isn't going to try to get Christopher as a trinket for Brenda—that's my stepmother, or rather, his wife—or a male someone to continue the sainted Carpenter line. Be sure Mary changes his name to hers."

Faith had so many questions, but Miriam was already untying the line.

"How can you be certain that he won't take legal action to get his grandson?"

Miriam hesitated for a moment, then said, "Because, good, kind Mrs. Fairchild, Daddy finished what Duane and Ralph started. I got there just in time to see him go nuts when Bruce managed to pull a knife on him, thinking he was their backup, and the knife ended up in Bruce. Self-defense? Helps to have a witness for that. What I did witness was the way he wiped his prints off and left in a big hurry. Believe me, he'll tell Brenda the baby was ugly and threw up a lot—something like that. She'll be happy with another fancy dog or a few more diamond tennis bracelets and there'll be no more talk of babies."

It was a scene Miriam would never quite be able to obliterate from her mind.

At first it seemed as if there was blood everywhere. Then she realized it was confined to a pool at Bruce's side and splatters on the wall he was slumped against. The wall she had painted a soft yellow in those early weeks of nesting when she first moved in. Those sunny, optimistic weeks that now felt as if they had been lived by somebody else. Like a book she'd once read. Fiction.

She knew he was dead. But he hadn't been dead long. Her fa-

ther was standing over him motionless, holding the knife and looking at her in horror.

"He came at me. It was self-defense. He thought I was some-body else. Somebody who was going to kill him. He'd been hurt. He was already bleeding. I didn't do anything. He pulled the knife out of his pocket and came at me. I grabbed it. He was going to stab me with it. I had to. It was self-defense."

Miriam had listened to the rush of words, barely comprehend-ing what her father was saying, and was struck by the incongruous thought that this just wasn't the real estate mogul's scene at all. A seedy apartment with a dead drug dealer. Not his scene, but his scene now.

She believed him. Bruce must have thought Daniel was there to finish what Duane and Ralph had started.

Blood. So much blood.

She was starting to pull away from the dock. The shadows were lengthening as the morning crept into afternoon; darkness was falling on the picture in her mind as well. Then she remembered something else.

"I took two thousand dollars from the money I left with the baby. Mary stashed it all in a bale of hay in the barn. She told me last night. I think she knew what I'd do. But I'll pay it back. Be sure to tell her."

Miriam had a lot of things she wanted to be sure Mary knew.

This wasn't the right ending, but it was the ending. There was only one more thing.

"I told you that you could get in touch with me if you need to," Miriam said.

Or *you* need to, Faith thought.

"The island newspaper is online now," Miriam said. "In July Mary and I joked about how high-tech the island was becoming and that she would be selling cheese on the Internet soon. We'll use the Personals; you know, where people put ads saying 'happy anniversary' or 'thanks for the cards' when they were in the hospital. I'll call you if I see one that says, 'Mother Mary, come to me.'"

Faith held Christopher up so Miriam could see him. She waved and left them, heading for the bridge, not far away, and a ride to somewhere.

Let it be.

EPILOGUE

The New Year's Eve sky was filled with stars when Mary Bethany brought her baby into their barn. The brief warm spell of the last two days had given way to bitter cold and she had bundled Christopher into his snowsuit and wrapped him in a blanket before putting him into the sling, which kept him close to her heart. Close to her heart. He'd arrived in this barn only a little over a week ago and she was already having trouble imagining her life without him. The nannies greeted them with a chorus that did not resemble "Auld Lang Syne," so she hummed the tune as she milked. "A cup of kindness"—she knew it referred to sharing a dram of something, but liked the image of a cup truly overflowing with some sort of ephemeral kindness. A vapor that even now she felt mixing with the warm, sweet hay smell in the barn. Miriam had asked her to raise Christopher to be a good man and to Mary this meant a kind man, a man who would do unto others, following the Golden Rule. When she looked at his face and into his bright, alert eyes, she was sure that she saw the man he would become and rejoiced.

When Miriam had placed the infant in Mary's arms and told

her he was hers, Mary knew she was receiving the greatest gift anyone could give. She felt as if her whole life had been a preparation for this trust and was glad that the fates had kept her from other paths. Christopher was meant to be her son. She had already started rehearsing what she would tell him when he was old enough about the night he arrived and the loving mother who cared so much about him that she knew she had to give him up. What she would say about his father, Mary wasn't sure, but there was time to figure it all out.

The baby sneezed and Mary stopped humming, quickly finishing her chores. She knew he wasn't cold. It was a tickle kind of sneeze, but she wanted to return to the house and put him in his crib. Faith had brought all sorts of baby things, some a marvel to Mary, like the little windup swing. Christopher Bethany had everything he needed.

She stepped out into the yard and looked up into the night sky. The moon hadn't risen yet, but she'd seen it last night—almost the third quarter. Some folks minded the early dark of winter, but Mary never had. It was part of the rhythm of the seasons and she embraced them all. Auld Lang Syne was now.

On the other side of the island, people were still arriving at the Dickinsons'. The house smelled of fresh paint—and all sorts of tantalizing food aromas. Jill had been baking and cooking for days, telling everyone simply to bring themselves, but nobody listened. Earl had extended the long dining room table with doors set on sawhorses, which Jill had covered with bright cloths from her shop. Every inch was covered with traditional favorites like baked beans and brown bread, an enormous baked ham studded with cloves, baking-powder biscuits the size of catcher's mitts, pickled beets, chowchow, watermelon pickles, three-bean salad, Jell-O molds, and pies of every possible description from blueberry to coconut cream. There was also a fair smattering of fare not usually seen at island suppers, such as the pâtés Faith had brought—a layered seafood one, chicken liver with Madeira, and a hearty pork country variety. She'd also made a large, nontipsy trifle in a glass bowl that displayed the succulent layers of fruit, ladyfingers, and whipped cream.

At ten o'clock, Amy conked out and Tom carried her up to the bedroom where everyone had thrown coats and jackets across the large bed. Two other kids were already nestled down. Faith had followed them up, and as Tom deposited Amy among the down parkas and woolen overcoats, she recalled similar, long-ago nights—waking with her equally drowsy sister, Hope, at their aunt Chat's apartment in New York, protesting at having missed seeing the ball drop before promptly falling back asleep in the cab that took the Sibleys across Central Park back to their side of that other island.

Ben was firm. He wasn't at all tired. He was with the group of teens watching television in the cozy den that doubled as Jill's office. Nan Marshall was there too, having confided to Faith that she was a lifelong Dick Clark fan. Amused as she was by the confession, Faith knew it was more likely that Nan couldn't bear to let her grandson out of her sight.

Jake Whittaker was totally in the clear so far as the police were concerned and the coach hadn't said anything. Wouldn't. Whatever punishment Jake deserved for breaking training had been meted out to him a thousandfold. Faith had been startled—and saddened—to see the change in the boy's face. A permanent change. He looked older, bitter, and utterly bereft.

The events of that night and its aftermath were becoming clearer each day. Lab results on Jake's hair had revealed that he too had been given Rohypnol, which accounted for his loss of memory. And then there was the letter Miriam had left for the authorities detailing Bruce Judd's drug connections and her belief that he was responsible for Norah's death directly or indirectly. When shown a photograph of Bruce, Jake recalled seeing him in the kitchen of the Temple Heights house shortly before Norah arrived. In Jake's mind, there was no doubt that Bruce followed them and overheard their conversation. Norah had been given the overdose and placed in Jake's car, along with Jake, himself unconscious. The car was then driven down to Sanpere by Eddie Sanford and a cousin of his. Miriam had named Eddie in her letter as Bruce's contact on the island and the person responsible for the break-ins that had occurred during the fall. He was a regular at the apartment in Orono and had amused Bruce with his scornful descriptions of what the summer people left lying about. A sometime fisherman, Eddie had proved useful the summer before in both transporting and receiving Bruce's caches. Faith remembered his grandmother Daisy and her comment that hearts on the island would be breaking over Norah. Daisy's heart was surely breaking over the grandson whose generosity was funded by a life of crime.

Ralph and Duane, Faith's captors, would be guests of the state for a very, very long time. Besides the kidnapping and weapons charges, the pickup had yielded a cornucopia of illegal drugs.

It was close to midnight and Faith went in search of Tom. He was crowded into the den with Ben, fighting sleep, on his lap. She realized it was probably one of the last times Ben would occupy this position. He would soon be a teenager, but for tonight he was their little boy still.

More people entered the room, their faces reflecting hopes, dreams, and all sorts of optimistic resolutions. Faith slipped next to Tom and took his hand. She hadn't tried to downplay what she had been through as she had occasionally with past tight situations. This had been the worst, and she could still feel the muzzle of the gun on the back of her neck at times. These days if she wasn't reaching for Tom, he was for her.

"Ten, nine, eight . . ."

Ben sat up and rubbed his eyes.

"Seven, six, five . . ." he chanted with the others.

"Four, three, two . . ."

Just one more second of this year. A difficult year. Never wish time away, Faith's mother had told her more than once. But if ever Faith did wish it gone, it would be now.

And suddenly it was.

"One! Happy New Year!"

The Fairchilds kissed each other. A long, lingering kiss, then sang along with everyone else:

> *Should auld acquaintance be forgot*
> *and never brought to mind?*
> *Should auld acquaintance be forgot*
> *and days of auld lang syne?*

She knew she was crying. The song always made her cry. "Auld Lang Syne"—"good old days."

Auld Lang Syne was now.

HAVE FAITH
IN YOUR
KITCHEN

By Faith Sibley Fairchild

(A WORK IN PROGRESS)

Seafood Risotto

5 cups fish stock

2 tablespoons unsalted butter

2 tablespoons olive oil

1 small yellow onion, diced

1½ cups Arborio rice

½ cup grated Parmesan cheese

2 cups small, cooked shrimp (shelled and deveined)

8 ounces crabmeat

Parsley for garnish

Pour the stock in a large saucepan and heat to a simmer.

While the stock is heating, melt the butter and oil in a pot (Faith likes a Le Creuset–type casserole). Sauté the onion until soft and add the rice, sautéing for 2 more minutes.

Using a ladle, add the heated stock approximately ½ cup at a time, stirring after each addition until all the liquid is absorbed. Whole Foods and other stores sell an excellent prepared fish stock if you do not have the time or ingredients to make your own.

When all the stock has been used, stir in the cheese and then fold in the shrimp and crab.

Serve garnished with chopped parsley. Serves 6.

This is tasty with just the shrimp or crab. Heavenly with lobster.

"The Annie" Breakfast Sandwich

2 large eggs (per person)

¼ cup crumbled feta cheese

1 generous handful loosely packed
    fresh spinach, stemmed

Freshly ground pepper

Unsalted butter

2 slices of grilled or toasted
    sourdough bread

2 slices tomato

Beat the eggs and stir in the cheese, spinach, and a pinch of pepper.

Butter the bread and set aside on a warm plate.

Scramble the egg mixture in a nonstick frying pan.

Place the tomato slices on the bread and mound the filling on top. Cut the sandwich in half and serve immediately. Good with rye also.

Kyra Alex of Lily's Café in Stonington, Maine, names many of her sandwiches and other dishes for friends—Ethel's Pulled Pork, Darrell's Muffaletta, Cecil's Chicken, and, in this case, Annie. I think of it as my sister Annie's, though!

Pumpkin Pie Soup

4 cups pumpkin puree (your own from
    a sugar pumpkin or canned)

4 cups chicken stock, preferably salt-free

3 tablespoons brown sugar

1½ teaspoons cinnamon   ½ teaspoon salt

1 teaspoon ground ginger   2 cups half-and-half or light cream

1 teaspoon nutmeg   Sour cream

Mix the first 7 ingredients together in a large saucepan and bring to a simmer. Simmer for about 10 minutes. Turn off the heat and add the half and half. Let sit for 5 minutes and reheat gently. Serve with a dollop of sour cream to cut the sweetness. Serves 4–6.

Children love this nutritious dish. For all ages, it's fun to use a mug, piping a rosette of sour cream on top.

Chocolate Bread Pudding

4 large eggs   Pinch of salt

1½ cups milk   5 thick slices of chocolate bread, cubed

1½ cups half and half or light cream   Butter to grease the pan

¼ cup white sugar   1 cup dried cherries

1 teaspoon vanilla   1 cup semisweet chocolate morsels

Mix the eggs, milk, half and half, sugar, vanilla, and salt together. Faith likes to pulse this in a blender, which makes it easy to pour over the bread cubes.

Put the bread cubes in a large mixing bowl and pour the egg mixture over them. Use the palm of your hand to gently push the bread into the liquid to make sure it absorbs evenly. Cover with plastic wrap and refrigerate for at least 30 minutes.

Preheat the oven to 350°.

Butter a Pyrex-type baking pan, approximately 12 by 8 inches. Set aside.

Mix the cherries and chocolate chips together in a small bowl.

Put a layer of the bread mixture in the pan, sprinkle the cherry/chip mixture over it, and cover with the remaining bread mixture.

Again, use the palm of your hand to press down, so the ingredients are evenly distributed.

Bake for 40 minutes.

Serve warm with vanilla ice cream or frozen yogurt.

This is a very rich dessert and this recipe will serve 12 easily.

Neither Faith nor I have ever met a bread pudding we didn't like. It's comfort food. Many bakeries make chocolate bread. When Pigs Fly, the bakery company mentioned in the text, is based in York, Maine, but their breads—including the chocolate bread—are sold at many Whole Foods and other markets. They sell the bread—you bake it in your own kitchen for the last 30 minutes—online at www.sendbread.com. They also sell a kit to make the chocolate bread.

Norwegian Christmas Cake—Mor Monsens Kake

1 pound plus 2 teaspoons unsalted butter, softened

2 cups white sugar

4 large eggs

2 cups flour

1 teaspoon vanilla extract

½ cup finely chopped blanched almonds

¼ cup currants

Preheat the oven to 375°.

Using a paper towel, spread a 12-by-18-inch jelly-roll pan with 2 teaspoons of butter.

Cream the remaining butter and the sugar together with an electric mixer. When light and fluffy, beat in the eggs—one at a time—and then the flour and vanilla. Spread the batter evenly onto the pan and sprinkle with the chopped almonds and currants.

Bake 20 to 25 minutes, until the surface is a light gold.

Remove from the oven and let the cake cool in the pan.

Cut the cake into diamonds, or squares, with a sharp knife.

This cake may be made up to 2 weeks before Christmas, but they must then be wrapped in aluminum foil or placed in an air-tight tin. Makes about 2 dozen small cakes.

Helen Barer was the high bidder at an auction benefiting the John L. Gildner Regional Institute for Children and Adolescents held at Malice Domestic XX, a convention in the Washington, DC, area for mystery lovers. The prize was the opportunity to submit a recipe to Faith's cookbook. When I received Helen's recipe, I was amazed. It's one we make every Christmas—the original recipe came from my Norwegian grandmother.

It turns out that Helen, then Helen Isaacs, was a researcher and writer for the Time-Life Foods of the World series, produced in the mid- to late 1960s. I have almost all of these large, beautifully illustrated hardcover cookbooks that came with a handy, smaller spiral-bound paperback with the recipes. They sometimes turn up in library or other book sales and are well worth having. Helen was working on the Scandinavian one and "had a delightful time reading through old cookbooks, talking to Scandinavian cooks, et cetera." She was "thrilled" to travel throughout Scandinavia on her first overseas assignment and was introduced to this recipe and others.

In the Time-Life book, the chapter in which the recipe appears is titled "Christmas: Antidote to Darkness"—an extremely apt description of this time of year with many bleak months yet ahead. Christmas Eve is celebrated in Scandinavia rather than Christmas Day, and I have wonderful memories of these gatherings with my grandparents, uncles, aunts, and cousins feasting on traditional foods and singing carols in both languages.

There really was a Mother or "Mor" Monsen. She owned

a hotel/restaurant on Norway's West Coast, which is still serving these treats as patrons gaze out at the fjord.

All these recipes, with the exception of the Norwegian Christmas Cake, can be made with heart-wise substitutions such as Egg Beaters, butter substitutes, and low-fat creams.

Author's Note

The Body in the Sleigh is dedicated to librarians and I want to write about them and libraries, but first a bit about how this book came to be written. In 2003 I wrote a short story, "The Two Marys," which was published in the 2004 Avon collection *Mistletoe and Mayhem*. Over the years I've heard authors talk about falling in love with their characters and said characters taking over. I had never had those experiences, although I'm extremely fond of Faith Fairchild and it would be wonderful if she *could* take over, saving me from the task of writing about her—some sort of automatic writing, perhaps? I'd have more time to read, for one thing. And then I did fall in love—with Mary Bethany and Miriam Carpenter. And, in a way, they took over.

By definition, a short story is short, but as I wrote it I kept wanting to write more about these two women, much more. I wanted to write about their childhoods and I wanted to write about the two of them together. I wanted to write Faith into more scenes. I was happy with the way the story came out and was honored when Malice Domestic nominated it for an Agatha Award, but I kept wishing I had been able to write a novel instead. When

I mentioned it to my agent, Faith Hamlin (serendipitous note: I wrote the first book *prior* to meeting this Faith), she said, "Why not?" Why not indeed and I was off, free to write about these two women, and all sorts of new characters, to my heart's content. What resulted was not simply an expansion of the short story, as I planned originally, but a completely new tale and one that has become very dear to me. This is because of the message of the season and the people whose paths crossed at that time of the year. I admit to getting choked up when I wrote about Jake and Norah and read the last lines in the epilogue.

And now to libraries.

Henry Ward Beecher, brother to Harriet, wrote: "A library is not a luxury but one of the necessities of life." My first library was housed in an old farmhouse in Livingston, New Jersey. Today, the town I grew up in bears little resemblance to the small farming community it was in the early 1950s when we moved there. The children's room in the Livingston Public Library had been the kitchen, and although it wasn't in use, the old cookstove was still there. Removing it would have been quite a project. Bookshelves lined the walls and there was a window seat where I would curl up to read while I waited for the rest of the family to select their books. Out the window I could see a few apple trees, remnants of the orchard, and beyond them, across the street, the first of what would be many new stores and offices. I worked my way around the kitchen walls, reading about the March family, the Moffats, All-of-a-Kind Family, *Ballet Shoes* and the other shoes, *Misty of Chincoteague* and the other horses, and all the Landmark books.

Mrs. Ruth Rockwood was the librarian, custodian not only of the town's library but also of much of its history. With my parents and others, she started the Livingston Historical Society. When I was about nine, I had exhausted the kitchen's offerings and she allowed me to enter the parlor and dining room—the adult section! Books did not line the walls here, but were arranged in floor-to-ceiling stacks. The wood floors were brightly polished, although the room that had been created was a little dark—the windows had been partially obscured by all the books. I thought it was the most wonderful place in the world. Each week Mrs. Rockwood would pick out a book for me to take home and read. The first was *A Lantern in Her Hand,* a tale about a Nebraska pioneer woman written in 1928 by Bess Streeter Aldrich. I loved it, and after reading that canon, I progressed to Frances Parkinson Keyes (including *Dinner at Antoine's,* her only mystery), and Marjorie Kinnan Rawlings—Mrs. Rockwood's favorite authors, I assume. My home was filled with books, and Ruth Rockwood didn't instill my love of reading, but fanned the flames. What she did instill was a lifelong passion for libraries and librarians.

Eventually the town built a fancy brick library that matched the other new municipal buildings. I was in high school by then and had transferred some of my loyalty to the LHS library and librarian, Mrs. Galford. I was a library aide with my friend Ellen McNaught. We never minded shelving books, since we got to see what had just been returned, discovering Conrad Richter—*The Trees,* such a great book—and Mary Stewart's *Madam, Will You Talk?,* which took us to the others of this vastly underrated writer. Even now, I gravitate to the "To Be Shelved" or "Recent Returns" in my town library. It's like a smorgasbord.

I'm sure Ellen and I felt very important stamping cards with the wooden-handled date device that had to be checked each morning to make sure it was accurate. I also recall we were not above leafing through *The Dictionary of American Slang,* which was kept behind the desk, not because Mrs. Galford believed in withholding information, but because a certain group of boys was destroying the binding and causing it to flop open at several juicy entries.

When I toured Wellesley College before applying, the beautiful lakeside setting was a plus; Professor David Ferry's poetry class and his recitation of Yeats's "Lake Isle of Innisfree" an inspiration

(I was ready to "arise and go," right then and there, wherever Professor Ferry might lead); but it was the library that sold me. The Rare Books Room actually has the door to 50 Wimpole Street with the brass letter slot through which Robert Browning slipped missives to Elizabeth Barrett! During exam times we used to try to get locked in the library overnight by hiding in the lavatories. The "libe" closed at an hour presumably intended to give us a decent night's sleep. The custodian always discovered us, but before he did there was a delicious sense of being almost alone with all those marvelous books.

I somehow find myself in my local library several times a week. Often it's to consult Jeanne Bracken, reference librarian extraordinaire, or I'm lured in by the thought of new books, new titles, although I have stacks of my own to read or reread at home.

Librarians are my favorite people, and libraries my favorite places to be. I'm a member of six Friends of the Library groups. I enjoy giving talks at libraries, especially at meetings of the American Library Association, the Public Library Association, the Massachusetts Library Association—what's the collective for "librarians," as in "a pride of lions," "a tome"? "A volume"?— library book festivals, or fund-raisers where patrons whoop it up all for the sake of words. Having just returned from Hagerstown, Maryland, and their "Gala in the Stacks: Let's Jazz It Up" benefiting the Washington County Free Library Capital campaign, I really do mean "whoop." Speaking to the revelers, I mentioned the fact that the access to libraries, and therefore information, that we enjoy in this country is rare worldwide. I can use my Minuteman Library Network card at over forty local libraries. Simply walk in, check out a book or some other material, use their computers with no questions asked, no fee required, and nothing under lock and key. In addition to their roles as providers, librarians are also protectors.

They're a feisty bunch. I've always thought so, even before the librarian action figure came out. It's modeled on Nancy Pearl, the Seattle librarian author of *Book Lust* and *More Book Lust*. The figure's hand comes up to her lips to shush patrons, a gesture I have never seen a real librarian use. More accurate would have been a librarian waving an arm in protest. In my mind's eye, I envision librarians atop barricades, protecting our civil liberties, guarding our rights to privacy, and unbanning books.

Ultimately librarians are matchmakers. They introduce us to new authors and subjects. They connect us with needed information and, if we like, will teach us how to find it ourselves. They embrace new technology and draw us in, as well. Traveling to libraries all across the country, I have been reminded how they also function as gathering places. New libraries have small auditoria that are available to community groups for meetings and events. Comfortable places to sit and read, yes, but many libraries are adding cafés where patrons can meet for coffee. I loved my little Livingston farmhouse library and the small, gray-shingled Chase Emerson Library in Deer Isle, Maine, but I admit to detours whenever I'm in town to see the McKim courtyard and Sargent murals at the Boston Public Library—the oldest municipal public library in the country and the largest—and the Rose Reading Room at the New York Public Library, pausing outside on Fifth Avenue to pat one of the stone lions, "Patience" and "Fortitude." Our jewel in the crown is, of course, the Library of Congress—again unique in the access it provides and its preservation of books and documents. (There is still a card catalogue as a backup to the digital one.) The Great Hall is splendid. Participating in a panel at the library was an honor and a memory I will always hold dear.

Libraries have functioned as centers of learning since Alexandria, but now more than ever in these economic times, they are providing instruction that individuals cannot afford to take elsewhere. Courses in ESL, literacy, computer literacy, taxes, writing of all sorts, and book groups for every taste are standard fare.

Andrew Carnegie suggested "Let there be light" with the rays of a rising sun be set in the stone above the entrances to his free libraries. It's as apt now as it was in the nineteenth century. Yes, librarians are keepers of the light as well as matchmakers—and it's a match made in heaven. The dedication of this book is long overdue.